LIES LEAD
TO
DEATH
Family of Killers

STEPHEN W. BRIGGS

Black Rose Writing | Texas

ISBN: 978-1-68513-010-7
PUBLISHED BY BLACK ROSE WRITING
www.blackrosewriting.com

Printed in the United States of America
Suggested Retail Price (SRP) $21.95

Lies Lead to Death is printed in Bookman Old Style

To Carolyn, the rock in my life.

LIES LEAD
TO
DEATH
Family of Killers

PART ONE

CHAPTER ONE

Caribbean Sea, Summer 1990

Cold water and ice struck David Grant's swollen face. His body stiffened from the shock as he regained consciousness. Pain radiated through his body; his head throbbed like Mike Tyson had used it for speed bag practice. Multiple straps held him to an old wooden chair where his forearms and shins were bruised and bleeding. Stale salty air hurt his throat as he breathed. He took in a deep breath, the pain in his ribs stabbed at his body. Duct tape covered his mouth, pulling at his facial hair and swollen lips as he lifted his head and tried to focus on the person who stood in front of him. His eyes adjusted to the lack of light in the room while his vision cleared.

He struggled with his balance as the floor moved, rolled, and pitched in different directions. The dull drone of a large diesel motor echoed through the walls. A thought came to him. *I am in the bowels of a ship.*

David surveyed the dark, damp room that imprisoned him. Steel walls surrounded him. There was a small, tinted window to his left where seawater lapped up against and over it. A ladder, old and rusty, fastened to the wall that faced him, led to an opening in the ceiling. Wedged through the rungs of the ladder was an AK-47.

David tried to move his arms and legs. The pain brought him close to passing out again.

The guard who watched David was large. His head was shaved, and dark curly hair blanketed his sweaty body. A tie-dye tank top, with Miami written across it in white comical letters, was wet and stuck to his body. He laughed at David and his confused state.

David focused on him and mumbled a sound. His captor dropped the plastic cup to the floor and walked to the ladder.

"The little shit's eyes are open, and he is looking around. He is awake and seems alert this time. Someone pass the information to Igor. I am not climbing this whore of a ladder again," he yelled in Russian to the opening.

A man peered through the hatch from above and answered, "I will get Igor. He will be happy to hear this."

David's mind, engulfed in a fog, continued to clear. He searched it for answers about how he got onto the ship.

•　　•　　•

David continued to look around and tried to understand the situation. He studied the man who stood at the bottom of the ladder but had an overwhelming desire to close his eyes and sleep. Like an old car engine on a frigid winter morning, David forced his mind to turn over and start. Finally, patches of his memory flashed before him.

He was in Venezuela on an assignment for The Family. The official name he gave the organization after the death of his granda.

At the local airport, he waited for his target, Sergio. When he was sure Sergio had missed the flight; he called John to update him on the mission. There was a lengthy discussion, but David could not remember all the details. Told the mission was a failure, John instructed him to come home. The fog returned, and his memories disappeared into it. Then another memory flashed in his mind's eye. He was in a taxi on his way back to the shantytown, where he stayed in Caracas. He entered his tent. After that, nothing… until now.

Was I drugged? he thought. *How did I get here? Where is here? Are John, Dad, or Phil aware I am missing?*

• • •

Through his swollen eyes, David stared at the man. He recognized the man spoke Russian, but couldn't identify him. To get his captor's attention, David grunted and moaned.

The man at the ladder walked back to David and bent down to look him in the eyes. "Not till da-boss gives the okay. When he comes, then maybe you can talk, but I doubt it," said the stranger in his thick Russian accent.

David grunted again.

"No, you little shit, not till da-boss comes down." He smacked David in the jaw with the back of his hand.

David noticed the stranger had a black eye, a large gash across his left cheek, and swollen lips. His right hand was bandaged, as if he had punched something hard. *I was obviously in a fight with this guy and who else?* David thought.

A shadow appeared over the hatch and a set of legs dropped into the hold, searching for a rung of the ladder. A tall, thin man in dark dress pants and a white cotton button-up shirt entered the hold. He climbed down the ladder, turned to look at David, and pulled out a handkerchief. With it, he wiped his brow and walked to David.

"I cannot adapt to this heat and humidity," he said.

Another man dressed in shorts and a white tee-shirt descended the ladder. He picked up the gun, checked the clip, then rested it on his shoulder. He leaned against the ladder and lit a cigarette.

"You had a good nap, David. Someone miscalculated your weight when they gave you the Diazepam," said the well-dressed man.

David recognized him instantly, Igor Volkov. A past friend of John, James, and Kenton, David's granda. He had worked with The Family on jobs in the U.S.S.R. back in the sixties and seventies. Trained by the Soviet Army and KGB, Igor had skills like David and James. Just like Kenton, Igor took all his military training and turned it into a successful business, working privately for various countries and underground groups. The relationship between Igor and The Family broke down on a job in 1981 when he betrayed Kenton and James and left them in a small village in China. On that job, if Kenton did not have an evacuation plan, Kenton and James would have died a slow, painful death at the hands of Igor's new allies.

David knew Igor was in the area. He, like David, was sent to hunt Sergio.

"Ruslan, carefully remove the tape from his mouth. No one can hear his screams in here," said Igor.

"Gladly. He has been wanting me to do it since he woke up. Well, careful what you ask for, you little shit."

He picked at the edge of the black tape on David's right cheek. With enough tape to get a firm grip, he pulled hard and fast. David screamed, but only in his head. The five days of hair growth on David's face and the cuts that had begun to heal went with the adhesive tape.

Ruslan rolled up the tape and dropped it on David's lap with the melted ice.

"Fuck you," David said to Ruslan. "I'll do the same to you later. Only it'll be your skin I will peel off, you oversized chimp."

Ruslan laughed and backhanded David on the cheek. "I don't see that happening, you little shit."

"Ruslan, that's not how we care for our guest. David, why were you in Venezuela?" asked Igor. "Who were you waiting for at the airport? Was it me? I heard you were waiting for me. What an honor to have you looking for me."

"Don't flatter yourself, Igor. I wasn't after you. You would've been a bonus, but it wasn't you. You're so smart; you tell me who I was waiting for."

"Well, I know a lot now. We found the key hidden in your backpack. The key to the locker at the airport? You know what I mean, don't you? We, and most of the civilized and uncivilized world, were after the same man, Sergio. David, you know I am right." He looked at David and smiled. "It looked like a convention of alphabet agencies, cartels, organizations, mobsters, and underworld goons. Everyone wanted that man. He holds so many secrets in his head and files. He gave us all the slip. Seems someone had deeper pockets than us. I love how your client, the CIA, pays you to kill their own. Land of the free, they say? The beautiful lady who followed him—Adoria? Yes, Adoria, she told us quite a lot."

"What did you do to her? If you—"

"Not to worry. She won't be messing up any more jobs for you or John. After three hours of questions, she gave us all the information I needed. Lovely lady, amazing how high-pitched her screams got when we cut off her hands. Could shatter glass. That lady should have been an opera singer. We didn't have time to dig the full six feet down before we buried her. But no one will be looking, anyway. Now, back to why we are all here. Who has Sergio? Did John say anything when you called him at the airport?"

"You still have the gift of gab, Igor," said David. "I don't know where Sergio is and neither do you."

"I assume if neither one of us does, then a cartel picked him up. If they have him, well, I would assume he is dead, or for sale. I need to speak to him as much as you do. We both know what he has hidden in that little brain of his."

"Igor, I don't look—"

"Please don't go into the details of how John runs the operation. You only take what you need from the prepared reports. Blah, blah, blah. I know all that, David."

David struggled in his chair.

"A little too close to home, David? Sorry. David, my team followed you for the last couple of days. Imagine that? You were a target while waiting for your target. David, friend, well, I guess I used to call you that. David, our families worked so close for so long. What happened?"

"You, know. Igor, you know what happened. You went bad, you went rogue and got greedy. Like an animal with rabies, you couldn't control yourself and now you need put down," David said, his anger clearing the fog from his thoughts.

"Now David, is this any way to talk to your host? You are my guest on this boat. David, I assume the lads back home will be looking for you. Your last check-in was a couple of days ago." Igor smiled at him. "Oh yes, I can see by the look on your face. Yes David, you have been missing for almost two full days now. You must feel rested. You slept like a baby." He placed his hand on David's shoulder. "Back home must be on high alert. We know how militant they are on matters like this. I bet your dad has not even told your mom you are missing. We all appreciate how she feels about the business we are all involved in."

"Igor, you know they are searching for me. When I'm found, you and your band of monkeys will suffer a slow and painful death." He took a deep breath to continue. The pain locked his body, and he lost his train of thought.

Igor broke the silence. "I assume they have all kinds of people looking for you on land. I bet they won't think to look on a ship. And how many ships are out at sea right now? By the time they get down here from Canada, we will be in Cuba. Me taking John and James's money maker is going to crack open the wedge between us even further. I think our days of partying together are well behind us. But I will sell you on the black market once we get you home to Russia. They will identify me as a legend for this little heist."

David felt his mind close again. He wanted to fight it, but the darkness continued to cover his thoughts.

"We took you right after your last check-in. Took the taxi driver too. He won't be seeing his family again. How do the Americans call it, collateral damage? You put up a good fight, but in the end, well, here you are. Ruslan took the worst of your beating, but he also returned the favor. David, I'm not what you think. Oh David, am I boring you? Hold your head up and look at me. Ruslan, please wake him up."

Ruslan slapped David across the face. "Pay attention. The boss is talking to you. Do not disrespect him again, you little shit."

David looked up and spit a mouthful of blood at Ruslan, then smiled. Ruslan cocked his arm to punch David.

Igor grabbed his elbow.

"Ruslan, settle," Igor said. "David, if your granda could only see you now. Maybe he is from above." Igor looked up at the ceiling. "How is your dad doing? Has he gotten over the loss of his father, the patriarch who started the family business? How are you as well? You and your granda were remarkably close. You did a lot of work together, not as much as I did with him, but, well, that was unfortunate. I guess no more, now you are on your own." He turned to Ruslan, who was behind him. "Ruslan, you might not know this, but a car bomb blew David's grandfather up last year. Terrible thing to happen. They accused me of the bombing. I can assure you I had nothing to do with it." A wave hit the side of the boat and Igor paused to secure his balance. "As much as our businesses have grown apart, I would have given Kenton a warning if I knew. I was in Afghanistan picking up old Soviet equipment to ship to my customers in Columbia when it happened." Igor bent to David's eye level. "I am sorry about your family's loss, David. I was heartbroken when I heard the news."

"Are you done talking? You're like a politician spewing shit no one cares about. You know why I'm here and you know who sent me. So go fuck yourself, Igor. History is just that, history. We were allies, but now, you should kill me now, because if I get the chance, I'll kill you and your mindless sidekicks. I might make a rug out of him. He's as hairy as a bear. Are most Russians fat and hairy like this one?" He braced for a hit to his body. His energy was diminishing quickly.

Igor tapped Ruslan on the shoulder and shook his head. Ruslan stepped away from David and spat at him.

"David, your family is no better than me and my associates. You and The Family run the same type of underground organization I do. You know that. That is the problem. We keep stepping on each other's business toes. With your granda gone, the world sees your family as weak, vulnerable, and most believe, now is a time to strike to end your reign. The gun and weapon sales, the hits, the connections with so many governments, and the cleaning up for others are all up for grabs." Igor swung his arms out dramatically. He stepped back from David. "I know John is the best in the world at hiding people, better than any country's witness protection program. He should use that for all of you before it is too late. Everyone knows John and your dad don't have the presence that your granda had around the world. And now, with the mighty and feared David tied to a chair before me, I will show my new government that I am still powerful and useful. David, I need a photo to remember this moment. Before we arrive in Cuba, I will need a photo. Ruslan, when we go up for dinner, find me a camera."

"Igor, you're sounding like an evil cartoon character. You might want to settle down a little. I'm a nobody. Just some punk that can use a knife. I'm just a minor part of the business," said David as he fought to stay conscious.

"Oh David, we both know that is not true. Your family has made mistakes since your granda's death. That last issue, with John and your Uncle Scott? I might have played a part in that ship sinking. If only they had vetted the crew better. Your granda would never miss little details like that. Well, let's just say I will be the leading arms trader for those who need large amounts of weapons and artillery in the future. As good of an assassin as you are, you can't be perfect. If you were, I would be the one tied to the chair." He chuckled at his comment. "I can not wait to show off the ultimate prize, you! They will tell stories of me catching the mighty David. Then sneaking him away on a ship. Brilliant, if I do say so myself." He turned and smiled at Ruslan.

Igor leaned into David. In the dim light, he had not seen David clearly.

"Ruslan, get him some water. Now that we have him, we don't want to lose him. We can have him sold for millions. Ruslan, his face is a mess. Don't touch his face, you stupid gorilla. I want him to be recognizable when we take photos of The Great David. Just like the one in the Bible."

"And just like that David, I will live to an old age taking revenge on my enemies. You are at the top of the list and this fat slob a close second. What about the clown at the ladder? He hasn't said anything. He just stands there with a gun. Tall cool one, I guess."

David ran out of gas. His mouth, the same one that got him in so much trouble over the years, hurt too much to continue talking. And the pain around his ribs intensified with each deep breath.

"David, I guess we haven't done formal introductions. You know me. You have met Ruslan, my bodyguard." Igor pointed to the man at the ladder. "He is the man who waited for you in your tent when you arrived. My top assassin, Alek. Nowhere near your skill level and I would throw him to the sharks right now if you said you would work for me. Maybe you two can talk and compare notes once we arrive in Cuba. The drugs should wear off by then. But as I have reminded all the people on the ship and as much as Ruslan wants to kill you slowly, we need to get you to Russia alive. Unlike most people in this business, you are worth a lot alive. Not so much dead." Igor turned to Ruslan, who was lighting a cigarette. "Ruslan, once we get our money for him, and once whoever purchases him has finished with him, you can do with him as you wish. Until then, hands off. If only I had Sergio tied to a chair beside him."

David stared at him. When his granda passed a year ago, there were organizations like Igor's who wanted to finish off the rest of The Family. The Family was the standard all others worked towards. Unlike the movies and television shows, David knew there was no getting out of this one alive. When the ship docked in Cuba, he would be a commodity.

The boat rolled heavily to the left, hit by an enormous wave. Igor dropped to his knees. David and the chair fell over. His head bounced off the steel floor and a new gash opened above his ear. The impact on his head caused David to black out again.

Igor stood up, dusted his pants, and cursed the captain in Russian. Ruslan grabbed David by the hair and righted him and his chair in one swift motion.

A punch to his stomach brought David back to consciousness. Winded, he threw up blood and stomach acid. Unable to pull in deep breaths of air, David floated between consciousness and unconscious. Staring at Ruslan, he smiled. "Remember, you need to keep me alive, asshole."

"Come on Ruslan. Our dinner should be ready," Igor said. He smiled at David. "Not for you, my friend. Tonight, you will go hungry. Ruslan, give him water before you come up. And keep your hands off him. If he dies before we get him to Cuba, so will you."

Igor and Alek climbed the ladder. Before he stepped back on deck, Igor yelled into the hold, "We will be in Cuba tomorrow. David, I will come to get you then. I hope you will smile for the photo. I know it isn't your first visit to the island, but it is likely your last. Castro might come to see you at the docks. What an honor, indeed."

Ruslan took a couple of bottles from the corner of the hold. When he returned, he found David blacked out again. Ruslan poured water over David's head to wake him. "Here, you little shit, drink your water," he mockingly said. "You might piss yourself, but that is not my problem."

Ruslan unscrewed the cap from the bottle and flipped it at David's face. He jammed the glass bottle into David's mouth. It reopened the cuts on his lips and gums. He choked on the water and coughed, but the bottle did not move. Water spurted out of his mouth and nose while his lungs received the rest. The bottle, now empty, was taken away from David's mouth while he continued to cough and then vomit.

"Can't keep up with the water? What a waste. Sit there. Well, I guess you can't go anywhere. I will get another bottle."

The little water David swallowed had a distinct taste of copper.

Ruslan went back to the corner and grabbed more water. This time, he allowed David to drink at his pace. David took in the full bottle of water without choking. Ruslan threw the empty bottle at David's legs.

"Don't die tonight. I guess we need you alive. Boss seems to think we can get some money for a little shit like you."

"Won't be me dying tonight," said David with a raspy voice.

Ruslan shook his head. "What a waste of talent. You should work for us. You and me, we would make an amazing team."

Ruslan climbed the ladder. From the top rung, he yelled to David. "I will see you before bed. You can have another bottle of water then, you little shit."

CHAPTER TWO

David struggled to stay awake. He could see it was later in the day by the colors coming through the hatch. The water he had taken in refreshed his body and mind.

Darkness replaced the daylight, and two dim lights came on in the hold. David looked around the room. The half-empty case of water sat in the corner to his right. Rope and a roll of duct tape lay beside him. On his right side were blood-stained clothes, his clothes, and an opened package of candy. With his clothes beside him, he looked down to realize he had track pants and a white undershirt on, wet and covered in stomach bile. *They stripped me looking for a tracking device,* he thought.

He wiggled and tried to loosen the ties. Each arm had three thick, black zip ties holding them to the arm of the chair. Starting at his wrists, they spaced the ties up to his elbows. His legs had three ties from his ankles to his knees.

With the tape off, he could breathe through his mouth instead of his broken, blood-clotted nose. His head pounded and his whole body ached from the beating. Whatever happened, he needed to figure out how he got on this ship, and how he was getting off. The last thing he needed was to land in Cuba and meet Castro.

Sitting quietly and fighting off sleep, he tried to remember how he got on the ship. His memory failed him, and his energy levels plummeted. The spurt of energy from the water dissipated as he fought off another blackout.

Searching his mind, he struggled for answers. *What happened? How did I get here?* Slowly, the veil lifted, and his memories came back to him like a lucid dream.

•   •   •

Two Days Earlier
David stood in the lobby of the Caracas International Airport waiting for Sergio's plane to arrive. The plane disembarked onto the runway, but Sergio Garcia, his target, did not exit the plane. Twenty minutes later, the flight crew disembarked from the plane. David knew the plane was empty and walked through the airport searching for a telephone.

This last minute emergency request was all because an ex-CIA agent, Sergio, went rogue three years earlier. Before Sergio left the agency, he gathered files, papers, and disks, full of information, enough to destroy the CIA, the United States, many free world governments, and the faith people had in their governments. Sergio, since he had gone into hiding, had released pieces of information that revealed secrets the FBI, CIA, and many other agencies in the United States and the world needed hidden from the public. An intelligence team from Britain traced Sergio's last information dump of documents to South America. The U.S. military attacked the group that had protected him in Columbia. So, Sergio was on the run again. The information David received documented Sergio's flight from Columbia would take him to Caracas. After a two-hour layover, his flight would land in Europe and then the last leg of his journey would be to the safety of the Middle East.

David found a phone.

"Hello?" John answered. The phone crackled and popped.

"John, the target didn't arrive on the plane. Have you heard anything?" David asked.

"Yes, I have. Adoria called about ten hours ago. Someone trapped her, and she lost Sergio. It sounds like a setup, the way she explained it, but she lost him. Right now, she has all her associates looking for him. I think we have lost him. We don't know where he is. She was to call me an hour ago to check-in. I'm still waiting for her call."

"What? How did this happen, John? How did she lose him? It sounds like everyone is on his tail."

"Yes, we weren't the only ones trying to run an extraction operation. She said there were a bunch of Russians, Israelis, Chinese, and about every other group in the area the last few days, and we both know the Russians want him."

"Okay, you have me scheduled for some deliveries of military equipment in a couple of weeks. I'll visit her. She's botched two jobs in the last few months. Time to cut her loose, I think."

"We can talk about that later. Right now, we need to figure out our next steps. Your dad is on the phone with Peter as we speak. Hold on a second, I need to talk to him."

David leaned against the wall and looked around the lobby of the airport. People rushed around and stood in lines, just like every other airport David had visited.

"David, are you still there?"

"Go ahead, John. I can hear you."

"Peter and his bosses in the CIA have pulled the plug. He has confirmed that it was all a distraction. Sergio bypassed you, and the others, and is heading to Iraq. Mossad confirmed with the CIA, it was a body double. He left the region two days ago. Everyone's intel was off. There is obviously some big dollars backing him. We are pulling you out."

"Okay, I need to gather my things back at camp."

"Of course. Just be aware that Igor is in the area too. If you want to bring him home as a gift, we would be happy to see him."

"Oh, I would love that."

"Your dad is jumping on a job in Texas. Some of our clients are behind on payments."

"Okay, John, what do you want me to do, head home, hunt down Igor, or meet Dad in Texas?"

"Pack up. Get your equipment and return to the airport. I'll start sourcing out flights. I'll see if I can get you to meet in Texas with your dad. Can you be back at the airport in four hours?"

"Yeah, that is plenty of time. I will call when I am back here."

"Take care David, talk soon."

David hung up the phone and headed outside to find a ride. A cab picked David up, and they drove to the shantytown where he had set up his tent.

With a large tip in his pocket and the promise of more when they returned to the airport, the cabby walked with David to his tent. The shanty was noisy and had a putrid smell from the lack of sanitation. Happy to pack up and leave the makeshift tent city, David opened his tent door. A large man was inside. Before David could react, someone from behind shoved him into his tent. The man inside grabbed him. The person who pushed David hit the taxi driver on the head. That was the last thing he remembered, until he woke, tied to a chair, in the bottom of a ship.

• • •

Ruslan climbed down the ladder. Cleaned up for supper, he had showered and shaved. A button-up shirt replaced the sweaty tank top, it was more Hawaiian than Cuban. From his chest pocket, he pulled out a film canister.

David watched Ruslan closely. He picked up a bottle of water and approached. Popping the top off the canister, Ruslan rolled four pills into the palm of his right hand.

"Good to see you are awake. How are you feeling? You still look like shit, like a little shit." He laughed at his joke. "Dinner was excellent, fresh fish caught from the side of the boat. Beautiful David, beautiful. There were no leftovers, so all you get are some pills."

David looked up at him and spit a mouthful of blood. It landed on Ruslan's shirt.

"What is the saying Ruslan? You can dress him up, but he still looks like shit, something like that. A shave and a shower do nothing to hide the lack of intelligence between your ears."

"You little shit, your time will come. Boss says not until he gives me the okay. Fuck it." Ruslan tossed the bottle of water onto the floor. He stepped to David and swung his fist. The large cut above David's ear was where Ruslan aimed and hit with his fist. It reopened and blood ran around David's ear. The force of the blow sent the chair backward. David hit his head on the steel floor and lost consciousness.

"Shit," said Ruslan. "Boss won't be happy with me. David, you okay?"

He put the pills back in the container and into his pocket. With both hands, he lifted David and the chair. Slumped over, David did not wake. Checking his neck for a pulse, Ruslan found it and smiled.

"David, David, try to be more careful with your balance. When the ship rocks, you need to be ready. David, wake up. I have some pills for you." He gently tapped David on the shoulder and cheek.

David gradually looked up; his head throbbed even more than earlier. He looked at Ruslan and spit again. This time, Ruslan didn't react. He took out the pills and opened a bottle of water.

"Here, you little shit, take some pills. They will keep you quiet. You will sleep until we get to Cuba. It should help with the pain, too."

He gently gave David water and attempted to put the pills into David's mouth. With his mouth closed, at first, David opened it to receive the pills. Ruslan rolled the pills onto David's tongue and gave him more water. With a huge smile, David spat the water and pills back at him.

"No thanks bud, I will suffer from the pain and deal with a logical mind," David said with a slight slur.

"Okay, we do it the hard way, just like everything with you. You little shit."

Picking the pills off the damp floor, he grabbed David's face. His large hand pushed David's head back, and he pulled down on his jaw. Ruslan's middle finger pressed into David's eye. Dropping the pills into David's mouth, Ruslan's large hands covered David's mouth and nose until he swallowed.

When he stopped coughing from the forced feeding, he smirked at Ruslan. "If I survive this, I will hunt you down and kill you."

"I don't know how, you little shit. Seems I am the one climbing the ladder and going to a comfy bed. You, well, you get locked down here for another night."

The pills worked swiftly. David slurred words at Ruslan that neither one of them understood.

"Sleep tight, you little shit. I will see you in the morning. Captain says we might have some rough seas tonight, so be ready to fall over and roll around a bit." Ruslan climbed the ladder and closed the hatch.

The pills fully kicked in. David tried to fight the fog that engulfed his mind. Most of the pain and his ability to fight off sleep disappeared, and he blacked out.

● ● ●

A full bottle of water crashed into David's chest as he lay on his side. Dried blood cracked on his skin when he lifted his head.

Ruslan laughed, "Wake up, my sleeping beauty. You were snoring. Looks like you fell over in your sleep. Were you dreaming of your freedom?" He laughed again. "Back to the nightmare of your real life."

The fall overnight caused David to land on his shoulder, dislocating it. Lifting his head, he looked at the hatch. The dim light of sunrise leaked through the opening. The old pains joined with the choir of fresh pains that sang throughout his body. Still strapped to the chair, the fog over his mind was as thick as the fog he could see through the hatch and the small window. By the light, he estimated it was early in the morning. He had slept all night. Laying on the floor, waiting for the pain of being righted, he wondered how close they were to Cuba.

Ruslan grabbed him by his arm and pulled him up. The chair cracked as the one leg twisted on the floor.

"Lucky you won't need that chair much longer, you little shit. We are almost to Cuba. We will be there by evening. So, time to take your pills for the last part of the trip. When you wake, we will be setting you and your chair on the dock."

"What day is it?" David asked.

"Doesn't matter for you, you little shit. Each day you are alive is a lucky day. That is what you should call all your days now, lucky day. Here, I brought you food. Eat up."

Ruslan fed David bread and cold, salty meat. To David, it didn't matter. He was so hungry he ate the food, even though the salt on the meat stung every cut in his mouth. He forced two bottles of water down his throat to wash down the food.

"What about the pills, you idiot?"

"Oh, I hid them in the food. You should learn to chew your food better. If you had, you likely would have found the pills."

David's head dropped in defeat.

The volume of people and their activity around the hatch was escalating. David could hear panic and confusion as the voices echoed into the hold. He heard Ruslan's name called a few times before a head appeared at the hatch. "Ruslan, Ruslan. Come quick. Igor is looking for you," Alek said.

"What's happened up there? Why is everyone yelling?" Ruslan asked Alek. "Tell Igor the little shit is awake. I stuffed his pills in the meat, so he won't be awake for long."

Alek's head disappeared, and Ruslan walked back to David.

"Da-boss wants another chat. Maybe to make sure your paperwork is ready for customs," Ruslan said.

"When will we be off this shitty cruise ship? I have a complaint about the service," said David.

"Not long now. I don't think the flight service will be any better for you."

Ruslan brought over a third bottle of water for David. The panicked noises from above continued as David downed the water. The voices grew louder, men yelled in Russian and a dialect of Spanish above their heads. Shadows rushed past the hatch.

"Ruslan, what is going on up there? Someone is in trouble over something. Is Igor mad at you?"

"Shut up, you little shit." Ruslan looked up at the opening. The calls from the others continued to escalate. The look of confusion on the Russian's face pleased David.

Standing on the top rung of the ladder, Ruslan looked around the deck of the ship. Seeing the panicked actions of the crew and the fear in Igor's face, he quickly lowered himself to the floor and ran over to the corner of the hold. He searched for the roll of tape. It had rolled behind David. The voices above were in a state of frenzy. More people rushed past the hatch as Ruslan tore off a strip of tape.

"Did I just hear someone yell Navy? I heard Navy. You might be right, asshole. Maybe today is my lucky day."

Ruslan grabbed David's head to place the tape over his mouth. David swung his head while he yelled for help. His throat was raw, and his voice failed him.

A punch to David's jaw stopped his movement, and he blacked out again. Ruslan placed the tape over his mouth and ran to the ladder.

CHAPTER THREE

Guelph, Ontario

John Clark sat at his desk in the basement of his plumbing wholesale business, the legitimate business for the other illicit operations, James, Phil, David, and he ran. Phil Clark, his son, worked at the conference table booking flights and motels for David's next job in Japan.

When Kenton died a year earlier, John became the senior member of The Family. During World War Two, they joined their countries' armies at the early age of seventeen. When their military companies joined in Europe after D-day, they became friends, assigned to night watch together. After the war ended, they stayed in Europe for an additional year to help rebuild ruined cities before they returned to their countries to work. John had a successful career with CSIS, The Canadian Security Intelligence Service. Kenton rose through the ranks of the SAS, The British Special Air Service, one of the most elite military special services. After two decades apart, they found a way to work together. That was the beginning of The Family. John worked the American side of the Atlantic while Kenton worked with the Brits throughout the British Isles, Europe, and the Middle East.

Kenton's sons, James, and Scott joined The Family in the sixties when they were teens. In the late seventies, James had to pack up and move his wife, Elizabeth, David and Amy, their children, to Canada. A man he was to kill identified him doing a hit in Belfast. For the second time in his career, he had a bounty put on his head.

Scott stayed in Northern Ireland, with Kenton, to help run their small machine shop. They used it to hide their side of the unofficial business. The machine shop they ran, built, and sold sub-machine guns. They shipped those guns and many other forms of weapons and military equipment from the docks of Belfast to customers around the world.

John was in his forties when he married his younger wife, Brenda. Together, they had one child, Phil.

David and Phil, just like Kenton and John, became close friends when they met. They were both the same age and grew up in The Family. During their early teens, their fathers identified their natural strengths; David trained to be a world-class assassin while Phil trained to work the books, hide people, and negotiate contracts with governments and organizations.

•   •   •

"Dad," Phil said. "I'm surprised David hasn't called back yet. It's been twelve hours. It shouldn't take him that long to gather his things and get back to the airport."

"Yes, I have him booked on a flight to leave in an hour and a half. I'm not sure where he is. My only hope is he bumped into Igor and is dealing with him," said John.

"This job in Japan, I think I'll book David and myself a week in Hawaii once it's done. He needs a break. Working with him, I can recognize when he needs some downtime. The signs were there before he left for this job. When is James..."

The phone rang on John's desk. "Hello?" said John. "Hi, James. No, nothing—I am too—okay, I'll have a car waiting for you. See you tomorrow."

John replaced the handset onto the base. "Damn, I hoped that was David. It's not like him to miss a check-in. It shouldn't take him twelve hours to pack up and return to the airport."

"I should've gone with him. If this is our future, then going forward, I need to be with him on every job. No more picking and choosing. I need to be closer. We can't be sending David around the world without a second set of eyes. I know his granda and dad always did it as individuals, but the world has changed. Dad, where is he?"

John's warehouse manager and bodyguard, Frank, knocked on the door and opened it. "Phil, are you coming with me? I have the van loaded. We should head out. The traffic is going to be bad through Mississauga."

"Yeah, coming Frank. Two minutes," said Phil.

Frank nodded and closed the door. Phil organized his papers and dropped the file on his dad's desk. "Okay, Dad, I'm leaving with Frank. I guess this delivery of guns will help take my mind off David for a while. At what point do we make some calls to see where he is? Who do we have in the area?"

"If he misses this flight, I'll make some calls. We have contacts down there. I'll call Peter to see if he has heard anything. He has four agents embedded in the area and hopefully, he can contact one of them. Get them to head to the shanty. James will want to head down too, so I better look for flights. Phil, don't we have a shipment of weapons heading south shortly?"

"I think so. I can check when I get back if you don't have time. Dad, I'm telling Frank once we drop these items off at the warehouse in Toronto, we're coming straight home. He'll be upset if he can't hit the nudie bar and Italian restaurant, but I need to be here. I was thinking, we need to look at outfitting the vehicles with car phones. It's the nineties, you know."

"You and David and your modern technology. How secure can that be? Pay phones are all around and can't be easily traced. We can talk about it later. Frank is waiting for you."

Once Phil left the office, John pounded on his desk. He wanted to hide his concern about David's safety. Phil and David had been closer than brothers since they were seven. This was the day John and James hoped they never had to talk about. The "what if something happened to one of their sons," moment.

•   •   •

The flight from Caracas left without David on board. John called Peter, The Family's CIA contact and friend.

Peter Thompson worked his way up the ranks of the CIA during his career. Now, the Deputy Director of National Clandestine Service, he worked out of Washington, D.C. That was his official job. His unofficial job was to have The Family, and others like them, do the work the United States government and many of their allies could never officially be tied to. Both of his jobs, official and unofficial, he performed with pride, secrecy, and attention to the minute details. The Family was his closest contacts. Their relationship began and grew back to the late 1970s. There was a mutual trust and understanding between Peter and The Family, and both parties benefited throughout the years financially.

"David should have checked in by now, Peter. After you and I talked earlier and agreed to kill the assignment, I sent him back to get his personal items. Plus, he would never go this long without checking in. He is well over the agreed time."

"John, don't overreact," said Peter.

"We have bloody rules, unlike you cowboys. There has been no update, he has not checked in. I have reached out to my contacts in Caracas. A couple are going to the shanty to see if he's there. Another couple are putting out feelers to see what comes back. Right now, no one knows anything about his location. What about your men? Do you have anyone who can get eyes on him quickly?" John yelled down the phone. "Supposedly, when MI6 identified Sergio's location from the last dumping of information, one of your guys, a guy he worked with, was seen in Columbia and spooked him. Peter, you need to get your damn house in order."

"John, I will do everything I can. Give me the night to see what my team can find. You know I want him back safe. We, I, need him now more than ever. I'll call you before noon tomorrow. I'm heading into a meeting. As soon as it ends, I'll make more calls. I promise. John, I am sorry about what has happened."

"Peter, you know what will happen if he's missing and we find out it was one of your guys that compromised his position and caused even one of David's hairs to be hurt."

"I don't even want to think about it. Goodnight."

John hung up, then called his primary contact in Caracas. There was still no confirmation of David's location. The latest information was about David's tent. It was still in the shantytown.

•　　•　　•

John didn't leave his office all night. James' plane arrived at the airport and he rushed straight to the office. John's office door swung open. With no pleasantries, James asked about his son's location. James sat down and sunk into the chair by John's desk. With a glass of whiskey waiting for James, John updated him on David's situation.

Phil worked the phone at the conference table. He tried to get news from Venezuela or Columbia about David. It had been thirty hours since David did his last check-in.

The strictest safety rule The Family had for all their jobs was there was a check-in required at a specific time daily. If David was with Phil, either could call the office, but they had to check-in. The time and frequency changed on every job and only the four of them knew the schedule. They had two reasons for a specific time; John or James would be in the office and if something happened to David, and he called in at a different time, then John would send help, knowing he was in trouble.

If Elizabeth, David's mother, knew her son was missing, there would be more issues to deal with than finding David.

John had used up every contact in every agency he could get a hold of. He even reached out to some of his competition around the world.

James' day was not going well; the news was bad, and so were the flight arrangements. The only flight available was one of their own. James called the airport, looking for his pilot. Knowing the plane would need to refuel in Grand Bahama before the last leg to Columbia, James booked a private plane from Grand Bahama island to Caracas. He called the hangar looking for the pilot, Teddy.

James, phone in hand, paced back and forth as far as the cord would allow. "I won't wait for your team to load the plane. I don't care whether the order is loaded, we will be wheels up in three hours. Teddy, you have worked with us for years. Have I ever made a request like this?" James tried to hide his anger with Teddy. Phil waved his arms at James and pointed to himself; he was going too. "Listen, Phil is coming too. Adjust your weights for the two of us and a couple of bags. If you can't load the completed order, I don't care. If anyone complains, I will gladly have a chat with them after this issue is resolved. Be ready in three hours." James hung up the phone.

John motioned for James and Phil to come to his desk, where he had his phone pressed to his ear. He waved his hand at James, signaling he needed to write something down. James tossed him his pen. In between "uh-huhs," he wrote on the notepad. *David was last seen leaving the airport in a taxi. My call? Possible kidnapping. Could be on a boat. Taxi was located abandoned at dock, driver in trunk dead. Possible on boat. Has not been back to shantytown in 24 hours. Missing. Sol Matutino fishing vessel. He was loaded on it???? Left a couple of days ago.*

James read the note.

"Okay, call in four hours with another update. Yes, have his items collected. I'll have someone pick the items up and reimburse them for the information. Goodbye." John hung up the phone.

"Who was that?" asked James.

"A lieutenant in the Caracas police. He called because they found a taxi driver dead at the docks. Unfortunately, it was his cousin. Our boy, José, told him to call me about it."

"Our José? He's new, right?"

"The very one. José had told his friends and family, who were also cops or emergency workers, to report any strange activity. We are lucky this guy was on duty."

"Story of our lives," said James.

"I guess a couple of shore workers saw three guys load a body onto the ship, Sol Matutino. They called the police. When the cops showed up, they found a taxi abandoned at the dock with the driver in the trunk."

"If David is on a boat, how the hell do we track that? And where would it go?" said Phil.

James looked at John. "Cuba, the fucking Russians. My gut tells me Igor took David. We believe he organized dad's death. Now he has David. What were his last words to us years ago in Berlin? *'I will take down your family of killers and those who support you!'*"

"James, I have confirmation that Igor was there to hunt for Sergio. Think about it. The job got called off, and he saw an opportunity to take David. Our David."

James pounded John's desk hard enough to make both John and Phil jump. The type of person who needed to control situations, James felt helpless, thousands of miles away from his son. His son was in trouble, and he needed to do something about it. He knew Igor's skills. They had worked together on other jobs when Igor was an agent for the KGB and plenty of jobs after he left the agency.

They were quiet, each one worried David could already be in Russia, hidden away by Igor. Sighing with defeat, James knew he would have to tell Elizabeth, David's mother, that her son had missed his last check-in.

"James, you see the notes. I hate to say it, but I don't think David will be there when you arrive," said John.

"I booked a private plane in Grand Bahama," James said. "When we get there, I will decide where to go."

"James, don't let your emotions control your actions. Remember when you had to live here when you were a lad? Control the situation, don't let it control you. Call me when you guys arrive stop for fuel. Be safe and smart. Watch out for each other. That area is now a hot spot of activity. James, I don't care how you do it. I don't care how many holes we will need to dig. Bring David home." The tremor in his voice exposed his fear and concern.

"Aye John, I'll call you from the airport for any updates."

The phone on John's desk rang. He answered the call on speaker. "Hello," John said.

"John, it's Peter. You seem far away."

"I have you on speaker with Phil and James. Any news?"

"Nothing John, sorry. You?"

"Yes, but I don't know what to do about it. We're almost completely sure David is on a fishing vessel. Somewhere in the Caribbean."

"Really? How do you know that?"

James sat down; the emotion of the moment caught up to him. He placed his head in his hands.

"Information from a police lieutenant and some shore workers. It's not good Peter. We won't give up but—"

"John, this is great news."

The three men looked at each other, confused by Peter's response.

"John, please, please tell me you have the name of the ship."

"Peter, he is on a boat. How can this be good news? I—"

"Ship name?"

"Hold on, Sol Matutino. I think that's how you pronounce it."

"Guys, give me an hour. Don't go anywhere." Peter ended the call.

"I don't get it," said John.

"He seemed happy by the news," said Phil.

"We have trusted Peter for a long time. He must have something up his sleeve. Let's let him work his magic, I guess," said John.

Phil left to pick up food. They hadn't eaten since breakfast the day before. Sitting in the office, they waited for the phone to ring. They struggled to eat the food despite the rumbles from their bellies.

An hour and a half after Peter hung up, he called back. "Lads, we have your ship and will be in contact by nightfall."

"Peter, what do you mean?"

"Boys, the best thing that could happen is they transported him by boat. It's a brilliant plan except for one thing." Peter stopped for a dramatic pause.

"Hello, Peter, are you there?"

"Yes, I'm very much here and happy as a pig in shit."

"Peter, we need more details. What the hell is going on?" James asked, excited but upset at the dramatics of Peter.

"Boys, we now have the USN or the United States Navy tracking that very ship you gave me."

"What the hell?" Phil said. Shocked, he said it out loud.

"My brother works in the legal side of the Coast Guard. He works on USN ships in the Caribbean as the LEDET or Coast Guard Law Enforcement. The navy can't just board ships in international waters, but with him on board, they can if they suspect drugs, human trafficking, stuff like that. My brother is deployed right now on the USS Carr a frigate. He spoke to the captain about our little tip. They are steaming towards the boat as we speak. He is working with his bosses onshore to receive the proper paperwork to have a visit, search, and board team ready to go on the ship at sun-up. He will call me before supper to confirm the operation is a go. I am calling in a bunch of favors on Capitol Hill to make this happen. I hope your tip is right."

James broke down and cried. John choked up, and Phil could not believe what he heard.

"So, Peter, the USN is now looking for our boy? I don't believe it but, thank you," said James.

"James, we have worked together for a long time. I would never forgive myself if we lost David. And selfishly, I need David for, well, you know. I will call you once I get confirmation from my brother, Tony."

John hung up the phone and stared at James.

"What the hell just happened?" Phil said.

"You two have a flight to catch," said John.

"Aye John, I'll call you when we arrive."

"Have a good flight and don't worry, I will not sleep until I have David's location and a way to get you to him."

"Call Scott back home. Let him know what is happening. He has a few weapons orders to ship, but we might need his help."

James and Phil headed to the airport. In the meantime, John continued to check with his contacts in Caracas while he waited for Peter to call.

Due to weather, James and Phil didn't leave until six the next morning.

CHAPTER FOUR

Ruslan climbed the ladder. He pulled himself out of the hold and closed the hatch.

Igor waited for him to come out. "Ruslan U.S.A. Navy or Coast Guard," Igor said in Russian to Ruslan. "The captain said they approached overnight. The night watch saw nothing through the fog, but the radar tracked them. They were there when the sun came up. Didn't you see them when you came on deck to go to David? Why didn't you say something?"

"What Navy? Where?" Ruslan asked.

"There, behind us. Look, that big gray ship chasing us. What did you think it was?" Igor yelled. He pointed to the stern of the ship. "We are being followed, you great ape. How did you miss this? How did you not see them?"

"It was very foggy when I came on deck, boss. I couldn't see past the edge of the ship. I headed straight down to deal with the little shit."

Ruslan looked around again, his eyes adjusting to the daylight. He could see a large ship had taken a formation behind the vessel he was on. The fog still hid a clear vision of the ship, but its ghostly silhouette was visible. He could see an inflatable rigid boat skim across the water, loaded with a group of heavily armed men.

"There is a craft heading to board us. They are full of Navy men who might not take kindly to us hiding our guest in the hold. We need to keep the hatch closed. They can't find David," said Igor.

"Yes, leave that to me. Where are Alek and Dmitry?" asked Ruslan.

"They are down in the galley, hiding our weapons. It seems we are not the first contraband the captain has hidden on this ship."

"Are we hiding too?"

"No, the captain said they had eyes on us all night, so they know how many are on board. There is a place for David, but we don't have time to move him. When they come on board, we need to make sure we are hiding the hatch to David. Get some of the crew to sit around it. I have to see the captain again."

"Radio communication, we are being boarded!" The captain yelled from his wheelhouse window. "Be prepared. We are being boarded starboard side. Get the ropes and ladder. No one talks to them, only me."

"Did they give a reason why we are being boarded?" Igor asked.

"Yes, they believe we are running a human trafficking ship. They have all the paperwork from the Coast Guard. They received a tip from somewhere in Caracas. People spotted us onshore when we lifted David onto the deck. We can't refuse. Well, we can, but it won't end well."

Igor turned to Ruslan. "What did I say when we were at the dock? Dmitry will die for this. I told you two we needed to be cleaner about the taxi. Ruslan, keep them away from David or it will be you I will torture to death. Protect our cargo at all costs," said Igor.

Alek and Dmitry came out through the companionway. They looked around and walked to Igor and Ruslan.

"Did you hide our weapons and product?" Igor asked.

"Yes, the captain has some excellent locations on this boat. It gave me a few ideas for later. Unless they bring in some form of x-ray equipment, we should be fine," said Dmitry.

"Listen, everyone remain calm. Let the captain do the talking. Blend in with the regular crew. We are close to American waters. Right now, we have no reason to believe they are looking for David or us. They are working on a tip from shoremen or something. Who knows how many enemies this captain has? Don't talk unless they speak to you, understand?" said Alek. He was a retired Senior Lieutenant from the Soviet Navy and Igor's right-hand man. This wasn't his first time on a ship that was boarded. He had also worked on a boarding team in the Soviet Navy and knew there was no way to stop this team. They would board the ship, either peacefully or with force.

Igor found the captain while the other three blended in with the crew. The South American crew did not match with three tall, pale men. The Russians watched with the others as the inflatable Navy boat made up on the leeward side of their ship. Alek noticed this was not a routine inspection when he saw the amount of firepower held by the Navy seaman.

The owner of the fishing boat, Captain Lyle, met the LEDET, Tony Thompson, once he boarded the ship. Tony shook the captain's hand as the naval team pulled themselves onto the deck. They quickly backed the ship's crew to the port side of the boat. Two of the naval team patted down the crew and instructed them to stand in line, hands on their heads.

"Do you speak English?" Tony asked.

"Yes, English, not well. But I understand. Why are you on my boat?"

"We have a report you are trafficking humans. An eyewitness reported a body being carried onto your boat. If we can go to your wheelhouse, I can show you my documentation for this search. I will need to see all your papers. My crew will search the vessel while we review the paperwork. Please, show me your wheelhouse?"

"Yes, I have nothing to hide, sir."

"Well then, we can do our search and let you get on with the day."

While two of the boarding team stayed with the ship's crew, the other four split into two groups. They instructed the first mate and the lead engineer to escort them during their search of the vessel. One inspection team began their review at the front of the ship, while the other team moved below deck.

The crew and the Russians stood and watched the activity on deck, disguising the hatch and seal to David's hidden location. The team assigned to the deck opened hatches and climbed into the lower holds of the ship's bow. They worked towards the stern of the ship. Once back to the vessel's crew, they gave the "all clear signal" for the bow and the front holding tanks of the cargo ship.

The Naval team that watched the crew lined them up and transferred them to the bow of the ship to allow the inspection team to check the aft deck. Those around David's hatch refused to move. Again, the search team requested all the crew move to the bow, having a mate make the request in Spanish. A few of the crew and the Russians, including Igor, steadfastly refused to move. Yet again, the crew was instructed to move to the front of the ship. The ship's crew did not move. There was one last verbal request, then the gunner's mate spoke into his radio. He removed his sidearm from his holster and lifted it over his head. Pointing his gun towards the sky, he pulled the trigger. The crew dropped to the deck. This time, his voice was loud and annoyed when he commanded them to move to the bow of the ship. He pointed his gun at two of the crew and motioned them to move. The men shuffled to the bow.

One of the ship's crew, in a desperate attempt to escape, ran to the edge of the boat and dove into the ocean. With the confusion on deck, a couple of men made a move to the door that would lead down to the engine room and a hidden stash of weapons. A gun jabbed into the back of one of the defiant men as he pulled on the engine room door. Scattering, the fishing crew tried to attack the search team. The piercing sound of a rifle ended the attempted rebellion against the naval team. They gathered the ship's crew and moved them to the front of the vessel. In English, then Spanish, they were told to lie face down with their hands laced behind their heads.

The gunners' radio came to life. "USS Carr to BT. Can I have a report on the gunshots? Is assistance required? Do you need support? Over."

"Curtis to Carr. No, we had a few heroes. We have the situation under control and put a stop to the mutiny. We are continuing the inspection of the ship. Over."

The pilot of the inflatable boat recovered the man who abandoned ship. Now a guest of the U.S. Navy, he sat on the inflatable, cuffed, and guarded.

"Well boys, looks like we have one more area to check. Why would they hide this one from us, do you think?" said Curtis, in his thick Texas accent. "I guess this is the hold we were waiting for. Twenty bucks says drugs."

"Na, I bet we have an entire load of illegals down there, just like the tip," said Dell, the Second Gunner. Dell swung his leg over the edge and started his descent into the hold. Halfway down the ladder, Dell stopped and looked around. He yelled up to Curtis. "Looks empty, just like the front one. What the—no, wait! There is—Curtis, get Tony, now. Right now!" Dell lowered himself further, then jumped off the ladder when he was four feet from the floor.

"Hello, hello. Sir, I am a member of the U.S. Navy. Hello, can you hear me?"

David sat motionless. Dell pulled off his leather glove and reached for David's neck. While he searched for a pulse, David slowly raised his head and looked at his rescuer. The light from above reflected off the tape covering David's mouth. Dell carefully removed it.

"Sir, can you see or hear me? I am Dell Goldstone of the United States Navy. We're here to help you; we have found you."

David forced a smile. "Thank you." His head dropped to his chest as he blacked out again.

Curtis and Tony climbed down the ladder, followed closely by the second search team. From the deck came the sound of three more splashes of water as more crew tried to escape from their ship.

Tony spoke into his radio, "Tony to Carr. I need a medical team. We have found what we were looking for. Prepare the helo. We might need to fly him to you. Over."

"Copy, medics on route. Helo team is heading to the bird. Over."

Tony turned to David and paused. "Curtis, Dell, stay with him. You two, I want the crew detained, cuffed, and moved to the berthing below. The Sol Matutino is now under the control of the USN."

Dell reviewed David's vitals while Curtis cut the ties to his arms and legs. David didn't move. The team stood around David in disbelief.

"Who the hell is this guy? He must be important. Those guys up there did not want this hold opened," said Dell. "I would have put a paycheck on this operation that it was bad intel. I'm glad we completed the search. He is beat up pretty bad. But he thanked me for being here."

Their radios came to life. "Medic team is ten minutes out; helo is being prepared if the inflatable is not an option. Over."

"10-4." Tony said. "Carr, can you ask the captain to make the call to my brother, please? Let Peter know I have a gift for him. It's damaged but should survive. His intel was spot on. Over."

The ship's crew moved to the berthing area and a Prize Crew arrived with the medics to commandeer the ship and navigate it to the Naval port in Key West.

Dell gave his report to the medics while they rechecked David's vitals. The medic cleared him to be moved off the chair and placed in their rescue basket. Almost three days of being tied up in a chair had stiffened David's body, like rigor mortis had set in. It took the team a half hour of careful work on David's muscles and joints to straighten his arms, back, and legs. Each movement brought him in and out of blackness. There were four large goose eggs on David's head and his shallow breathing was a clue that he had broken ribs.

The team reviewed their options to get David out of the hold. They called off the helo. The medics decided they could transfer David into the inflatable. With the large hold doors opened, they dropped four ropes down.

In the hold, David continued to float between the two states of consciousness. The third time he woke, he fought. He swung his arms and kicked anyone close to him. He pulled out his IV and threw it at a team member. After a flurry of actions, he blacked out again. They tightly strapped him to the basket for his and the crew's safety. Each time he woke, they tried to gather information from him, but with the continuous supply of meds from Igor, David could not tell them his name or how he ended up on the ship. Secured in the basket, they lifted David from his prison. A flood of sunlight and warm moist air covered David. The bright sun woke him again. He struggled to protect his eyes from the brightness. His body ached as he fought the straps that held him. He cried out in pain and frustration as they carefully lay him on the deck.

The medic inserted a second IV in his other hand. They started a saline solution to rehydrate him. As one man worked on the IV, the other checked his vitals. They were faint and hard to track. David woke. His eyes hurt as they adjusted to the bright sun. He looked at Tony. "Help me."

"We are, son. What is your name? Are you David Grant?"

"Let me out. Who are you guys? I don't want to meet Castro." David said with a hoarse, dry voice. "Don't take me to Castro, please."

"Tony is my name. I am Peter's brother. Do you know Peter? Son, stay with me. We are the U.S. Navy. Who are you? Do you know your name?"

"How did you find me?" said David.

"We followed the ship you were on last night. We received a tip from two shoremen. Son, you are going home."

"Where is Igor and, and—" David went silent, back to blackness.

Tony reached for his radio. "Someone on this ship goes by the name Igor, I believe. Sounds Russian to me. Our guest asked for him by name. Over."

"Igor," David said, then was back into the blackness.

Tony gathered his team. He demanded they search the ship again, this time with a lot more attention to details. Identified during the second search, they separated Igor and his team from the crew. The first inflatable took the four Russians, the captain, and the first mate back to the frigate.

They examined David one last time before they lowered him onto the inflatable. The sun was blistering hot on his skin as he rode the inflatable to the frigate.

It took six hours to complete the second search of the fishing vessel. The Prize Crew took command of the ship and pointed it to Key West. The frigate left and charged with David to port. He was stable, but needed a proper hospital. When the USS Carr was within fuel range for the helicopter, the Navy medics and crew flew David to the Naval base in Key West.

CHAPTER FIVE

Key West, Florida

David fought through the fog that covered his mind. Opening his eyes, he looked around the room. The coldness of the off-white paint, the dimmed lights, and the closed curtains over the window played tricks with his eyes. From his left arm ran plastic tubing. Air blew up his nose from more tubes. His upper body was elevated as he lay on a bed surrounded by stainless steel rails. Draped over the bed, wires ran from machines to his body. Rhythmic beeps and bops from the machines played a crazy polka beat in his ringing ears. Shelves of medical supplies helped his slow mind process that he was in a hospital room and bed. The only difference between this room and any other hospital room David had been in was the two large military men dressed in camouflage that stood outside in the hallway. A high back leather chair at the foot of the bed held a man in a white lab coat.

David took a mental inventory of his aches and pains. Head, the throbbing pain and pressure made it feel like his skull would crack open and his brain would splatter on the walls. Arms and legs, strapped to the rails on the bed and little strength to move them. Body and ribs, not good when he breathed. Face mouth and teeth, all hurt. He moved his jaw to make sure it wasn't wired shut.

"Hello. How do you feel? I am Doctor Pine. Don't try to move, please. You are in Key West, Florida. At the naval hospital, to be exact. You are under the care of the U.S. government and military. You have had a rough few days, but my partner and I have been working to put Humpty Dumpty back together," he said with a firm, caring voice.

David jumped a little in the bed. The constant ringing in his ears made it hard to hear the doctor clearly. He slowly nodded at the question.

Doctor Pine stood beside David. "Don't move too much. You have four cracked ribs and one broken rib. But you are safe. You are under my care. We are on a Navy base in Key West. We rescued you from a ship yesterday. You are safe. Do you remember that? Do you remember being rescued?"

He watched the monitor on the other side of David's bed. David's heart rate slowed back to a resting pace. "I need some information from you. I will keep the questions simple, yes or no, if possible. Let's start with a simple one. Do you know your name?"

David stared at the doctor. He searched his mind for an answer. *Name, what is my name?* He thought. He looked at his cuffed wrists and shook them.

Through the fog and blankness, he spoke slowly, "Daaavvviiiid, David is my name. Why am I—I can't think of the word—locked up?"

"Hello, David. You let me know if you need a break. I locked you up because you were floating in and out of consciousness. Sometimes, like on the ship, you get violent. You broke a lieutenant's nose. But that is for later. I can let you out now that you are talking. Let me just finish my questions, then I will get the keys. What happened to you? I don't expect you to know any of these answers. It's okay, don't worry."

"No, I don't know."

"Your brain is swollen. If you need to sleep, then just lay back down. We can continue this conversation later."

"Last name, David. David is my name. Where am I?"

"David, I just told you that. You are in Key West." Doctor Pine wrote a note on his clipboard. "David, you are showing signs of short-term memory loss. That is normal. We see it with soldiers after an explosion. Again, ask as many questions as you want. You are safe."

Doctor Pine reviewed all of David's monitors. "Okay David, I am going to ask again. What is your name?"

"David."

"David what?"

"David—David—Grant."

"Good, good. Where are you?"

"Umm, I know this, lock west."

"Good, David. You are in Key West, but you associated key with a lock. That is particularly good. Okay, one more question, then you need to rest and I will remain with you. But I have to ask, someone cut off your ring finger and sewed it back on, either a terrible doctor or someone that had no clue what they were doing. I remember hearing years ago, while they stationed me in Germany, of an old ritual. The story told to me was there are a few marked men on the planet that have their fingers cut off and replaced as a sign of circumcision to the gods of chaos. With the way we found you and the people that had you, it almost makes sense. But it was just a crazy myth I was told at a bar. Does any of that ring a bell?"

David lay his head down; his neck couldn't hold it up any longer. He stared at the ceiling tiles, the reverse of night. Instead of a blackness with lights poking through, he looked at a sky of white with black darkness breaking through.

"David, just nod if what I said made sense. Also, there is a strange scar on the inside of your thigh. I almost didn't see it when I examined you. It's a strange place for a scar if it is a scar. It almost looks like a tattoo, but I can't confirm that."

"How did I get here? And where is here? Are you going to help me or kill me?"

"David, please, focus. Again, I have some questions; can you think of a phone number, where you came from or why you were on that ship? They only gave me medical information from the medics on the ship."

David continued to stare at the negative of a night sky above him. His mind was blank and muddled. Thoughts and answers appeared but never clearly and never long enough to allow him to say what he was thinking.

"David, it's okay if you don't know. You have been through a lot. Go to sleep, I'll be here. If you wake and I'm not around, Doctor Jacobs will attend to you. She is my partner and is incredibly good with brain injuries. Okay, David? You are safe now. I don't know who, but someone has been contacted about you. I am just trying to assess the brain damage."

"Thank you, doctor. Can I go home soon?"

Doctor Pine smiled at him. "You will go home, David. Like I said, they gave me limited information about you. They told me to keep your location quiet, but I think there must be someone back home worried you are missing. Together, we need to figure out who those people are. I think the crew on the ship contacted your handler. I want to talk to your family."

"Wait—wait—yes, no, it's gone. No wait, the mark on—mark on leg—black light, a black light. I got with Granda. Granda did it. Black light—I think. It's a phone. It's there so I—so I—be able to call home if something happened. What happened again? Granda made me get it when I started to work. Top secret technology from somewhere. Never mind, he is dead. He gave me my knife. Where is it? Take a black light, look again. Call, please. Cana—" David moved and squirmed on the bed. "LET ME OUT OF THESE FUCKING CUFFS!"

A guard entered the room. He watched David fight against his cuffs and shackles.

"Conner, we're fine here. Go see what you can do about finding a black light. There must be one on the base somewhere. Bring it back right away. I don't care if you need one hundred people looking. Bring me a black light now!"

David let out a breath and relaxed his body. He was exhausted. His brain, body, and face hurt from the conversation.

"David, good job. That was incredibly smart of your granda. I am going to give you a little something in your IV. It will help you sleep."

"No, NO!" David fought with his bindings. "No more poison. I need to think." The rattling of his cuffs on the metal bed rails hurt his head. He relaxed and cried. "Please, please, no more medicine. Please let me go. I want to go home."

"David, I want you to sleep. Your brain and body need to rest. You might not think about it, but you have done plenty. I will get the information from the tattoo and get your family here. A black light tattoo, who would have thought."

"Granda and his friend in, in—"

"David, you are okay. I will do nothing to hurt you. I will give you half a dose. It will help you sleep. I will get a black light and call the number. Either I or Doctor Jacobs will wake you in twelve hours. Hopefully, we can give you some answers and you will give us some more."

"Doc, one more thing. How did I get here?"

"David, you need to rest. I promise when you wake and are feeling better, I'll bring you the team that brought you here. It's one hell of a story from the parts I have been told. Please relax and sleep. I hope I can call your family to talk to them."

The doctor pressed a syringe into the Y-port of David's IV and discharged the chemical. David closed his eyes and slept.

CHAPTER SIX

Guelph, Ontario

John had dozed off at his desk with his head cradled in his arms. The ringing of his phone woke him. "John here."

"Hello? Who am I speaking to?" the voice on the phone asked.

"Hello, you're talking to John. How can I help you?"

"John, do you know a David Grant?"

"What? Yes, I do. Who is this? What do you know about David?"

"Sir, are you related to David?"

"Yes, I'm like a second father to him. Who are you? Do you have my boy?" John was alone in the office. He needed someone to call his team of Israelis in Toronto to have the phone traced.

"Okay, John, I'll take your word for it. I will likely get moved to Alaska for what I am doing, but just hear me out. I was told not to contact any of David's family. I don't want to be on the phone too long, so I will skip the details. You probably have a million questions. But unfortunately, I don't have the time to answer them right now."

"What are you trying to tell me? Is David okay? He is alive?"

"I am Doctor Pine and David is under my care. The USN brought him to the base at Key West. I have been taking care of him. He is in rough shape, but I have him stabilized, and he will live. We just had a wonderful talk. Can you get here to see him?"

"What? You have him and the USN rescued him? Who told you not to talk to his family?"

"I don't know their names, sorry. I was told to treat him and get him healthy. Once I thought he was healthy enough to move, I was to call a, hold on," John heard papers being shuffled, "A Peter, Peter Thompson. That's all I have and a phone number."

"Let me guess, a Washington government number. To confirm you are who you say, what are the last four numbers of the phone number?"

"Yes, sir, I understand. The numbers are, 1271."

"Well, that confirms you are legitimate. His father is on a flight to Venezuela; I'll tell him the good news when he lands. Thank you for this. I can't believe Peter would keep this from me. Okay, we will get there. Thank you. Whatever you need, we will give you. If you lose your job, we will help you. I'll give Peter a call and chat with him."

"Okay, I will call you when my shift ends at this number. I'll get more details from you about him and about his father arriving. I should be able to talk more too. I'm staying by his side twelve hours a day and my partner switches with me. He is someone special from what I can gather. Oh, by the way, the tattoo, fucking brilliant. I mean amazing. Luckily when David came to, he remembered it needed a black light. I should get back to David. I will quietly let him know his family is on their way. He will be fine. When I call later, I will have time to get into the details of his injuries."

"Thank you," John said and hung up.

John got up and paced around his office. He needed to call Peter, but didn't know how to discuss his call with the doctor.

John dialed Peter's office and waited for him to pick up.

"Peter, any word on David? Did your brother find him on the ship? It has been twelve hours since they were to board the ship."

"John, how are you? I, well, I just got off the phone with— Yes John, we found David. With everything going on, I guess I didn't call you. He is in awful shape. The medical team doesn't think he'll survive his injuries. I was just planning to fly up to Guelph to talk to you about it."

"That's strange Peter, I just spoke to the doctor at the naval base. He seems to think he will recover."

"What? Who did you talk to? His doctor? How? Well, yes, that was what I was going to say. I was giving you the report from my brother Tony when they found him. But yes, our medical team did amazing things when they got him on shore. The doctor contacted you? Good, good. Is James there?"

"No, he isn't. He's on a flight to Venezuela. They need to refuel at Grand Bahama, and he's calling me then."

"Oh, good. Hold on."

After a couple minutes, "John, I'll plan to meet him there and bring him to David. Sorry about the confusion. There's a lot going on in the office. Looks like the war drums are sounding again. John, I'm sorry I didn't call sooner. This is good news, though."

"Peter, we go way back, and I know how busy things are. But how would you forget to tell us this? The good news is we have David."

"I'll call you back in a couple of hours with the flight arrangements."

"Please do Peter, I look forward to meeting his medical team. Especially the doctor who called me. I assume he will be there to meet us?"

"I hope so John, they have medical personnel coming and going, you know, on and offshore work in the navy."

"Peter, let me be clear. I am saying you pull strings or whatever is needed to make sure I meet that doctor," John said and hung up.

●   ●   ●

A category three hurricane marched northwest, determined to impact the South Carolina coast and the lives that lived along it. The plane, with James and Phil on board, had to divert around the massive cloud cluster created by the hurricane. It delayed the flight's already late schedule. James and Phil slept most of the flight. The stress of David missing, the knowledge they likely would not sleep until they found him, and the situation they might happen upon when they found him all ran through James' head as he dozed off. The plane landed on the island of Grand Bahama, on fumes.

James was the first off the plane in search of a pay phone. He entered the airport terminal, pushed his way through excited travelers ready to start their vacations, and located a bank of pay phones. Plunging into the crowd, he waited for an available phone. A lady hung up as James stepped behind her. He grabbed the receiver before the person next in line had a chance and dropped a handful of coins into the phone. The phone rang four, five and a sixth time.

"Come on John, answer," James said to the wall.

"Hello, hello," said John. The phone reception was poor. John sounded far away and there was a repeat to the line.

"John, I can hardly hear you. It's James. Have you heard anything? John, can you hear me?"

"James, we got him. Not in the best of shape, but we got him. He's alive. James, we got him!"

James teared up as another man pushed into his space to use the phone beside him. He took in a deep breath. "Where is he? How can I get to him?"

"James, are you there? James?"

"Yes, I can hear you, John. Where is he?"

"All arranged James. Sit tight. Get Phil off the plane and send it on for its next leg of the trip, then home. I canceled the other plane for you. Peter has a plane, but because of the hurricane it's grounded for three hours. He will pick you up this afternoon. They are coming to you, James."

"To go where?"

"Back to the States. They have him, James! The Navy got him, of all things, the Navy! Peter's brother got him and Igor. I think we will want to chat with Igor and his team once we see to David, if you know what I mean. He is on the Naval base in Key West. He's in rough shape, but he is getting all the medical attention he needs. So, a jet will land there later. Go grab some food, then call me back. Peter said he needed a couple of hours to finalize the flight path and a few other things. They got him. I'm getting a flight down right away. Should we bring Lizzy or leave her here?"

"I didn't even tell her about me leaving. No, leave her there. I'll take that beating later. I don't think the U.S. navy is ready to handle David's mother just yet."

"James, there is more, but we can talk about it when we are together. Until then, keep your eyes open and only trust a Doctor Pine. If he is not there, demand to see him. I have told Peter we all expect to meet him."

"Okay, this sounds interesting. I'll grab Phil. Thanks John. See you shortly."

They hung up. James turned and drove his shoulder into the gentleman who bumped him earlier as he headed back to his plane.

James announced the good news to Phil and the crew. With their belongings in hand, they disembarked from the plane.

With the plane back in the air, James and Phil waited inside the terminal for their next flight to arrive. In a bar, they discussed the conversation James had with John. Neither one of them could believe the news. They had both secretly, like John, assumed they would never see David again.

James checked his watch. "I will call home and see what your dad has found out."

Phil watching a soccer game on the television, nodded.

Ten minutes later, James returned to the bar. Phil could see by the look on James' face the call had gone well.

"All good, James?"

"Yes. Peter will pick us up in four hours at the same place we got off our plane."

Four hours later, right on schedule, a United States government plane landed and parked just as John had said. James and Phil boarded the plane, where Peter and Tony greeted them.

Back in the air, Peter said, "This is my brother Tony. He led David's rescue."

James and Phil both shook his hand.

"Okay, we have some time to talk. First, do you want a drink or something to eat?" asked Peter.

"Peter, I don't want anything but the updates you better have for us," said James.

"Yeah, spill it Peter," said Phil.

"I guess it thrilled you guys when Peter called to say we had your son?" asked Tony.

"Yes, we were shocked," said James as he glared at Peter. "It wasn't Peter that told us. A doctor called the office in Guelph. What the hell happened? How is David?" asked James.

"David is okay. He has some issues," said Tony.

"What issues?" said Phil.

"When we found him, he was beat up pretty bad, real bad," said Tony.

"He is under good care now, James. We took care of him. We ran scans, did blood work, the full monty, so to say. He is recovering and will be fine," Peter said, refusing to meet their eyes. "He has severe brain trauma. There is swelling of his brain and some memory loss, but both are improving. He has four cracked ribs and one broken rib." Peter scanned his notes on the clipboard. "Sorry, not sure which one it was. It was close to puncturing his lung and heart. If they had transported him without a full triage of his situation, he would not have survived the transfer to our ship."

"What? What happened?"

"Let me finish the rundown of injuries, then we can get to that. He has ringing in his ears, severe enough to hinder his hearing, but it should go away as the brain swelling goes down. Let me see, obviously with what I told you, he has cuts and scrapes, oh a broken nose, again according to the report. Swelling and blackness around his right eye and bruises on his arms and legs. Plus, the one thing we used to identify him, a tattoo on his inner leg. It was coded, but he had enough sense to tell us the meaning. We might do that with our higher risk agents. We are working on a microchip but a tattoo, rather good idea. Especially where it was on his inside leg."

"So, he's awake?"

"Yes. We are trying to let him sleep to let his brain reset, but when he is awake, we have him talking and eating. He is using the washroom on his own and, no longer pissing blood, medical term, I believe. We have him on pain meds through his IV. That is all I have on his condition. Tony here can debrief you on what they did."

"First, let me say thank you for finding him. You probably didn't know he was lost," James said.

"It's my privilege, sir. It sounds like your family has quite the history intertwined with military service and assistance, so thank you. Now for our part in this. We were on patrol of the Caribbean Sea, regular patrol. Looking for vessels not running the proper lights or radar, low-flying planes, or rafts full of people. As you are aware, that area has creative drug runners and human traffickers moving their supplies to the States. The day before we boarded the vessel David was on, Peter called me and asked if we could locate the Sol Matutino. The information he gave me was enough for us to take it as a serious kidnapping. Plus, he is my older brother. How could I say no?"

"Thank you, Peter," said James.

"With the name of the vessel, we located it through one of our destroyers that has been outfitted with new, secret technology. While I was working my channels on the ship and with Southern Naval Command in Mayport to receive permission to send a boarding team, Peter was burning up his phone trying to secure the proper documentation and permissions from his bosses in the upper levels of our government. I am not sure who gave the go ahead, but I believe they brought this issue to the Vice President?"

"Yes, yes, it was. Tony, once you get to know this family, you will understand. They are incredibly good at their job, but they don't accept no as an answer. If I was to tell them that I didn't turn over every stone, well, I would be under a big one, myself." He laughed at his comment but knew there was truth to what he said.

Tony methodically reviewed the boarding and search procedures, from how he picked the team to what they found when they stepped on the Sol Matutino. He noted the crew's reaction and how his team found David and four Russians.

"Was one of them an Igor?" James asked.

"We will get to that," said Peter.

"With David on the Carr, our medical team stitched him up, popped his shoulder back in place, then hooked him up to our machines. Through his IV, he was hydrated and loaded with nutrients."

Phil and James both sat in silence with their mouths wide open.

Tony asked. "I would love to know how David and Igor ended up on a ship together. Well, I know how, but what led up to that moment."

Peter went to the cockpit, then returned. "We have forty-five minutes until we land. The back story to get you caught up will take a lot longer than that and would be better over a few beers."

"Oh, more CIA top secret, need to know, stories?" said Tony, grinning.

"So, what about the ship's crew? Where are they? Who were they? And most importantly, when can I meet them?" asked James.

Peter and Tony looked at each other.

"Well, that's a story in itself. Let me grab food from the galley. Do you two want anything?"

"I would love a pop," said Phil.

"Whatever is back there will be fine," James said.

Peter headed to the rear of the plane. After a few minutes, he returned with drinks and finger foods. "Let's eat, then we can talk about the crew," said Peter.

They downed their food while Tony and Peter talked about growing up together, how they became employees of Uncle Sam and where Tony hoped to be in the future. Once they ate, the food and the plates returned to the galley, they returned to the issue at hand.

"Okay, the crew," said Phil.

"This is top secret knowledge, so it goes to your team and no further," said Peter.

"Aye," said James.

"Understand," said Phil.

"Our Navy took control of the ship. It should arrive in Key West later today with a Naval escort. They detained the crew on the ship and have them under guard. We interviewed them and found the crew were South American workers that had no real ties to David being on board. They use the ship primarily as a fishing vessel, working around many islands in the Bahamas and Caribbean. So, their stories checked out. There were nine of them on the ship, all documented and with proven jobs, mostly long-term employees. They are still in custody but will, after a second interrogation, be released and flown home. When we identified four Russians, we took them to the USS Carr in custody. We also transferred the captain and the first mate to our vessel. We will interrogate them. The U.S. government will not release them until they have answered all our questions. Now for the interesting part, the four Russians; these four gentlemen were the ones that were babysitting David."

"I want all their names and information. Not just Igor's," interrupted James.

"Oh, don't worry. Let's just say your team is still on the clock," said Peter. "The only identification we found on them were fake passports issued from Greece. Once we did proper background checks, we found none of the passports were real."

"So, how did you identify them?"

"Well, the Russian accents were the first giveaway. David asked for an Igor when he was being transported. Sure enough, once we began the interrogation, we learned their story. John's theories were all correct. Once Tony sent their photos, my team, in a matter of minutes, were able to get their real names. They are demanding lawyers and diplomatic immunity. All the same shit we hear from most people that become guests of the government." Peter fastened his seat belt. "Buckle up, we are starting our approach. Once my bosses heard of this operation, we had to contact the Russian embassy. The Russians we found are still in custody, but there is substantial pressure from above to release them to their consulate. The Russians called to have them released into their custody. There are two officials and four lawyers in discussions right now. We might only have them for a brief time. Seems we have someone in our ranks who is also talking. I might have some rats in my office. I will need that dealt with once we have the proper information."

"Don't worry, time and place, I will do it myself if it comes to that," said Phil. "Did anyone ever locate Sergio, or did he make it to Iraq?"

"He is safe and sound in Iraq, with his new sugar daddy, a minister in Saddam's government," said Peter.

James turned his seat to face forward. With all this information, his primary concern was still to see his son and make sure he was safe. He was also looking forward to hearing from John about his concern.

CHAPTER SEVEN

James burst out of the elevator on the fifth floor of the hospital. Phil, Peter, and Tony were close behind. He ran down the hallway. He didn't need to look for a room number; the two large military police officers in front of a door were evidence enough to where David was. The one MP reached for his sidearm as James quickly approached.

"Sir, you cannot ent—," the MP began.

"It's okay, let him in. We are all going in," Tony said.

The MPs looked and came to attention immediately. James opened the door with Phil on his heels.

"I will give you a couple minutes," said Peter. He retreated to the far corner of the room.

Tony continued down the hall to the nurse's station and asked for David's doctor.

Inside the room, James leaned over the side of his son's bed while Phil went to the far side. They both rubbed his arms, then stood and watched him sleep.

"David, David, it's Dad, I'm here. David, Dad, and Phil are here. John will be here soon."

"James, I'll go find a doctor to see what's going on," said Peter.

"Yeah, bring him in here. We need to know what is wrong," said Phil.

David's eyes fluttered open. Reaching for Phil's arm, he said, "No, stay. Doc will be here soon enough. Just give me a minute. Doc never leaves except to get me meds or make a phone call. Just hold on. It takes a few minutes for my brain to start back up."

"Okay, son, I was so scared. Thank God you're okay," said James.

"Dad, I'm fine, just a couple of bruises and a headache," David said. "Granda's tattoo worked, I guess. It's so good to see you two. Is Mom coming with John?"

"No, we haven't told her yet. I don't need to be lying beside you, son. We could fill the floor with injured people if she knew we had lost you. When we left home, we were heading to Venezuela to search for you. John stayed behind burning up the phone lines, trying to get any information."

"Wow, all alert on this one, I see. Can I get a drink of water? My mouth is dry."

Phil poured the water into a plastic tumbler and tried to put it to David's lips. "Bud, I'm a bit beat up, but I can drink my own water," David said.

"Right, sorry," said Phil. "So how bad are you?"

Tony, Peter, and Doctor Pine walked in and heard Phil ask his question. "I can answer that, David," said the doctor. "Hello, I am Doctor Pine."

"James, David's father." He reached out and shook the doctor's hand.

"Phil, his handler, and best friend, most of the time."

"David is resilient, to be sure. Tough lineage, I would say. I'm optimistic David will make a full recovery. Either here or back home. He has internal issues, but they are all healing. Once I feel he is close to having those issues cleaned up, I'll give you the option of taking him home. The U.S. government will gladly take him on one of our jets. He has broken and cracked ribs and a bunch of cuts and scrapes. My biggest concern is the brain issues. He suffered multiple severe concussions. Real bad. His brain is almost back to normal size. And he is working through it. Toxicology shows they drugged him, a lot, at some point. That is mostly out of his blood. My team and I believe he will fully recover from all his injuries. We are lucky we found him when we did."

"Thank you doctor," said James. "Could we have a few minutes alone to talk?"

"Yes, of course. I need to do a couple of tests, but I can come back in fifteen minutes. I will check on my two other patients in the meantime."

"Thank you," said Phil.

Everyone left the three men alone. Phil stood by David's head while James looked out the window.

"You have a marvelous view from here. When John arrives, we will do a debrief. Until then, just relax and rest. Did you say much about the job you were on?"

"Not that I know about, but honestly Dad, I was in and out of it. I'm pretty sure we're safe here. They're all military and from what the other doctor told me, they both carry a high clearance with the government and military. They have been great too. What have you guys found out about my assignment?"

"Not much," said Phil. "We focused on finding you. Sergio is in Iraq. The government is holding Igor, and the CIA might have dirty agents. The doctor was the one who reached out to us about your location, not Peter."

"So just another day on the job, I guess," said David. "So, are we telling Mom? I guess she knows I'm on an assignment. She doesn't know how long it was to last or where it was."

"She'll just worry if we do," said his dad.

"I can call her and tell her I'm going home to see Uncle Scott for a bit. She might ask some questions, but we all know she won't dig too deep."

"Aye, we can do that. We can call her later. Once we talk to Scott and John."

"Oh, are Scott and John coming here? Where are we?"

Phil looked at James, then at David.

"You might still have some memory loss, David. We already told you that."

David laughed. "Just seeing if you guys are keeping up. I'm going to have a nap if you guys don't mind. I go in small sprints, it seems. Seeing you two is great. But I need another nap."

"Of course. Son, we'll talk to the doctor some more. I want to get information about the team that found you. I think we have bills to pay there. We will let the medical staff do their thing and wait for John to arrive. We'll be back in a few hours, with John."

"Okay, Dad. I'm so happy to see you guys. I never thought I ever would again. I thought for sure I would arrive in Cuba, then Russia, and then a shallow grave. Granda was watching out for me, for sure. I'll see you when you come back. Tell the doctor no sleep meds this round. I want to be alert when we have our talk. I love you two," said David.

Before long, David dozed off and dreamed. His dreams had been very vivid since the head injury. In this dream, he was back in time on a job with his grandfather, Kenton, in Ireland.

• • •

John's flight landed at 3 p.m. Outside the arrivals door, Peter waited for him in a rental car. The passenger door opened, and John slipped into the vehicle.

"No luggage?" Peter asked.

"What the fuck are you up to, Peter? I didn't want to probe too deep over the phone, but I need some answers from you."

"John, I couldn't say much on the phone. You have every right to be angry. I think the only thing that kept James from killing me and my brother on the plane was he didn't know where David was on the Naval base."

"Peter, skip the bullshit. I want answers. Right now, our professional relationship is in jeopardy, as is your life. Why did you keep finding David from me? What were you going to do with him?" John rolled his window down. "Peter, we have worked together for a long time. I have never doubted you or considered you a threat. But this, this has taken all my trust away. You will have one opportunity to explain yourself. At that point, we will need to reassess our business and personal relationship."

"John, the hospital is a couple of minutes away. But believe me, you have no reason to doubt our relationships. I explained some of it to James and Phil. Believe me, John, I would never do anything to betray your trust. I had my reasons to hide David. I believe I have dirty agents in my group. They might be after your family. I wasn't sure if someone bugged the phone in my office. I was planning to fly to Guelph to talk. Something is not right. Once I find out who it is, I will need that person disposed of. We can get into the details now, or you can go see David. It's up to you."

"I am glad you told me that, Peter. I knew you were stressed, and I'm sorry for doubting you. We are both stressed and emotional right now," said John.

The car pulled into the hospital parking lot and John jumped out. "David is what matters right now. We can talk later."

• • •

Doctor Pine reserved a meeting room down the hallway from David's room. The medical staff used the room to update or console family members of patients. While David was a patient, the team could use it to meet, conduct business, and rest. James and Phil waited in the room for John.

Peter and John entered the room and joined Phil and James at the round table. Before everyone could settle in their seats, Peter's pager chirped. He slipped the pager from his belt and read the text.

"I have to go. I now have a meeting to attend about our Russian friends. Why don't we meet back in David's room at nine tomorrow morning and begin the debrief? I think I'll have some answers after this meeting. My concern is we are running out of time. The Russian embassy has stepped up their demands for their men's release. You guys settle in, spend some time with David, and get some sleep."

"Agreed," said John. "I want to see David and talk to my partners about our next steps. Peter, I assume Doctor Pine is available to talk?"

"I will send him in, John."

"Thank you. We will see you in the morning."

The trio went to David's room and stood around David, who was sleeping. As John stood beside David, thoughts of betrayal played in his mind. *When was the last time I talked to Igor? Who in the CIA is out to get us?*

•　　•　　•

A nurse entered the room with a couple of bags of saline to add to David's IV pole.

"Another guest? This kid is extremely popular or very wanted."

"Popular and family," said Phil. "This is my dad, John. He was delayed in getting here."

"Nice to meet you, John. I am Annabelle, but people call me Annie. I'm one of only a few people taking care of David. Doctor Pine will be in shortly to see David and answer any more questions you all have. Should I expect anyone else to arrive? Would David's mom be coming too?"

James looked at John. "No, she's stuck at home. Maybe later in the week if he isn't released."

"Okay, you guys can show John around the place when you're ready."

She walked to the head of David's bed and woke him. "David, time for some blood work and your regular questions. She asked David a series of questions, took a vial of blood and replaced the saline bags with the new ones. She moved David's bed up a couple of inches and adjusted his coverings so he could comfortably see his guests.

"Nice boy, good manners, not sure what he did to deserve the beating he took." She looked at the others. "Not the talking type, I see. Well, he'll recover. Don't stress about it. Time heals all things at that age." She winked at John and left the room.

They sat with David until the moon was the brightest light in the sky. No one talked. When David slept, they just sat and looked at him. When he was awake, he asked about his mom, sister, Igor and when he could leave. None of them wanted to call Elizabeth and explain David's situation, but they all knew one of them, James, should.

James stood. "I'll call Scott, then let's find somewhere to eat."

In their meeting room, James told Scott that David was alive. After thirty minutes on the phone, he hung up, gathered Phil and John, and they headed out to find a place for supper.

A Denny's restaurant was a five-minute walk from the hospital. John tipped the server three hundred dollars to keep her section closed while they were there. He didn't want her to come to the table unless she was serving food or drinks. James updated John with the information the doctor had told him, and the concerns Peter had about a leak in the agency.

With an arm full of plates, the server approached the table. Everyone went silent. She dispersed the meals to the hungry men and left. With his fork in hand, John told James and Phil how relieved he was to hear that Peter had a potential leak. His thoughts that Peter had turned against The Family were silenced, thankfully. They completed their debrief and meal, then headed back to the hospital so they could take shifts watching over David.

John and James took the first watch beside David's bed while he continued to sleep.

"So, what's the plan now? Do we hunt those fuckin' Russians?" said James.

"I hope we get some answers on Igor in the morning. I want him and the other three brought home with us. He doesn't get to do this a year after your dad dies and live to talk about it," said John.

"Aye, I just hope they don't release them all to the embassy. And here we sit in this situation while Sergio is living it up in Iraq, still wanted alive, or dead now. Remember when they wanted me dead or alive?" said James.

"I believe it was more than once, James. You were a full-time job for your father and me when you were David's age."

"Now look, we have our own sons in the business. We have plenty of work coming up. I'll have to do most of it. Scott will need to pick up some extra work, too."

"Yes, but we found David. That's what counts. The tattoo worked, but there is better technology, according to Peter. He told me they can place a microchip under his skin. That way, their satellites can track him anywhere above ground. They say it's safe. They say that, I don't. But they also have car phones that don't need a car. He says everyone will have one by the year 2000. We can have ours now. It might not be a bad idea; he is trying to get a few released for us. But I don't trust it. The method of pen and paper, in my mind, is still the most secure."

"Let's head to our room. Phil can take watch till the morning. David doesn't need to wake to us chatting about Star Trek technology," said James.

•   •   •

Phil sat in David's room. He had a crossword magazine on his lap but couldn't concentrate on the clues. He usually knocked off a large crossword in less than an hour, but his mind just didn't want to work through those riddles while he sat across from his best friend and all their additional problems.

Rousing, David sat up in his bed and smiled at Phil. Phil smiled back as he unconsciously tapped his pen on the armrest of his chair.

"You sound like a herd of elephants trying to be quiet. Morning, Phil, how are things out there?"

"I thought you would still be sleeping. Sorry, I guess the tapping woke you. Things are fine. Doctor said you had a good night. Dad and John are in the other room. I'll let them know you are awake."

David lay back down. "No, don't wake them. I'm so glad to see you, Phil. Sitting in the bottom of the boat, I thought we would never bike together again."

"Dude, I was having a tough time holding it together. When you were late calling in, this was the last thing I was thinking about."

"I think we are going to be busy when we get home. There was this one guy on the boat. Ruslan, I want him. Like Alf wanted cats," said David.

James entered the room with John trailing behind. "Morning. David, you are awake?" said James.

"Morning Dad. John, you came down too?" asked David. "Oh, that's right. We talked yesterday. Duh—memory is still a bit off. I hope I remember all our lessons from when we were kids. Imagine going to my first job and forgetting my knife, or worse yet, forgetting how to use it."

"I don't think you need to worry about that. We keep those skills deep down in our brains," said James.

"Hello, son. How are you? I hear you are healing and improving," said John.

"So they tell me anyway," said David. "I need to get out of here and find those assholes. I have some unfinished business to do. Did anyone find my knife?"

"We had all your stuff sent to the office. A new contact in Caracas Police returned it. It should be there today. I'll have Frank make sure it's part of the inventory that gets returned."

"Do you feel like talking now? Peter will be here around nine to review where we are with our Russian friends. Until then, we have our own business to discuss, and how we handle your mother," said James.

"Sure. I feel better every time I wake up. I don't remember much. They kept me heavily drugged. I would like to sit in a chair for a while. Could someone help me? And when Peter arrives, can we do the meeting in your room? I would love to walk down the hallway for a change of scenery. As for Mom, dad I think you should call."

The team had an hour before Peter would arrive. They discussed the last few days, the next few days and how they would handle Peter, Igor, and the team that rescued David.

Peter knocked on the door, then entered with breakfast. "Oh wow. You're out of bed. That's progress, David."

"Yes, everything still hurts, but I need to get vertical at some point. Thanks for coming back."

"I brought coffee, English muffins and donuts for everyone, especially you, David. I assume you're already sick of hospital food. We can use the meeting room down the hallway. I figured we could eat and talk there. I have a wheelchair coming for you, David."

"Thank you. It's funny no matter the quality of the hospital, just like airlines, the food is always shit. No need for the wheelchair. I will walk. It has only been a few days, but I can see my legs already getting smaller. I can't have Phil beat me up the hills around home on our bikes," David said, looking at Phil and his legs.

The group headed to the meeting room. David dragged his IV bag on the pole as his bare bum hung out of the hospital gown.

"You're supposed to keep your underwear on, David. I haven't seen that bare butt since you got a good hiding when you were eight," said James. The comment caused the group to break out into full belly laughs.

"Yeah, you can probably see the marks," said David. "Just another spanking to prepare me for things like what I went through a couple of days ago."

"Well, little boys should not be running through the shop with a loaded gun, even when they are playing cowboys and Indians with their friends," said John.

Phil looked at David and they both laughed harder.

"Oh, stop. Don't make me laugh. It hurts too much," David said. He wrapped his free arm around his ribs.

James helped David sit in a lounge chair with pillows behind him. Everyone had food and coffee while they chatted about the last few days, the emotional roller coaster of losing David, and the things they wanted to do to Igor.

Peter sat quietly. He listened to their concerns. With most of the food gone, he spoke. "I wish I wasn't the one to bring this news to this group. Please remember, I'm only the lowly messenger. Never shoot the messenger, right?"

"We don't want to shoot anyone. We prefer our own hands. Then you know the job is done right," said James as he smiled at David.

"Rule number one from Granda," said David.

"Hilarious, you guys. Anyone else want to take a stab at me?" said Peter.

The room burst out in laughter. David spit out his mouthful of coffee on the floor.

"All right. Now for the unpleasant news. I checked in with my bosses last night and again this morning before I came here to see what was happening with the crew and our Russian friends." Peter cleared his throat. "We have released them."

"What?" said John. "How were they released so suddenly and weren't they here on the military base as spies against the country?"

"Yes, you're right on both accounts. It seems last night around 3 a.m. a team flew in from the Russian embassy with more lawyers. After a couple of hours of discussions, they released all the Russians to the consulate members. The agreed terms were, transport them to their embassy in Washington and have them off U.S. soil and back to Russia within forty-eight hours."

"What? This guy has his entire team with him. How could we just let them go? How does that team have diplomatic immunity? Why? He kidnapped me. Doesn't that count for anything? How did his people even know they were in custody?"

"Remember, do not shoot, strangle or knife the messenger. I brought you food, remember that. This just proves I have someone dirty in my office. We will need that handled once we identify him. As James knows, I suspected this. I hate to admit it, but this is the proof I needed. Yes, I was the one who told the doctors not to call you guys. I was hoping whoever was my rat would make a call to have David taken out here in the hospital. Guys, I am sorry, I should have told you and David. I shouldn't have used you as a pawn."

"Okay, so we have multiple problems, the way I see it. Bad agents, Igor and his team heading home, and Sergio in Iraq with information that could collapse western governments and all their connections, including all of us sitting here. Maybe I'll take some of the meds David gets and try to sleep through this one," said James.

"Yes, I know. We have a busy couple of months ahead of us. Back to Igor and his team. They have diplomatic immunity. Seems they picked up jobs working for the Russian government on the ship. Russia knows what Igor has done and what he does. They still wanted him home. Maybe they wanted to be there when they put him down. There is no way they want him rotting in one of our prisons. I assume their biggest fear would be we trade information for freedom. He has plenty of it packed away in his memory. They should be at the embassy now, I guess, and should be on a plane by tomorrow morning. I am sorry, we all are. We know what this guy has done and what we need done to him. I think there will be other opportunities to get our hands on him. A guy like that doesn't just sit in a rocking chair on a porch."

"Well, I guess this also proves his country still needs him around," said John.

"Yeah. So, we know he is still a threat to us. I guess we'll have to deal with this one. I assume he will continue to move weapons, people, and drugs for them."

"What about Sergio? Any news there?" asked Phil.

"He obviously released some intelligence once he arrived in Iraq. Some of our assets in Europe and Asia are now compromised. We sent cryptic messages out to all our field agents to be aware of their surroundings. We pulled six teams back to embassies or friendly countries. Sergio needs to be dealt with, if anyone can find him. Losing him has set us and others back years. While we wait for the air to clear on this matter, there is one job we could use The Family for if you guys are ready. It doesn't need to be done for a few weeks. We need time to prepare. David, you'll have to sit this one out, I think. You still need time to heal. Why don't you guys get David home and take a few weeks off. I will get the job package sent to you, John."

"Okay, so I have a lot of unanswered questions. But we likely don't know the answers and maybe won't ever. But the biggest one I have is how was I compromised. Was it one of your team who talked? If it was, he or she won't be talking much longer," said David.

Peter stood. "I'm going to leave. I have to fly back to Washington for a bunch of meetings today. Some will not be pleasant. If I hear anything new, I'll call on that phone. It's secure and so is the fax behind the table."

"Thanks, Peter," said John. "Let me walk you to your car while these guys get David back to his room."

While Phil helped David walk to his room, James made the phone call he had been putting off to Elizabeth.

James and John returned to David's room. James looked like he had just fought a battle and lost. He reported to the team that Elizabeth was concerned but mostly angry about David being put in a position where a commie could take him. She wanted to come to see her boy, but James stopped her. They didn't need her drama in the hospital. Before she handed the phone over to Amy, David's sister, Elizabeth yelled, cried, and yelled a bit more at James. Amy also wanted to come down to visit David, but James needed her to stay with her mom. Unlike Elizabeth, Amy wanted to speak to David. James told her to call later.

After David had his dinner, Amy called his room. She had a lot of questions for him. Except for the death of her grandfather, by a car bomb, she knew nothing of her family's actual history. Elizabeth and James had tried to keep her away from that part of the family's hidden past. Since the car bombing, David and

Phil had spoken to her and told her bits and pieces of the family's other businesses.

• • • • •

After a full week in the hospital, Doctor Pine cleared David to travel home to Canada with minor restrictions. The doctors recommended he not fly because of the pressure changes and the potential issues he still had with his brain from the multiple concussions.

The American government delivered a large RV to the hospital. John planned to fly home but decided even he could use a few days off. They spent one last night at the hospital to allow John access to their room. Preparing for a large shipment of weapons to Saudi Arabia, Scott and John wanted to finalize the details over the secure phone. The next day, John felt he had most of the business' loose ends tied up and the group of men headed out on their adventure.

The trip home took a few days longer than they planned. They stopped in Bristol, Tennessee, for a NASCAR race. In Cleveland, the Toronto Blue Jays were playing a weekend series, at a stadium none of them had been to before.

Phil got a bad sunburn at the second game and skipped the third one. It had been a long time since the four of them had taken time away from the business and just relaxed.

They made one stop in Buffalo to visit a bike gang, The Warlocks. David did not attend the meeting with John and James. John had to remind the executives of The Warlocks, they needed to plan out their weapons orders better. John reminded them. "The Family would not be involved in gang wars and they would ship weapons to any paying customer. The Family didn't take sides."

During the meeting, they asked James to deal with a gang member who turned snitch and was working with an FBI agent. For a fee, James made the problem disappear. Just one of the many services The Family provided.

You can take a vacation, but the business always needs tending to.

CHAPTER EIGHT

Guelph, Ontario,

The Family arrived back in Guelph, and John put David up in a hotel. He was healing, but his face and body still exposed the bruises and cuts. The nurse shaved his head again before he left the hospital to keep the stitches that held his wounds together clean. They all decided before he went home to see Elizabeth, he would need to heal a bit more. If she asked where David was, James would tell her that Scott needed help with work in Northern Ireland.

The next day, while Elizabeth prepared for choir practice, Amy cornered her dad in the kitchen. She had questions about David. "Dad, can we talk? I need to know what is going on with David. I want to know what happened to him. He was down south on our phone call."

"Amy not here. Never where your mom can listen. Let's go for a drive."

They drove around the outskirts of Guelph and stopped on York Road for Guelph's best hotdog. Sitting in the car eating, Amy asked, "Dad, what do you really do? What does David do? Do you have another family you are hiding from me?"

"What? NO! your mother is more than enough." They both laughed at James' honest quick reaction.

She took a couple bites of her hotdog and after a drink of pop asked, "Are you a terrorist like Granda was?"

"Amy, we do a lot of things. Your Granda was not a terrorist. But don't you worry about it. School and church should be your focus."

"Dad, he died in a car—" James looked at her. The sadness and pain in his face caused her to stop talking.

"Sorry Dad. I wish I had known him better."

"It's okay, honey. I wish you had too. But we had to move here."

"Dad, can you take me to the shop at least?"

"Okay, I'll take you to the shop. I will show you a few things, but Amy, one word of this to your mother and…"

"Oh, I know dad. I have heard you two talk and I have my own ideas. Not a word Dad, I promise."

James showed her more of the plumbing and wholesale business than the other side of his work. He invited her to work with them in the office, after school and during the summer break.

Hoping to find out more about what happens in the business and an opportunity to spend more time with David and Phil, she accepted the job.

The next day after school, Phil picked her up and brought her to the shop. Her first job was to put plumbing fittings away in the bins for Frank. Once she completed that task, Frank taught her how to enter the contractor purchases into the financial logs for billing.

While she worked in the shop packing fittings, she saw Phil leave with a person in sunglasses and a hat. Looking a lot like her brother, she ran to catch up to them. By the time she was outside, Phil's van had left the yard. She returned to the shop and continued with her tasks.

Later in the evening, James drove her home. "Dad, I'm sure I saw David today with Phil. He was wearing sunglasses and a ball cap. I know I ask this a lot, but what's going on?"

"Oh, Amy, I wish you would just turn a blind eye to all this. You can't tell mom anything, right? Nothing about the shop, me, David. Nothing."

"I know, Dad, you sound like a broken record. We both do, I guess. I will leave it alone, for now. Tell me when you're ready."

They drove home in silence. When they pulled into the driveway, James said, "It's nice having you at the shop."

"Dad, will I ever know the truth?"

"We are home. Mum's the word, yeah?"

"Yeah."

•　　•　　•

Phil picked David up to head to the shop. It had been three days since David was back in Guelph. There was a meeting scheduled to discuss business items, Igor and what to do with him, and who was a threat to the team.

David decided he was well enough to drive to the shop. Waiting at an intersection for the green light, David noticed, in his rearview mirror, a white car approach them. He watched it in the mirror. "Phil, the car behind us. I am sure it followed us from the hotel. If not then, definitely since we picked up coffees on Stone Road."

The light turned green, and they pulled away from the intersection. Phil looked through his side mirror. "It's hard to see who is in the car. The sun is bouncing off the windshield."

"Maybe I am paranoid, but do you think it could be more of Igor's guys? Did he put a price on my head?"

"Only one way to find out. Pull into the mall parking lot and see if the car follows us."

David waited until the last minute before he turned into the laneway that led to the four-level parking garage. The car followed.

"What do we have with us, Phil? They are still tailing us. I still can't see how many people are in the car."

Phil opened the glove box. There were two loaded Browning pistols on top of the owner's manual for the car. "Will these do?" he asked.

David nodded and headed to the ramp; he made the sharp left turn. They snaked their way up the ramps to the roof. Over the rough expansion joints, the car kicked and bucked, but David kept the pedal mashed. A level below, the car followed them. David could hear their tires squeal when they jumped an expansion joint. On the roof of the parking garage, David pulled the emergency brake and spun the car to face the ramp they just exited. He threw the transmission lever up to park and jumped out.

"Where are they?" said Phil. "We didn't imagine this whole thing, did we?"

"I thought they would be up by now," David said, looking at Phil.

Over Phil's shoulder, David noticed the stairwell door open slightly and close. "Phil, come over here, quick. The stairwell door just opened. They are on foot."

"How we doing this?" asked Phil.

"I'll go back down the ramp and head for the stairwell. If they are watching from the door, they won't see me with the position of the car. Once I am down, you jump in the car and drive over there." He pointed to the corner of the parking area. "Only shoot if absolutely necessary. We want this person or people alive."

"Did you see how many were in the car? Or who was in the car?"

"No. I can't be sure. This would be a good time to have one of those car phones," said David.

"Yes, I think that needs to be brought up again today."

"Are they waiting for us to make a move? What the fuck is going on?"

"They have us trapped up here. Maybe we didn't think this out."

"Okay, don't move the car until I am sure I can continue down to the next level. Don't leave me exposed. I'll clear the stairwell back up. So don't fucking shoot me when I come out the door, right?"

"Right, don't shoot till I see the whites of their eyes. Isn't that the saying?"

"Just don't shoot me. That is all I'm asking. I have taken enough damage this month."

David crawled to the ramp and looked to the level below. Beside the stairwell door sat the white car. David could see no one in the car or on the level. Cautiously, he made his way to the car. Above, he could hear Phil move their car to the edge of the lot. David looked in the car, a rental. It was empty except for a pair of sunglasses sitting on the dash. He looked around the level again. *No one to be seen. What the hell is going on?* He thought.

He turned the door handle to the stairwell and slowly opened the door. With his pistol leading him, he cautiously walked up the stairs. On the landing, he turned and noticed a figure, small and shapely, looking through the window in the door. David crept up behind the person dressed in black Levi's, and a black hoody. They had the hood pulled up over their head.

There was no weapon in the strangers' hands. He stepped closer and pushed the person into the door. The individual fell against the door, then regained their balance. Another push from David and the stalker fell on the crash bar. The door opened, and the stranger tumbled out to the lot. David dropped on the assailant lying prone on the concrete. He knew Phil would be nervous and held his breath, waiting to hear the bang of a pistol releasing a bullet.

With his gun pointed at the unknown person, Phil ran towards the two people struggling on the ground. Controlling the situation, David sat on the person's lower back. Firmly, he placed the muzzle of his gun on the back of the intruder's head.

"One move and the crows will eat your brains. Hands flat on the ground, not one twitch of a muscle," said David. His ribs ached and the old cut over his ear opened and bled.

"David, Phil, don't shoot. Please, don't shoot me."

David recognized the voice. "Amy?"

She cried out, "David—yes—me, your sister. It's Amy. Don't shoot me, please. David, don't kill me, please, David."

Phil and David both lowered their guns. David stood up, and Amy rolled over onto her back. Cut, and with swelling already appearing where her face smacked the ground, she cried, and her whole body shook.

"What the fuck Amy. You almost died. What were you thinking? David rarely allows people to land on the ground without having a new hole somewhere in their body. You are lucky he had a gun instead of his knife," said Phil.

"What? That's exactly why I followed you. What is going on with our family? David, what happened to you? Your face, your arms? And Dad said you were away on business? There is so much more going on than I have been told. I want to know, want to know it all. This has been going on for too long. Dad told me some things." She sat up and hugged her knees. "Every time I ask Mom, she loses her mind. Tells me to stop asking questions about the business. So, that makes me believe there is more to this family than what I am being told. You guys are more than plumbers. I have been doing my own digging and getting some answers. Why was I always kept in the dark, David?"

"Amy, I was told never to tell you anything. I am sorry I, we." He looked at Phil. "We wanted to tell you."

"I found out Granda died from a car bomb because of his past with the government. It was an actual hit, a hit!"

"Yes, Amy, I know. I saw it happen. I was right there when it happened. Dad was too."

She looked at David. The shock of his reply shook her reality. "Granda was an assassin and gun runner, David. Did you know that? Of course you did. The car bomb that killed him, it didn't happen by chance that night, David. They targeted him. I assume you know all that, too. What about you Phil? Do you know all this?" She buried her face in her hands and sobbed.

"Amy, David has argued with your mom and dad many times. He always believed you should know the truth. We both do. Amy, listen, you are like a sister to me. We are all so close, but some stuff you might not want to know. Believe me."

"What? What stuff? Dad took me to the shop yesterday. Maybe I have asked too many questions. But, David, I thought I saw you yesterday at the shop, all beat up. That was when I did more digging. I asked Frank questions. Believe me, I have never seen that man so quiet. Dad insisted you were away. When I told him I saw you at the shop, he told me I needed to take a break from working there and concentrate on my marks at school. When he drove me home last night, I asked again if you were at the shop. Were you, David? His response was he enjoyed having me at the shop and not to tell mom. David, I don't even know what he means! Tell Mom what? They had a big fight last night, biggest ever David."

"Amy, settle down. You are right, so right, you don't even know how right. But let me ask you a few questions. A rental car? You don't even have your license. What the hell are you doing? Does Mom know any of this? Amy, I can't give you any more answers. What we just told you will upset dad. We would love to say more because I always thought you should know. Phil and I have stories, but unless we're told to talk, they stay with us. Mom will be furious at both of us if she finds out you are driving a rental and I had a loaded gun jammed up against your head."

"David, tell me something, please. You almost killed me. Why don't we start with why you have a gun with you?"

David looked at Phil and shrugged his shoulders. "Amy, the stuff our family does requires us to carry guns and sometimes use them. I was kidnapped and almost ended up in Russia. When we talked a few weeks ago on the phone, the U.S. Navy had just saved me."

"What? The U.S. Navy? Who are you?"

"Honestly, Amy, some days I don't even know who I am. This brief event today. I thought you were someone who was sent to finish the job. Meaning, have Phil and me killed. We all live looking over our shoulders. So, when someone pulls a stunt like the one you just pulled, we rarely have chit chats with them after. You don't know how lucky you are right now."

"What? What happened to you?"

"I got hurt on a camping trip, fell off a cliff, rock climbing," said David.

"I call bullshit David, bullshit."

David and Phil both laughed. It was the first time they heard her swear. It broke the tension of the moment.

"Amy, that is the story you have to tell mom and dad. Understand? Okay, I assume my coffee is cold, so you owe me a story before you hear mine. Phil, you take the rental to the shop. I'll grab some fresh coffees and meet you there."

Phil took the keys to Amy's rental and walked down the ramp. David walked to his car. Amy didn't move.

"What really happens in the shop?"

"Listen, Amy, I can't tell you anything else until we are back at the shop. But you need to answer all my questions."

"I am not leaving here until you answer my questions."

"Suit yourself, sis. Do you have bus money?"

"You're not leaving me here, David. If you do, I will tell mom you held a gun to my head."

"Amy, that immature attitude will not get you the answers you want. If you say that to Dad, he will close the door and never open it for you again. We have a lot going on right now. The best advice I can give you is to do what you are told, keep quiet and don't ask too many questions. I'll talk to Dad. You'll get answers. You might not like them, but if you're asking, one of us will fill you in. I'm running late. Dad will be worried, so get in the car."

David started the car and waited for Amy. Once she was in, David caught up to Phil and followed him to the ground level.

"Amy, I could've killed you. The only thing that stopped me was your figure and shoes. I wasn't one hundred percent sure, but I thought it was you when I saw it was a female, and I was sure those were your runners. The ones I trip over every time I enter the house," said David.

"You and Phil talk like killing people is as common as putting shoes on to go outside. David, I know there is shit going on with our family. Mom, Dad, you are all hiding stuff from me. I hear the rumors in school and at church. I listen to Dad's calls when he's at home. And now I get thrown through a door and have two guns pointed at my head by my brother and really, my other brother. David, either I'm going crazy, or we have two lives in this family."

"Amy, you might be the only sane one in the family," he said. "Let's go to the shop. We are all meeting there to discuss what to do with the guys that tried to take me on a cruise to Cuba. I doubt they will let you stay for that part, but you and Dad can talk after."

•　　•　　•

David and Amy drove to the coffee shop. It was the first time the two of them had been alone in a while. Elizabeth didn't like to give them a chance to talk together.

"All right, I don't want to say much until you talk to Dad. We had our talk back home after Granda's funeral."

"There, that's my first question. You call Northern Ireland back home, but yet, we've only been there twice since we moved to Canada. You and I have now spent more years in Canada than we did living in Ireland, sorry Northern Ireland."

"Amy, please."

"Just answer that for me. Then we can... Wait, how many times have you been home over the years? When we were home for Granda's funeral, you seemed comfortable. Like you knew the town and area and spent a lot of time there."

"Okay, but you need to bottle this up inside and not let anyone know I told you. Yes, I have been home. I don't know, actually, I don't know how many times. Huh, a lot. A lot more than you can imagine," said David as he pulled into the drive-thru.

"What? To do what? With who? Why is it all a secret to me?"

David picked up the coffees from the drive-thru window. "Quiet, we don't discuss that stuff when people are around. First rule!"

Amy sat back and took the tray of coffees from David.

"Wait, there are rules? David, what have I been missing?"

"How about this? I promise once you talk to Dad, I'll answer any other questions you have. Until then, you answer my questions. Deal?"

"Okay, but David, promise me, please. I think I'm going crazy. I hear things and can never be sure if they are real or just rumors. David, I feel I have two families, the one at home and the one I hear about through rumors and whispers. Please, am I going crazy? I have thought I was for a while now. So, the camping trips, I assume, they never happened? You were going to see Granda and our family?"

"Yes, let's just leave it at that for now. And calling them visits wouldn't be accurate. I promise, you might not like what you hear. It isn't glamourous. Now my questions. So, explain to me how you got a rental car. You don't even have a license."

"It was weird actually and kind of cool. Stuff like this makes me think I'm living in a movie. I know we rent cars from Kelso Car Rental. I wanted to follow you. So, I had a friend get me a fake license a couple of months ago. Don't ask, maybe it is just in our blood." She smiled at David. "With it, I thought I would try to get a car. The worst they would do is call Dad and then, well, I thought that might lead to some answers for me. I took the bus this morning to Kelso. The guy at the counter knew me from visits with Mom and Dad. He knew me by name, kept calling me 'Little Amy,' I said I needed a plain car for two days. The guy at the counter—"

"Gene, Gene is his name," said David.

"Okay, Gene. He said he wasn't aware of a pickup, but he had one that wasn't clean. I said, I didn't pre book one. I told him if it was a little dirty, that was fine, I guess."

David pulled the car over. He laughed so hard at the innocence of Amy's story he couldn't see the road with tears.

"Why is this so funny to you, David?"

"Because—Oh wait till they all hear this. I can't say right now, but we will all fall off our seats laughing when you tell your story at the shop. Just keep going with the story. I have one question after you're done."

"Gene told me to take a seat and he would get the car. I assumed he went into the back to call Dad. But after five minutes, the white car pulled around. Gene got out and said to keep it as long as we needed. David, he didn't ask for any ID or money. Just gave me a car, no questions asked, nothing, just handed over the keys."

David slapped the steering wheel as tears ran down his face. His ribs ached as he breathed.

"Amy, you have to tell everyone at the shop the story just like you did to me. Please, keep that innocent tone. That's the funniest story I have ever heard."

"David, why is it so funny? I don't get the joke. And this is why I think I'm going crazy."

"Amy, you are fine. Hopefully, we can give you more answers at the shop. Okay, so who did you get the ID from? And can I have it, please?" David asked. He pulled into the plumbing shop parking lot.

"It's in my purse, in the other car. I can get it."

David picked up the tray of coffee and opened the car door. "Okay, get it and then wait in the car until someone comes to get you." He exited the car. "Won't be a minute." David entered through the service door. Two plumbers waited at the counter for their orders. David waved and headed to the office.

"You guys ready for me to bring Amy in?" asked David, poking his head through John's office door.

"Aye, let her in," said James.

"Okay, she is still in the car. I'll get her."

•   •   •

Before David arrived with Amy, Phil sat at the conference table and told James and John of the activities from the morning. He kept them under suspense, leading them to think Russians were in town and not revealing it was Amy until the end.

•   •   •

David directed Amy down the stairs to the office. "Okay, sis, when this door opens, your life changes. I just don't know if it's for the better," said David.

He opened the door, and she followed him into the office. The size of the office and how everything looked expensive stunned her. Her dad came over, hugged her, and pointed to a chair at the large conference table. Once they had all sat around the table, she told her story about her new ID and picking up the rental car. A roar of laughter filled the room when she finished. David laughed even harder the second time. When the men had settled from her first story, she told her side of the morning's activities on top of the car park. She ended her story with a question. "How do we hide the marks on my face from mom?"

"I have the same question," said David. "Can we see the fake ID, Amy?"

Digging through her purse, she found the card and passed it to David. He passed the card to John, the expert.

"Who made this for you, Amy?" John asked. "It is very good. Incredibly good."

He handed the ID to James.

"Wow, real good," James said. "Hon, where did you get this and how much did it cost? You're not in trouble; we just need to know. We haven't seen work like this before."

"What does that mean, Dad?" she asked.

"Amy, we ask the questions first. Remember our talk in the car. You need to answer our questions first," said David.

"I don't want to cause any issues, Dad. But I bought it from a kid at school. He is Eastern European and been around our school for a year. I think he came from Poland. He lived in Montreal for a year before he moved here. I can show you where he lives."

"Not right now. But we will need that information. So, we are having a meeting shortly, and you're not invited. Actually, shouldn't you be in school?"

Amy smiled at her dad. "I thought I could miss a day."

"Amy, you can't skip classes. Frank will drive you to school. Tell Mom, David and I will both be home for supper, and a talk."

•　　•　　•

James and David opened the door. The smell of roast beef filled their noses.

"Hello, we're home," David yelled out.

Amy came to the door. "I told Mom about tonight, and told her David's face was a bit messed up. I tried to prepare her so we could get past the yelling and her concerns quickly."

"Good thinking Amy," said James. "Where is she?"

"Are you three going to stand at the front door all night conspiring, or are we going to gather and talk like a family?" Elizabeth yelled from the kitchen.

They all sat at the table while Elizabeth took the roast out of the oven and made the gravy.

She turned and looked at David. "What the hell, forgive me for my language. What happened to you? Did Amy do this to you this morning when you scarred her beautiful forehead?"

"Yes mom. Amy did this to me. All this time you thought I was the bad one in the family, but really it was Amy. I owed her twenty dollars, and this is what she did to me."

"James, I'm not having supper with him if that's going to be his attitude."

"Mom, you started it," said Amy.

"Now you have turned on me? Help me bring the food to the table. I don't want to know anything about David and his marks. Amy told me to expect something, but I was not expecting this. She told me about her adventure too. Looks like you two have finally got your claws into her."

"Okay, stop everyone. We can get through this as a family. Mom, you knew this was coming. Amy, you don't know what is coming. Dad, you'll have to lead the conversation," said David.

Elizabeth and David brought the roast beef, potatoes, Yorkshire puddings, baked beans, roasted vegetables, and gravy to the table.

After grace, they served the food, and the discussion began.

"So let me start Mom," said Amy. She placed a slice of beef on her plate and reached for the gravy. "At Granda's funeral, I asked Nannie what happened. I found it strange Dad and David were 'camping' when Granda died. She got noticeably quiet and nervous. Seems everyone fears you, Mom. She told me she couldn't say, but there was more to it. So, I asked Aunt Sarah. She said talk to David. At that point, I knew there was more to our lives. I was being bounced around the family like a ball in a pinball machine. Mom, the funeral alone had more people with weapons than not. Plus, when I saw the military and a representative of the monarchy appear, I knew we were doing something wrong, or maybe right. I had my questions before, but I just kept them to myself. But really, the vacations, the houses, the shop and all the trips camping, hunting, or fishing. I'm not stupid. The comments at school and church. I turned a blind eye to it all, but I knew. I just stayed quiet and asked David. He said nothing at first."

"That was when I asked Dad if there was anything I could tell Amy," David said, taking over the story. "Dad told me and Phil to take her for a drive and have a talk. We went to Bangor for lunch. She came prepared. She had a notebook full of questions. I either answered them or referred her to Dad."

"With that bit of information, I talked to Aunt Sarah, Nannie, and finally Frank. Obviously, the more I learned, the easier it was to ask the right questions and get even more details. Finally, I talked to Dad. Dad took me out for a drive and then brought me to the shop for a real tour. He offered me the job with him. So now I would like to know more, all or any part of what my actual family is involved in."

Elizabeth pushed her plate away and glared at James. James started with his family's history. They finished their meal and dessert; made a pot of coffee and drank it. Wine was poured, and they emptied the bottle. David drank a pop and water. Finally, at midnight, with dry throats, wet eyes, and shocked minds, they finished filling Amy in. Elizabeth had some knowledge and understanding of what the organization did. She knew the reason her family was living in Canada, the connections to many agencies and governments The Family had and the sales of weapons. It shocked her to learn about the battles The Family had and continue to have with others like themselves. Amy, who had been protected from all the things her brother and father did, was in disbelief. The stories she heard were an edited version of The Family's history. She was not told her brother was an assassin. They told her about the weapons they sold, the people they hid for protection, and the businesses they used to launder money. Amy and Elizabeth learned a lot. They had both asked many questions, not all of them were answered.

When James concluded the conversation, Amy responded. "I want in. Mom, I know what you are going to say. I am not like you. Dad said you had the chance to help, and you didn't. I want to help. I want in. How can I help, Dad?"

"Amy, no. You don't—Amy, please, no. For me. No," said Elizabeth.

"Mom, you have hidden this from me. You caused me to grow up in a world of lies. I barely know David, my brother. He was always on trips with Dad. What I thought were camping trips were jobs for The Family. Well, I want a piece of it too. Dad, can I be involved with planning and organizing? Maybe go on some trips? Maybe not right away, but later. You said David started when he was fourteen. Well, I am older than that."

"Amy, no. Please. I worry about these two all the time. Now my little girl. James, I won't have this." Elizabeth stood up and went to her bedroom. They could hear her sobs in the dining room.

David had no regrets about the talk. His sister still didn't know about his unique skills, but she was told about many other things, some he could use her help with. There were operations David ran, where a female partner, Amy, would be beneficial. She could even join him on trips back to Britain. He looked forward to having Amy around the shop more and closer to him. At some point, she would need to learn that David, her brother, was a highly skilled and popular assassin.

James, always worried about his children's safety, no matter how old they were. He was glad that some of The Family secrets had been revealed to Amy. His little girl was just too observant not to see things happening in the background of their family's lives. She received the PG13 version of The Family business and history. Now the whole family could move forward with a few less secrets. They got up from the table and cleaned up the dishes before heading to their bedrooms.

CHAPTER NINE

David's first trip on a plane after being rescued from the hold of the ship was a private jet to Florida. Traveling with his dad, they planned to meet and thank the crew who rescued David. Forever indebted to the people in the U.S. Navy, David offered them cash and trips. Unable to take money or gifts for what they did, each man knew, when they left the Navy, there would be a retirement package waiting for them.

During the visit, they offered David a ride on a jet. He asked if he could get a ride in an A-10 Warthog instead of a Naval jet. A day later, he was flying over Florida and the Gulf of Mexico in a Warthog. The pilot couldn't believe he would turn down a ride in a Tomcat for a Warthog, but David always loved the ugliest plane in the United States military. A two-seater attack plane had to be flown in from Myrtle Beach Air Force Base in South Carolina for David's ride.

The ship he was a captive on was still at the naval base. Scheduled to be released the next day, along with the captain and the first mate, Peter had arranged for David and James to meet them and have a tour of the ship before it departed.

Standing in the wheelhouse of the Sol Matutino, the captain and the first mate met David and James. David still couldn't swing his fists because of his ribs, but James could. The price they paid for assisting in David's kidnapping was a beating from James. The best David could do was kick them when they fell to the floor. James took photos of them, wrote their personal addresses and other information. With their beaten and broken bodies, they set sail for home. For over twenty years, the captain had run a trustworthy company with a good reputation across many ports, but one bad decision, one afternoon for the greed of money, now caused him issues with the USN, the loss of his trusted customers, and worst of all, David now had his name and address.

David and James returned home after three days in Tampa. They both took time to relax on the beach and meet with a new client.

•　　•　　•

Gathering around the table in John's office, The Family sat down for a proper business meeting. With everyone seated, John began the meeting by announcing Igor was back in Moscow, safe for now, and protected by the new government that secretly ran Russia. They had disciplined him for failing to get David into Russia and then creating a diplomatic nightmare between the governments.

David wanted to get to Moscow and locate Igor. The intelligence John received was fresh, and the same contact who passed the information to him could track Igor until David arrived. As much as they agreed with David, until he healed, hunting Igor was not part of their plan.

"David, we all know Igor will be on high alert right now. Sending anyone to take him out could be risky. Russia is not stable. If they catch you within their borders, I don't know what would happen. I don't think any of our contacts in the government could help," said John.

"I know John, but... Yeah, you guys are right. We need to be better prepared, and I still need to heal. Just promise me I will get the opportunity soon," said David.

David's body was still healing. Although not as frequent, the headaches from the concussions were unpredictable. They were debilitating and sapped his strength. If one occurred during a confrontation with Igor, or any other target, he would be vulnerable and weak. Until cleared to work and travel, they assigned David to his plumbing truck, the shop, or diplomatic visits with Phil. None of his jobs would involve physical force. For the near future, the roles would be reversed. David would assist Phil on his trips.

Deciding to use his down time to give back to the community, David wanted to volunteer his plumbing skills to Habitat for Humanity. He wished to return the good fortune he had during his rescue and time in the hospital. The team agreed, some volunteer work would be a good idea as he healed. David and Phil would donate their time and do plumbing rough-ins and finishes for the charity. With the rest of their free time, David and Phil cycled around southern Ontario.

John cut the meeting short when he received a call from a man The Family supported and hid from the South African government.

•   •   •

David watched his father and his team do the jobs originally assigned to him. No matter how much he protested, James and John kept a short leash on him and his jobs, plumbing or otherwise.

Around the shop, the other plumbers asked David what happened. He answered, "A poor decision mountain biking in California." Knowing David and his addiction to cycling, that answer satisfied the plumbing shop staff.

Pulling into a driveway on Carey Crescent, David reviewed the job order. Change a kitchen faucet. David thought, *I wonder what this customer would think if they knew I was an assassin, doing plumbing in their house.*

•　•　•

Two weeks later and after multiple doctors' approvals, James okayed David to return to his other job.

David's priority was to get to Russia and locate Igor. Peter scheduled a meeting at the shop. The first one at the table was David. He patiently waited for everyone to arrive. He could not wait to get Peter's update on Igor and travel to Russia.

John started the meeting once everyone was around the table. "David, you now are able to work and speaking to Peter on the drive from the airport, he has an abundance of work for you to do."

"Where is Igor? I don't care about the other stuff, Peter. I want Igor. Where is he and when can I get to him?"

"David, I fully understand what you are asking for. We all want Igor. He has been a thorn in my, and your, family's side for years. But if you head to Russia, you go alone. Sorry David. I can't support you on that trip." Peter squirmed in his chair. David gave him a look of disgust that bothered him.

"Son, what have I always taught you? Patience, you will get your chance. Let it come to you. You can't force it," said James.

"David, you will get your opportunity. I think the word is out on Igor. He will be in hiding for a while. In the meantime, I have a few jobs coming up. I need a President in Africa to remember who butters his bread, if you know what I mean. That is a job for Phil and John, but if David can travel too, I have a small side job that needs done at the same time. We know there are three government officials from Russia paying and supporting

Moi's opponents in the upcoming election. He has asked me to have them removed."

"Done. I need to get out of Guelph. I need to travel and make money for The Family," said David. "What about the issues in your office? Have you found any information on a potential rat?"

"Yes, and no. As you know, they record everything in my building except for a handful of phones, mine being one of them. One desk in my department has been making a lot of offshore phone calls. I had the recordings sent to me, quietly. The problem is, I can't identify the voices on the calls. It would have shocked me if it was Roger, the agent who sits at the desk where the calls came from. I know it's not his voice." He paused and shook his head. "It just confirms that we have a bigger problem than I first thought and means I have a lot of work ahead of me. Other than that, nothing new. I have a small team I trust, investigating the issue, but I had to assign them to some cartel work in Mexico. My office is busy with the sound of war drums. It's the worst time for any of this to happen. All eyes are on the Middle East."

"Okay, I am a phone call away if you need anyone dealt with. And even less if you have any tangible information on Igor."

The team continued the conversation with updates on mob issues in New York. Peter had thoughts on digging up old friends in Africa to help stabilize the area for democracy and to line The Family's pockets with cash.

With the meeting over, The Family and Peter enjoyed a meal out, then Peter was back on a plane to Washington.

• • •

With the prospect of war within months, it focused the CIA on the Middle East. They prepared for what the history books would call 'The Gulf War.'

James was in Northern Ireland. He was there to help Scott ship weapons to countries in the Middle East that became American allies, or puppets, depending what side you were looking at it from. James and Scott also had a job to complete against a couple of Ulster sympathizers who caused havoc in a town north of Londonderry. They went into a catholic run school, after all the children went home, and killed the principal and the head nuns. The bishop for that district hired Scott to deal with them and ship a small box of pistols to a church for the safety of his people.

James had escorted shipments of weapons to small groups of Iraqi nomads and Turkish militants. The United States hoped they would assist from within if the Americans decided to take Iraq after freeing Kuwait.

PART TWO

CHAPTER TEN

There was a large shipment of guns that needed to be flown from the shop in Northern Ireland to Kenya. The Americans had quietly, or not so quietly, supported President Moi since the seventies. During the Cold War, Scott's operation in Northern Ireland shipped weapons, supplies, and money to Kenya. With talks of a national protest and the threat of President Moi being overthrown, the Americans wanted to be sure President Moi knew where his real support came from. The weapons, money and gifts that were constantly sent to him would end if he could not get his people under control. David and Phil were to remind him of the agreement and his responsibilities. The United States had other "Jackals" set up in the Soviet run countries like Ethiopia, Sudan, and Somalia. The Americans tried to buy the support of those leaders and build new relationships. With the support from those countries, Kenya and President Moi would not be seen as an asset to the U.S.A.

The CIA confirmed to David that the three Russian diplomats were still in Kenya, having meetings with Moi's opponents.

Loaded with supplies, and the boys, the cargo plane took off for Kenya. After a couple of refueling stops in Europe and Northern Africa, they landed on an airstrip behind the Presidential Palace in Kenya.

President Moi, with an entourage, greeted Phil and David. They welcomed them with food, beautiful women, and jewelry. David didn't wear jewelry, but he accepted the gift of women and food. David's grandfather, Kenton, had made the original trip back in 1979 with many weapons, money, and promises. The president's house welcomed him as a guest and friend.

Moi's crews stood ready to unload the plane once the presidential party left. His specialty foods and ammo supplies were dwindling; he loved a good Maine lobster.

Once Moi's crew unloaded the plane, with other deliveries and pickups, they would return two days later to bring the boys home, unless they called for an immediate evacuation.

David's pager chirped. He stepped away from the group to read the text. *Birds have flown the coup—enjoy your down time.*

David ran to catch up with the group. He stopped behind them and watched Phil work. Phil oversaw the peacekeeper missions. He was already working over Moi with his talk and charm. Two skills David lacked in. More comfortable holding a weapon or interrogating a prisoner, David did not negotiate. He was the person people called when talks broke down. On jobs with Phil, the customers treated him like a prince with all the benefits of a presidential guest. On his own jobs, he hid from his targets and lived in cheap motels or on the street.

Peter had briefed the boys on the political concerns and issues President Moi faced in his country. They knew Moi's leadership wavered with each day and his people were starving and mistreated. Phil had his agenda and talking points. He also knew what guarantees he needed in return for more weapons and supplies.

With the Russians out of the country, they had two items on their agenda. One; supply Moi with his regularly scheduled money, guns, and words of support. The second was to watch the news. If a series of code words appeared in the credits, on the BBC six o'clock news, they were to leave the country immediately, leaving one last gift from the United States state department and CIA.

Sitting in Moi's office, Phil reviewed the schedule of meetings and public gatherings they needed to attend. He requested a couple of engagements be rescheduled.

During the day, David and Phil sat in meetings with Moi and his upper staff. The recommendation from the United States and President Moi's handlers was to have his opposition leaders arrested and kept quiet. Phil stressed they did not want him to have others on the election ballots, especially one's backed by Russia. They knew there was an underground uprising and if he wanted to keep the United States' support, he would need to shut down any political challenges. When any protests broke out, he needed to act quickly and ruthlessly to get the point out to the people in the poorer areas of the country. This was not an option but a demand from the West. They reminded him, with the political changes in the countries around Kenya, Moi needed the Americans more than they might need him. He was to control his media and any international news teams that entered the country. The United States would not tolerate the news spewing sympathy for the people of Kenya. Knowing David's family history and David's actual skills, Moi had his staff leave the meeting. He stood up and removed his sidearm and placed it on the large wooden table.

"If you, David, are here to kill me, I ask you to do so. I wish to die with honor. So please take that sword off the wall. I will look you in the eye as you pierce my heart with my family's sword. You can leave without a fight. You do not attend these meetings, David. These types of trips for meetings and political negotiations are not what you do. Phil, we have met many times before, with your father. We have shared meals and good times. Why did you bring David if not to kill me?"

"No, he is not here for that. He will not kill you unless you give him a reason. They did not assign him to any hits on this mission unless you request and pay for them. We are here to help support you during the attempted overthrow of your government. Why do you think we brought all those weapons and firepower? If anyone is to die, you will be the one giving the order, not us," said Phil.

"Then why did you bring him with you? I have served the establishment faithfully and now, what do they want, to have my head on a pike? To have my family destroyed? I could have an army in here and they would never find you two."

"You could, but to what end? If we don't return home, then next thing you know, there are large planes dropping bombs all over your country. If you think killing millions is worth killing us, then do so. Like you, we are prepared to die for what we believe in," said Phil.

"Phil, why are we talking like this?" Moi said, upset by Phil's aggressive tone. "I'm nervous he is with you. I am sorry David, your reputation, how do you say, precedes you."

David said, "I'm not here for anything like that. It upset me when I discovered you bugged our rooms. But we all know that happens, and that is why we check. Moi, I'm here as an observer and to take advantage of your hospitality, that's it."

"Again, let me apologize for my General and his desire to keep me alive. Bugging rooms is just our standard procedure. David, give me your word I will live through this visit, and we can put this behind us."

"You will live. To be honest, sir, two months ago I had some issues and busted up ribs and my head. I'm on a bit of a vacation, you could say. Relaxing here has been great; the food, the women, the weather. I just came along to see what Phil does. You know we all work for the same boss, just different departments. I wanted to see what he does, that's all. No need to be nervous. You have my word."

"I see what is happening in the other countries. Now is not the time for unrest in my nation, while those around me are in turmoil from the fall of the Soviet Union. I will have Kenneth Matiba and Charles Rubia arrested, as you asked," said Moi.

The meetings ended. Phil and David went back to their rooms to prepare for more relaxation and entertainment. With their free time, David and Phil did a little sightseeing, but the beat up rough roads were tough on David's ribs. Then they relaxed by the pool while Moi's personal staff ensured they had the best time possible. On the last night of their stay, the coded message came through the BBC news. In the credits of the show, under Researcher One and Researcher Two were the code names, Wilson Kill, John Best.

"There it is Phil. Did you see it?" asked David.

"Yes, it goes by so quick, but I saw it," said Phil.

"Okay, we're scheduled to fly out tomorrow. Looks like the team in Ethiopia was successful, so they don't need this guy anymore. Wow, how the world is changing, the fall of the wall, George Bush President, and the end of the Soviet Union. And now we're changing political systems in Africa. What next?"

"It's a good time to have a business like we do. We can't sell guns quick enough. With the trips to the Middle East lately too, there is some big stuff coming from there."

"Oh, yeah. Our future is bright. I'll call Teddy and confirm his arrival time tomorrow. I want to be wheels up by noon."

"Agreed. Now, we have a busy day tomorrow."

Phil and David headed to the main area of the house, where they met dignitaries and beneficiaries from the United States' funding over the years. After a feast made for kings, President Moi had a party to celebrate Phil and David's family and another successful visit. David and Phil spoke with many that were thankful for their support and the backing of those who sent them. Finally, at 2 a.m. they headed back to their rooms. Each had a couple of guests to keep them company, and neither slept that night.

President Moi had a large breakfast ready for David, Phil, and the air crew. After last minute discussions and a confirmed scheduled date of the next delivery of goods, the team headed to the plane.

"Teddy, can you walk with us, please?" asked Phil.

"Did you pick up anything for us while you were on standby in Yemen?" asked David.

"We have twelve skids on board to be used. I was told we are a go with the plan. I have briefed the crew and have a flight plan prepared. All I need is some strong backs," said Teddy.

"Okay, let's get it done and get home," said David.

The team boarded the plane; they lifted off, and David checked the skids of pamphlets.

"Okay, when we hit the smaller cities and villages, we can release the pamphlets," said David.

The plane flew over towns, large and small. Released to the people below, the pamphlets invited those who read the document to join the protests set for three days later, on Saba Saba Day, July 7th. The protests were to support open and free elections in Kenya. Funded teams, dispersed busses and vehicles across the country to bring people to the capitol for the protest.

The supply of money, weapons, and support between the Americans and Moi concluded when David and Phil dropped the pamphlets. Even though President Moi stayed in power for many years, he knew the visit by "the boys" ended his powerful career and the control of his people. President Moi believed David did kill him on that visit, just not in the flesh.

David believed he was ready to return to his regular duties.

CHAPTER ELEVEN

David, Phil, and James all returned from jobs, and as usual, the team had a debrief of each job. They reviewed the steps they took and what they could improve on. John confirmed with everyone, he received substantial deposits into The Family's bank account for their work. There was still a backlog of work from Peter and other customers that needed their help. David was getting his groove back and wanted to keep going.

The office phone rang. John answered while David continued with the rundown of his job. With a smile on his face, John hung up the phone and returned to the conference table.

"That was Peter. He says he is getting to the bottom of his leaks. Says he knows who told Igor where you were located when you were taken. I assume you would like to meet him, David? Phil?"

"Name and address, that's all I need," said David.

"As soon as I know, you guys will too. Until then, there is an issue we need to deal with immediately. Seems all the turmoil with the falling of the Soviet Union is now hitting our business," said John. "We have lost several weapon shipments to groups in Russia, possibly Igor and his group or maybe the new mafia that's growing over there. Sometimes I make the wrong call. I thought with you out of commission, and not having any backing from Peter, we should wait. I won't make that mistake again."

"How is that happening? He only sold small soviet equipment from the seventies and some light weapons from the eighties," said James. "There is more to this. I believe they tailed Scott and I when I was back home. When we loaded the shipment containers in the warehouse, someone watched us. I tried to find the person, but they got away."

"Well, I guess we know what we need to do. I need to find Igor and his team and dismantle them," said David.

"Aye, David, we need to be careful. We already have enough enemies and don't need to start another war. Our resources are limited right now. We're not set up for a full out war with our competition. I think we all need to remember; we were not selling this much equipment a couple years ago. We are moving into their territory," said John.

"I know, but we need to chip away at them slowly, like they are trying to do to us and our specialty work. We need to have a plan to fight back. There are too many organizations seeing us as weak since Granda passed. We need to make a stand and show some force because others are picking up my work while I am sidelined. They aren't as good, but they are getting the job done."

"David, we almost lost you a few months ago. I agree we need to show we're still a powerhouse and are back to normal business. That's different from a war with the Russians backed by their government. Igor seems to have found favor with what looks to be the new government over there."

The phone rang and John answered the call. "Hello," John said.

"John, is James or anyone else there with you?" said Scott.

"Scott, what's wrong? Yes, we're all here."

"They took out our last shipment. Those bastards, they got our plane."

"Who got our plane? What happened Scott? The line is terrible. You're echoing and distant. I'll call you back," said John,

"Aye, right away."

John hung up and dialed Scott's number. "Scott, is that any better?"

"Aye, much better. Can you hear me?"

"Yes. I have you on speaker with everyone. What happened to our last shipment?"

"I got a telegram ten minutes ago. It said, *'We might not have David, but we will get one of you. Ethiopia is our customer and territory, we now own the airfield, stay out.'* I called my contact in Ethiopia. He saw the whole thing. He was trying to call me, but the long-distance service isn't great there."

"What are you talking about? Scott, what happened?" asked James.

"Lads, I think we are under attack. They see an opening with losing Dad. They are taking advantage of it and us. We need to stop this. James, the guys you thought were following us while you were here with me, they were Russian. I have proof from the hotel owner after I did some knocking on doors. I assume they were the same guys who took down our plane. They left when the plane did."

"We were just saying the same thing," said John.

"Scott, what happened to our shipment?" asked James.

"Aye, this is a story. I got the call from Abere. He said his team was at the airfield with him waiting for the plane. They had done their security checks around the field and had flashed the pilot the 'all clear,' on his fly-by. The plane circled the field one last time and started its approach. At approximately seven hundred feet and three quarters of a mile out, someone launched a missile or RPG. They saw the trail of smoke leave the tree line."

"What? Surface to air missile?" said David.

"Aye, David. Then boom, it hit the plane. The plane lost its wing and engine on the one side. I think he said the right side. The plane pitched to the left then nosedived into the trees below."

"Was that Teddy and his crew flying the plane?" asked David.

"Aye David, the very one."

"That's it. We need to make this right, fellas," said David.

Scott continued to reveal the attack. "They all reacted immediately and headed to the crash site. There was a clearing through the trees in the crash's direction. His team had to abandon their vehicles about a quarter mile away there. As they approached the plane, they heard multiple gunshots. It looked like the co-pilot survived the crash but was shot. At the crash, they were engaged by a group of men. He thought at least seven of them. There was a gunfight, and he lost two men. The others abandoned their location and left. When his team arrived at the plane, they found three unidentified dead bodies. He believes two of them were eastern European or Russian. They searched the area but didn't find the weapon that took down the plane. There were tire tracks on a road about a mile away from the crash. Luckily, the plane didn't have much fuel, so there was only a small fire. Once they secured the area, they retrieved most of the shipment. Some of the larger weapons and the two pickups were not worth salvaging."

"What the hell? Who would know the location of that airfield? We had the airfield built from nothing. Only a few people are aware of it. Then there's the arrival time of the flight. Besides Peter, and us in the room and our men on the ground, no one else has our schedule or flight path. It sounds like they tracked the shipment the whole way from Northern Ireland to

Spain, then the flight to Ethiopia. But how? Does Igor's team have that many people involved? I need to call Peter. I just lost one of our best flight crews. If this is because of his dirty employee, well, he needs to clean up his house now. Or we will."

"Aye, you need to pass this back to Peter. I know they have their hands full right now, but we lost a plane and our best flight crew."

"Teddy's crew," said David. "That's bullshit."

"We have six more shipments to head out over the next fortnight. How are we handling this? We need to get another plane. The guys on the ground in Ethiopia are now extremely nervous. This is the last thing they need, more attention brought to their operations. Those Americans are fucking this up."

"I'll call Peter as soon as we hang up," said John.

"Oh, and whoever it was, camped there for a few days. They found a tent. There was a novel in what they believe were Cyrillic letters. There must have been a radio base there, too. They found batteries but no radio. But how did they know? This was our second shipment for the Americans to that location. Something is off. Dad being blown up, David being caught, a plane shot out of the sky, loss of business; we are under attack, brothers. They are coming for us, whoever *they* are."

"Okay, we need to stop all business and reassess our entire system. Fuck me, they knock down a wall in Berlin and now they want to be involved in our capitalist system. I guess we need to take back what is ours," said John.

"Scott, let us talk here. We will call you in the morning, or better yet, we might come for a face-to-face. Listen, Scott, get Sarah, Eric and Doris and head to the farm," said James.

"Already there. I had them picked up and brought out there the minute I received the telegram. I didn't want my wife, son, or Elizabeth's mother anywhere in public. Who knows how long they have been watching us?"

"Okay. Be careful. Keep the house guarded. We will talk tomorrow. You call us from the farm at noon our time. We will be here waiting for your call."

• • •

John called Frank and told him to come down to the office. The group sat in silence. Frank was the plumbing shops manager, and since the seventies, John's personal bodyguard.

"So, we know they are coming. We don't know where, when or at this point who," said John.

"We need to move up to the farm with our families. From there, we can run the business safely," said James.

"What's up, fellows?" asked Frank from the office door.

"Frank, come in here and close the door. We're in a bit of a situation. Looks like people believe we are weak and are looking to attack us. We were just hit overseas. We need to secure the building. Call in some help to man the other businesses. I don't want anyone in this building unless it's one of our plumbers or a known customer for the warehouse." John stood up and paced. "I always want someone at the counter carrying and someone in the warehouse packing. As for our plumbers, let's be careful where we send them for calls, only existing or vetted customers. No unknown emergency calls right now. Same for the warehouse truck drivers. I want them doubled up in the vehicles and at least one guy armed. If you need to shut down today to get organized, I understand. Let payroll know everyone gets full pay. If things slow down, we will still pay everyone their forty hours."

"Well, we always wondered when we would get into a situation like this." Frank paused and took out a notebook from his shirt pocket and wrote a note. "Okay, I think we're fine to stay open today. I will have a couple of staff meetings this afternoon. One with the staff who knows some of this and a second meeting at the end of the day with those not in the know. I'll spin it so we don't reveal our true business to those guys. Do you think we have a leak, internally?"

"Right now, I would assume we might. But who and how?"

Frank walked over to the back wall and entered a code on a hidden keypad. A door opened to reveal a secret room. He flipped the lights on to the room inside.

The room looked like a movie star's walk-in closet with shelves, drawers, and racks, with one exception, there were no expensive shoes and clothes. This closet held all kinds of weapons and ammunition. Frank picked up four Browning pistols and a bag of spare clips loaded with hollow point bullets. They organized the room with the larger rifles and automatic weapons hanging on the wall. There were cabinets on either side of the room, each with a black-and-white marble countertop. At the rear of the room was another door, which was the secondary exit from John's office, in case there was a need to evacuate the lower building.

"Okay, Frank. Is that all you need for now? Take what you want," said John.

"I will take the Browning pistols to start with and extra clips. I want to be a bit more strategic with the rifles."

"Just make sure the guys and girls are on guard. We don't know the extent of this issue yet, but we need to be prepared. I think we might pull out and move up to the farm by Orangeville."

"I was thinking the same thing. It might not be bad to take the families up there for the time being," said James.

"Dad, I can fly home to support Scott. I'll take Phil with me if that's okay, John. I have a job to do in France next week, anyway. Some guy from Syria. It's a full job too; identify, kill, and set up the scenario for the police to find him as a suicide victim. So that'll keep us busy," said David.

"Yes, the packet just arrived today, so you can take that with you. Phil, you prepared to travel?" asked John.

"Of course, Dad. What about Mom? Do you want me to pick her up and bring her up to the farm first?" asked Phil. "Or will you have time to move her?"

"Yes, I'll get mom, you get yourself ready to travel," said John.

"I guess I'll get your mom, David. Another conversation I don't want to have. No, I have a better idea. We could send the wives on a vacation if Brenda wants to go. When we call Scott tomorrow, we can ask if Sarah would like a couple of weeks away, too. Frank and a few of his guys can watch them at our place in Grand Bahama. It's secure."

"Good thinking. Brenda will be up for it, no questions asked," said John.

"What about Amy? Farm or Bahamas?" asked David.

"She can decide. I think she'll want the farm. She wants to see what we do. But I think we, specifically you, David, need to encourage her. She needs to go south," said James.

"Let's get ourselves sorted and be back for Scott's call tomorrow. Prepare your families. David, I will review the packet and have it ready for you tomorrow. Are you two coming to the farm tonight?" John asked David and Phil.

"No, we can stay at the condo and get ready for our flight tomorrow night if you can get us booked."

"All right, we all have a busy day ahead so, I'll see you guys tomorrow. James, I'll see you and Elizabeth at the farm for supper? We can discuss the trip south then. Let's all meet back here tomorrow around ten. We can get our plans out of the way before Scott calls."

Everyone picked up a pistol and clips from the safe room. They were going to war for their families and their business.

James left the office and searched for Amy. She was working with Glenn, the plumbing manager. "Dad, Glenn is showing me how he schedules jobs for the plumbers. When he leaves for vacation next month, I can cover for him. If that's okay?"

"Amy, can we talk?"

"James, is everything okay? She is picking this up quickly. She might replace me if I don't come back," Glenn said, with a growing smile on his face.

"Everything is fine Glenn. Frank will fill you in at a meeting later."

Amy followed James to the basement office. "Amy, I know I say this more than I should but, I need you to listen and not ask questions."

"Okay, now what's up, Dad."

"Frank is going to drive you home. When you get there, pack an overnight bag. Then Frank will take you to the farm. I will meet you there later. We can take the horses for a ride and have a real talk. Okay?" James told Amy.

"Why can't David drive me home? Doesn't he need to pack?"

"Later, hon, later, I promise," said James. "There is too much going on right now. Please, just do as I ask."

• • •

Scott called at noon, and the team was ready for his call. What they did not expect was the information he had recovered.

Scott started the meeting by requesting David come home right away. Fortunately, David confirmed he and Phil had plane tickets for the flight to London that night at 10 p.m. Their connector flight would arrive in Belfast at 7:30 p.m. Scott's time. Scott offered to pick them up. He felt it was better than having a vehicle waiting. That way, there were fewer people aware of David's visit.

"This next bit is disturbing. I got a call from the cemetery about Dad's grave." Scott paused. "Someone kicked over the headstone. They crossed out Dad's name in red and drew a tricolor flag on the dirt. A note was on top of the flag held there by a knife."

"What the hell?" James said. "What did the note say, Scott?"

"Just an idle threat. *All The Family will be lying in a grave soon.*"

"Anything else?" asked David.

"No, nothing."

"Where is your family?"

"Sarah, Eric and Doris are at our farm in Banbridge. What about you guys? Have you moved everyone out?"

"Aye, the wives and Amy are at the farm outside of Orangeville. We are thinking of moving them to the house in the Bahamas. Do you think Sarah and Doris would go? It might make things easier for all of us if they were out of the country. We can send Frank to set up security for them," said John.

"Aye, fully agree. I will let Sarah know when I go back to the farm. I hate moving my wife, but it is for the best."

"Yes, right now it makes sense."

The meeting ended and they agreed Scott, James, and John would stay in their respective countries, David and Phil would travel. James wanted his brother in Canada with him, safe. He knew the next best thing was to have David with Scott.

John continued to reach out to his contacts around the world. He had them search for any answers about who was after them and where they were located.

Elizabeth put up a fight when they told her she would be transferred to the Bahamas. When James explained her mom and Sarah were meeting her there, it took the sting out of her protest.

Before David and Phil left for the airport, there was one last meeting. They reviewed the jobs that were scheduled over the next few weeks. John reminded them. "Boys, you need to keep your heads on swivels, always looking around and taking care of each other. I want you carrying weapons all the time." Before the meeting ended, John received a call from a long-term customer in Turkey.

A group of young Russians paid him a visit. They killed his two German Shepherds and held his family hostage. He was told that any deals for weapons, hits, or any other business of that manner were to be done through a new group, Rodstvo. Throughout the conversation, at gunpoint, he was told The Family and Igor's group would be out of business, and most would not survive. The Rodstvo was his new suppliers and business partners. Before they left, they took his son's baby toe as a reminder of where his loyalty was now to lie.

John told the group about the conversation. Things were worse than they feared.

CHAPTER TWELVE

Portadown, Northern Ireland

David and Phil arrived at the shop in Portadown. It was eerily quiet; Sarah was not at her desk behind the counter to greet them, and there were no staff on the shop floor. David and Phil walked through the shop to Scott's office. They entered and sat at the table.

Plans had changed and Scott could not meet them at the airport.

Scott put down the phone. "David, Phil. I am so glad you are here. I am getting too old for this cloak and dagger shit." He hugged them and motioned them to his conference table. "Okay, I don't have much time. I need to get to the farm and get Sarah, Eric, and Doris to the airport. But here is a quick rundown of what we have coming up. I just confirmed a new shipment of weapons to Syria. This was a request from MI6. Our regular shipments are all on schedule. We can talk in the car. I need to go."

"No, I am staying here at the shop, Scott. I don't hide."

"Not a bad idea, David. Having someone watch the shop would be a benefit," said Scott.

• • •

The next morning, David was up early. He wanted to get out to the grave and see the damage to the headstone for himself. They parked the car beside the old church and entered the graveyard. The age of the headstones always amazed Phil. This graveyard had been in the church's service since 1410. The first patron to be buried in the graveyard was the architect of the church.

David walked straight to his Granda's grave while Phil wandered through the rows of headstones. David kneeled by the grave marker. Luckily, it did not break but was lying on its back. A crimson red filled the white lettering of David's grandfather's name. Written below Kenton's birth and death date were words "Fuck you and your queen." The marble stones covering the ground had the tricolors of Ireland's flag. Faded from the rain, David could still see the outline.

"I can't believe they found Granda's grave. We were so careful. Fucking guys," said David.

Phil walked over to David. "I'm so sorry to see this. What are the chances we—"

A piece of marble to the right of David exploded, and the sound of a rifle echoed through the graveyard. Phil and David dropped to the ground and crawled behind a couple of headstones.

"You, okay?" asked David.

"All good. You?" said Phil.

"Good. The shot came from the hill. I guess graveyards are fair game now? We need to get to the car, or at least the church walls. Do you have a gun on you?" said David.

Phil shook his head. "Damn, I left it in the car, under the seat."

Another shot rang out. The bullet ricocheted off the headstone behind them and imbedded itself in the ground a foot behind David.

"Whoever is shooting isn't too far from us. They're likely behind the cemetery wall up on the hill. If we do this right, we might catch him. Head to the church wall, use it for cover to get to the car. I don't care if you destroy the car, just don't let this guy get away. I'll try to get closer through the graveyard and take a few shots as I go. It'll buy you some time. If I can chase him onto the road, I want you there. Good?"

"Rock and roll, baby," Phil responded.

Phil crawled between the headstones to the church wall, then sprinted to the car. When David saw he was in the car, he distracted the assailant by jumping up and shooting in the direction he believed the bullets came from. Then he ran to the next row of headstones and crouched down.

Phil, in the car, headed up the hill. From behind a headstone, David jumped up, took one shot, and ran full out towards the hill and the edge of the graveyard. Running and weaving between the old gravestones, they fired a few shots in David's direction. Granite from a headstone cut his upper arm. He sprinted up the hill to the wall where the shots originated.

Phil raced up the hill. The car bounced over a gully and came to a stop inches away from the men shooting at David. With his gun drawn, Phil jumped out of the car. The older man with the rifle placed it on the ground and turned to Phil. "On your stomachs now. Arms out wide." David hopped over the old stone wall and stood beside Phil. Both men looked up when David arrived.

"I thought I said don't fucking move," said Phil. He was sweating, shaking, and his voice had a note of uncertainty.

"What did you find, Phil? A couple of sharp shooters?" said David.

David patted them down for other weapons, then lifted them to their knees. "I guess you know who we are. So how about introducing yourselves?"

Both men sat silent. They stared at the ground in front of them.

"Phil, go see if there is any identification in their car." To the men lying on the ground, David said, "So, you're the quiet, shy types. No problem. I love my prisoners like that. Because when they do talk, they spill it all."

Phil returned empty handed. "The car is clean. Just two pistols in the glove box and a packed lunch, ham sandwiches and those Hula-Hoop chips you love. Looks like they were expecting us at some point today."

David stepped in front of the older man. He was bald, there was not a hair on his head. "Name?" he said. He grabbed the man's chin and raised his head to look at him. "Your fucking name? Do you speak English? English?" David drove his knee into the man's chest. He fell backwards and landed close to a rifle. Rolling to reach for it, he stopped suddenly when David pulled his gun from his pants belt and shot once. It was enough to make the man recoil and tuck his hand under his chest. Phil helped him roll over on his back and get back to his knees. David moved to the blonde man.

"Do you speak English? English? Now?"

"Fuck you, David."

"We have a winner. Oh wait, that's a Dublin accent. Nice. I have a lot of questions for you."

David turned to Phil. "Let's pack these assholes in the car and take them back to the shop. We have a special area for people like this."

"I'll get the sacks and ropes. I assume we are blinding them and tying?"

"And gag them too," said David.

• • •

Elizabeth, Brenda, and Frank arrived at the property on a remote island in the Bahamas.

On the flight, Elizabeth was quiet. Even when Brenda tried to engage her in conversation, she stared aimlessly out the plane window. Now, in her vacation home, she relaxed a little. But she was still furious with James and The Family.

Here she was on another trip, hidden away from danger, only this time she was alone. She had Brenda, her mother- and sister-in-law, but not Amy. Unlike home, where she had to show people she was a middle-class wife and mother, in the Bahamas, she had a maid and chef to pamper her. Two positives on the list of many negatives.

This was her first trip away without Amy. The fight with Amy was at the level of fights she would usually have with James and David. And like those fights, it was another fight she had lost. Amy had questions and was now at the age, like David was, where she wanted answers and truth about her family. In the end, James decided against Elizabeth's demand to have Amy leave with her. Amy could stay at the farm for a few days, get more of her questions answered, and then head down to stay in the Bahamas.

Brenda called the shop. "Hi, honey. We have arrived at our place. Frank is setting up a security detail," said Brenda.

"Good. I am glad to hear that. How is Elizabeth? Has she settled yet?"

"When I told her I was checking in, she sternly reminded me to tell you she expects Amy to be on a flight by the end of the week. Honestly, I don't know how James puts up with her."

"Love, Brenda. Love."

They laughed, and after a personal conversation, hung up.

• • •

David called the office in Canada and received a busy signal. He and Phil had secured their new guests in the back room of the shop. Gary, their mechanic in Northern Ireland, was dealing with the guests' car.

When he was young, they forbade David from entering the interrogation room. When he was older, his first interrogation in the room was with an SAS member. He showed David a few tricks to convince an Argentinian spy to talk. Kenton had shown him plenty more after that. There were chemicals and tools available to encourage people to talk or die in the room.

David smiled as the memory of his Granda faded. He tried to call the office again.

"John here."

"Hey John."

"David, how are you? Hold on, let me get your dad, he's upstairs."

There was a pause. They put David on hold.

"Go ahead son," said James.

"Hey, we need to get on-hold music for the phone." David said with a sarcastic tone. "I have Phil with me. Is the office clear?"

"Aye, all clear."

"I assume Mom, Brenda, and Frank are gone now?"

"Aye, they just called. They are secure, and Frank reached out to some acquaintances for help."

"Good. I haven't seen much of Scott. He is getting them ready to leave. I'll spend more time with him once he gets his family to safety. So, we had an interesting morning."

David and Phil told their fathers of the visit to the graveyard and the guests they brought back to the shop. After a coffee, they would change and begin the interrogation with the lads in the other room.

"So, what do we do with these two once we are done with them?" asked Phil.

"Get me their names, fingerprints, anything I can use to identify them. Once I know who they are, then I can tell you if we need them or we feed them to the pigs," said John. "Actually, I just picked up a job for you two in Belfast later in the week. You can put the bodies in the car and when it explodes, we solve our disposal problem. That will confuse the coppers too."

"Okay, I am going to start with the mind games. I will call you once I have something worth reporting. Stay safe."

"Boys, take care of each other."

They hung up with the promise to check-in around midnight, Northern Ireland time. Phil made the coffee while David changed into his work clothes.

They sat and drank coffee, dipped digestive cookies into it, and reviewed the interrogation process. Phil had never seen one before, and David did not need to be dealing with him during the torture part of the exercise. They decided Phil would stay outside the room while David did his work. As close of friends as they were, Phil never liked the "Mr. Hyde," side of David.

• • •

David opened the door into blackness. He flipped the light switch, and the room became engulfed with white, bright lights, too many for the size of the room. The first thing the SAS taught him, keep your guests off balance. Going from darkness to bright light was always a good start. Three lights hung on the wall and shone directly on the prisoners' faces. The only relief was when their interrogator stood directly in front of them. From the ceiling, red heat lights hung behind the prisoners. The lights radiated heat onto the backs of their heads, neck, and shoulders. The color red also gave the room a tint, the color of blood. It tricked the mind, especially in a highly stressful situation.

Behind the prisoners' seats was a large workbench. The countertop was wooden, with multiple coats of lacquer on it to protect the wood from stains. Above the countertop was a pegboard wall. Hung from the pegs were tools, knives, utensils, and other items used to help people answer the questions. The wall and shelves in the prisoners' line of sight held larger tools. They suspended speakers from the ceiling. Sometimes music played to soothe the soul and other times to drive the mind crazy. The speakers also worked as a communication system for interpreters or others outside the room. At the end of the room was a one-way window.

"Hello, gents," David said. He stood before the two men cuffed to charred and bloody wooden chairs, all part of the illusion. "So, I have questions and you have answers. I just need to figure out how to get them out of there." He tapped on the blond man's head. "Are we all going to play nice, or do I need to get some tools off the peg board?"

"David, we know what you do. You're going to kill us no matter," said the blonde man.

"Yes, probably, unless you can give me a good reason to keep you alive. What about you? You're very quiet. Cat got your tongue?" David said. He leaned in to look the other man in the eyes.

"Not the cat, the bear, Russian bear, actually. He doesn't speak a word of English, from what I have been told. Oh wait, I do. So maybe we can negotiate for my life. I give you what you need. I walk away. Deal? You can do what you want with him. I will work with you to get the answers you need."

"How about you tell me how you got involved in all of this and we can negotiate after that."

David took a claw hammer from the pegboard. Then, from behind, swung the hammer at the countertop. The noise from the work bench rang in everyone's ears. The blond man screamed.

"Do I have your attention now, you commie piece of shit. I took a short cruise with a couple of your comrades." He turned to the blond man. "What's your name?"

"Ian, Ian. Put the hammer down, David, please, it doesn't have to happen like this. Please. No more. I told you I would work with you. He doesn't speak English; I speak Russian. That is why I am here, because I can speak Russian. So how about we negotiate together? I get whatever you need out of him, and then I head home to my family."

"No, no, that's not how this works. I ask the questions. I do the negotiations and I decide who walks out of this room and who gets carried. So let me start over. Tell me how you're involved and who the fuck is he, Ian?" David asked. He pointed the hammer at the Russian.

"Mate. You won't get any answers from me, not while I'm locked up in this room. I need to know I'm going to see my family before I help."

"Okay, so I gather you are a nobody. I can dispose of you and bring in someone I trust to interpret for him. Seeing you killed slowly might help him talk. Again, who are you and who is he? We have already taken your photos and my partner is burning up the phone and fax trying to identify you two. If he finds out before I do, he is crazy enough to get your family and bring them back here. Watching your wife and kids get hooked up to car batteries usually makes the hardest of people become Chatty Cathy. I know you're from Dublin. Your accent gives you away."

The Russian laughed at David. Both David and Ian looked at him, confused. David left the room, he turned the lights off, leaving them in complete darkness.

• • •

David entered the room with Phil. He took a different approach with Ian from Dublin. Phil cuffed and blindfolded the Russian before removing him from the room. Phil placed him in a corner of the shop and watched over him while David stayed in the room.

"Good news. I have an interpreter coming in the morning. Looks like I don't need you after all," said David as he sorted through tools on the workbench. "I think you should start with your name. And then his name. We can figure out the questions as we go. So, what's your full name?" He stood in front of Ian with shearing scissors. They were intended to cut sheet metal, but they could easily snip off a finger. "Nothing? It isn't a trick question. Your name, Ian?"

He grabbed Ian's right pinky and bent it up. He placed the shear at the base of Ian's finger. "It's a lot easier to talk than it is to scream." David closed the shears onto his finger.

"Okay. Okay. Stop! Stop, you fucking psychopath. I'm Ian O'Reilly. Stop! I'm from Dublin, as you said. The Russian, I don't know much about. They hired me to travel with him because I'm fluent in Russian. They, the IRA and Sinn Fein, use me when they need to negotiate or talk to their Russian customers or partners. It has become a full-time job. He wanted to see your shop and where Scott lived and needed access to guns and C-4. He needed to get you here, so he went and disrespected your Granda's grave, knowing you would be here in no time. I guess he was right. I don't know anything else about him. Honestly, I don't know why he wanted to meet you or why he is even in the country. I don't ask those questions. McGinnis hired me to be his guide. Listen, I have a wife and four kids. I just want to go home. If you need a finger, take one if it gets me home to my family."

"You guys are always using your family as an excuse not to kill you. Everyone has a family, asshole. They did not give some of my friends the option to see theirs again. So, you can stop using that line thinking it will soften my heart. What other business do you have with the IRA?"

"None really. My cousin got me in years ago once I graduated from college and traveled to Russia twice. I have never shot a gun or done any acts of violence. I just show up in a suit and translate. They pay me well for it."

"Okay, you will stay here for a few days. I think you might have a lot of secrets that might be useful for my bosses. I'll be checking your name and story. You better be as squeaky clean as you say. We'll bring you water and food later."

David left and instructed Phil to return the Russian and feed them both. He had calls to make. His first call was to John and then Scott. He needed information on Ian and wondered if there was an appetite for his knowledge.

$$\bullet \quad \bullet \quad \bullet \quad \bullet$$

John had just hung up the phone, and James could see the phone call did not go well.

"All right, John?" asked James.

"Yeah, we just lost a three-million-dollar weapons and gun deal. Seems Igor, or this new group, Rodstvo, can sell the equivalent for a million less. What is happening to this world?"

"So, they are undercutting us on sales and attacking us. We need to send David after them. Either he goes alone, or I go with him. But this needs to end, John. Igor or the Rodstvo are making a mockery of us," said James.

The phone rang in the office at the farmhouse.

"Hello," John said.

"Hey John. I need you both on the line."

"Standby," John waved James over to his desk and clicked the speaker button.

David reviewed the start of his interrogation and the name of the IRA interpreter. John agreed to do some research on him and find out if anyone had questions for him or if any of the agencies wanted him shipped out. Once David completed his information dump, John told David and Phil how they lost a large weapon, vehicle and equipment deal and that someone from Russia, likely Igor, was behind it. With all the activity going on, John admitted he still hadn't researched their newest threat, Rodstvo.

"Oh, wait before we go. Dad, how did Amy take the news?" David said.

"Well, fairly good. She's in her bedroom processing it all. Her whole life has been a lie. I think she is continuing to accept it all. I told her when you came back, we would all sit and chat more. She wants to be like your Auntie Sarah and help. I didn't make any promises, but we can all talk. She'll never be part of the inner circle."

"Did you ask her about the fake ID she bought?"

"Yes, just an additional problem we will now have to deal with. Sooner than later. We could go to the police for this one, but I think we need to take care of it in house. With the information Amy gave us, we made some phone calls. There are three companies the government uses to print government IDs. The staff are heavily screened and interviewed before they are hired in one of these factories. They are the same places that make a lot of credit cards."

"So very high security businesses," said David.

"The highest, right up there with the Mint. Seems there is a lady who works for the one company in Mississauga. She can sneak out small amounts of the ID's and credit cards."

"We need her on our payroll," said Phil.

"Well, boys, when you get back, that's the plan. The guy this woman was selling the ID's to, would then customize them to his clients' needs. He will need taken care of, or maybe put on our payroll. That's why the quality is so good. He's using authentic cards. We know the government and the banks are changing them to be harder to fake, so having her on the inside is what we need. Plus, we can also get blank credit cards. Again, they will upgrade them soon, too."

"Well, this is good news. Who would have thought that Amy would be the one to lead us to this? We should use her for some work. We can talk when we're all together. Mom's going to kill you, us, all of us, you know that, right?"

James replied with a laugh, "Oh yeah, well if she does, hopefully she uses our services, keeps the money in house."

"Well, we all have work to do. One of us will call you when we have more information from our friends in the room. You two take care."

"Boys, keep your eyes open."

They hung up.

•   •   •

David instructed Phil to remove Ian from the room and prepare him to be picked up. He decided he was going to make the Russian bleed or talk before he came back out. Phil removed Ian and David entered the room.

"Hello, David," the Russian said.

"What did you just say?" asked David. "You speak English?"

"Yes, I do."

"Name?" David asked.

"Aleksi."

"I think the meds are kicking in. I stuffed them in your food. A little trick one of your commie comrades taught me on a ship. Why are you here?"

"David, people see your family as weak right now. They see an opportunity to destroy it, to destroy all of you. To end your reign as the greatest."

"Well, that's not happening."

"The great Soviet Union is for sale. We are collapsing inside, rotting from the inside out. Our military is falling apart. The men are scared and don't know if they will be paid. We can sell what we want to the free world."

"Who are you working for?" asked David.

"David, what will you do with Ian?"

"Why would you care?"

"I would like to know he'll die. The things he said to me not knowing I speak English, kill him, David. For me."

"What? I won't be the one to decide if that happens, but I hope I am told to."

"Ah yes, John will make the call. Good old John. David, I volunteered for this job, and I have my reasons. I knew you would catch me. You are too good for a, how do you say, old fuck like me. I am dying of an illness. I knew you would kill me and save me from the suffering ahead. I am a coward. A few days of torture is nothing to the death I have ahead of me."

David looked at him. This hardened man of the old Soviet Union was about to cry. The Soviets never showed emotion, well, maybe one, anger. What David saw in the man's eyes was a need to speak and then be put down like a sick animal. David left the room and found Phil.

David revealed his conversation with Aleksi to Phil. Phil told David that the MI6 were coming to pick up Ian. They had questions for him.

Phil brought Aleksi food and water, then left the room. David removed Aleksi's restraints that held his arms to the chair. Aleksi refused the food. He sipped his glass of water. "David, thank you for this. I have done a lot of dreadful things in my life, but your grandfather, he was always good to me. We worked on jobs in eastern Europe together. I would work as his interpreter. We met way back when he was in the SAS and I was in the KGB."

"What? You two worked as a team?"

"Yes David. The grave, the paint will come off the headstone, don't worry. I would never disrespect him. Your family isn't easy to get hold of, so I thought this would get your attention. I am sorry for doing it this way, David. I had a final meeting with the IRA to close a deal. Before I even traveled, I knew this was how my trip would end."

"You worked with Granda?"

"Yes, David, a brilliant man. Today isn't the first time I was in this room. I worked in here before you were even a little boy."

"Okay, so why did you come?"

"Promise to kill me when we are done here. You must promise. Kenton would have done it for me."

"I can't promise that. I will call John. If he confirms your story, then I'll do as you request."

"Call John. He knows my story. See, I was in Chernobyl the day the explosion happened. Now, I am rotting from the inside. I have seen other comrades die. David, I don't want to die like that. I am a, how do you say, I am a pussy. Please finish what you started here. I beg of you, Kenton, my friend would do it for me. Know that."

"I will," David said. "But why are you here? You said you had information to tell me. So..., get talking."

"You have learned your trade well. Things are not what they seem in my mother land. Igor is not who you think. He is weak. There are others, they are growing with the new political leaders. There are rats everywhere. David, I saw a trade deal. A general sold a couple fighter jets with the pilots. Another captain is trying to sell a submarine. It is a new world. You, you and Phil need to lead your family. They are old and stuck in the old ways, the old rules. Everything is new, David. Everything. Kenton always stayed on the leading edge of the business. Your dad and John are comfortable, too comfortable. You need to look to the future; they are stuck in the past. David, you can lead The Family into the new century. I wish I could give you details, but I only follow orders and am told what I need to know. But be careful. Trust only your closest friends. Everyone else could be an enemy."

He coughed; blood splattered on the floor in front of him. "David, I have a note in my pocket. It is a few contacts for you, or John, to look up. The men I worked for. They are ex-military and ex-KGB. Good men. They want to meet you. They want to work with The Family."

"To sell me subs and jets?"

"You can trust them. They sent me to talk to you and anyone else from The Family."

David reached into Aleksi's pocket. The names he read were unknown to him. "I will make sure John gets this. What do you mean by rats? Who? Do you have names?"

"David, you will figure it out. I just know there are rats. That is it. Just whispers and ghosts, but they are real."

"Where is Igor? How can I get to him?"

"I know some things because I have been in the game for so long, but I don't know the details. I wouldn't be here, except I felt it was one last thing I owed Kenton. He loved you so much, and I want you to have a long life because it was what he wanted. David, watch your back. Not all your friends are looking out for you. Igor is in Russia. Leave him there. His ego will be his downfall. Since the fall of communism, there is a more powerful group, they are growing their numbers daily. Their name is the Rodstvo. They are ex-military, ruthless, hardened men. They might get to Igor before you do." He laughed at his own comment. "Igor will beg for you if they get him. One last thing, Sergio, I believe he might be in Iran now. I can't confirm it, just a rumor. You need to find and protect that man."

"Protect him? You mean kill him."

"David, remember what you think you know and what the truth is might not be the same thing. Don't be misled."

"Okay, I understand."

"One last thing, you have a staff member in the shop who is talking to Igor and others, rough, deep voice. He is one problem but, not your only one." His head dropped; he was pale. "David, you must kill me. That was the deal. I am done. Just be quick. There isn't much of me left to kill."

David stood up and left the room. The emotion of the conversation bit into David's heart. He called John and told him the Russian's name. With emotion and concern, David revealed to John what Aleksi had said. John told him to kill Aleksi, an old friend, respectfully and quickly.

Standing behind Aleksi, David prepared a needle. Trained by a military doctor, an old friend of Kenton's, David found a vein and injected twenty milliliters of Fentanyl into him. It took Aleksi six minutes to pass peacefully to the next world. David made a call back to Canada to confirm the job was completed.

The next day, two morticians collected the Russian and a note David needed passed to Aleksi's old handler. Aleksi's sister, his next of kin, was called and informed of his passing. She requested his body be cremated and returned to her in Russia.

Conner from MI6 called Phil. "Ian will not be returning to the shop or anywhere. If he left personal items there, dispose of them. We appreciate the hand off. He was extremely helpful in answering our questions. I believe his information might have saved many lives from a bombing in Manchester." He hung up before Phil could respond.

• • •

John needed the boys back in Canada. David and Phil would need to return to Guelph for three days before being back on a flight to Northern Ireland to help prepare a large delivery of weapons and other items for a client. The boys had traveled non-stop, but there was plenty of work in Guelph to clean up.

They had done their customers' bidding and neglected their own house.

The boys entered John's office, tired and hungry. The stress weighed on The Family and the added information David had gathered from Alexi didn't help make the future any clearer for them.

They discussed the last couple of days and what Aleksi revealed to David. David didn't know whether any of what he had heard was true or just an old man who wanted to play with David's emotions to get killed quickly.

John and James confirmed Aleksi's Chernobyl story and history. He had been a KGB security member most of his career. The government was nervous about how four staff members in Chernobyl planned to sabotage the nuclear plant. Aleksi and two other KGB men investigated the suspects who intended to melt down the power plant. Aleksi and his team prevented the explosion, but missed a secondary plan that caused the meltdown on April 26th, 1986. The men he identified as the saboteurs stood before a KGB firing squad. There was no mention of them in the official public investigation. The Soviets never revealed the truth to their people, or the world.

John had known Aleksi long enough to know that he had tremendous respect for Kenton and Igor. "I have no reason to mistrust this information or the names on this list. We need to act on it. We need to find these men and talk with them. If they need protection, well, we are the best in the business."

They discussed the leak in the shop. They all had an idea who it was but had no evidence but the dying words of an old adversary.

James wanted to put pressure on Peter, he needed to tighten up his team too. He also wanted Scott to speak with Russell, his MI6 contact. He wanted to be sure Russell's team was secure and on the right side of the line. They all decided they needed to continue to keep their circle small and tight. They needed to be better at their communication and dealings with others. If they were going to pick apart their clients' practices, they needed to look at their own internal processes. Everything would need to be compartmentalized with all their staff and contacts. Only the four of them and Scott, through face-to-face discussions, would know the full scale of each job. They would only give the others the absolute minimum information to make the operation a success, which included Frank.

They spent the day in the office reviewing how they would run David's jobs, Scott's shipments, the multiple businesses they ran and laundered money through, and the other smaller jobs they would continue to do. James and John admitted they were stuck with too many old ways of doing things. A big part of the discussion was about Amy and her illegal license. That group who created it would need a visit. For the first time since Kenton's death, the team sat and reviewed themselves. They discussed their weaknesses and strength. They looked at the business and what needed to change. That day, night, and morning, they talked and discussed many things. Once the sun came up, they had their notes. It prepared them to be better and stronger. There would be many more meetings and talks, but for now, the foundation of the new business model and its chartered goals had been reviewed and improved. Scott would need to fly over for a few days to discuss the new procedures.

CHAPTER THIRTEEN

John had done some digging and found that the student who sold Amy the fake ID bought it from a bike gang in Hamilton. While David and Phil had worked in Northern Ireland, John, Frank, and James visited the bikers, previous patrons of The Family. The bikers revealed, after a heated conversation, where they purchased the IDs. Before the trio left, they made an agreement on future purchases of weapons.

• • •

David and Phil headed out at 1 a.m. to a house in Scarborough. With all the travel over the last month, time had no meaning to the boys. It was either dark or light.

In Scarborough, David parked the car a street over from the house they were targeting. Approaching the house, Phil noticed the only lights on were coming from the basement. They walked to the front door, hidden behind overgrown bushes.

"Well, this is better than having to climb a fence into the backyard," David said. "I will clear the back of the main floor and basement. You do the front and upstairs."

"Got it."

David wished he had Frank with him, but he was in the Bahamas for a couple of days to make sure the ladies were happy and safe.

Standing at the front door, they pulled their balaclavas down. David picked the front door lock. Entering the house, David cleared the kitchen, then the dining room area, while Phil searched the powder room and living room. Silently, they both acknowledged the floor was secure.

Phil climbed the stairs. He found four empty bedrooms with only mattresses spaced out on the floors.

Standing at the top of the basement stairs, David heard four different voices. He stepped back and waited for Phil. "There are at least four people down there. We need to go together. Stay behind me," David whispered.

"Okay. Strange thing, up there, no furniture, only mattresses covering the floors. Each door had the lock reversed. They lock from the hallway. You know what that means?"

"These boys are more than forgers. Okay, we shoot first, ask questions after. We still have the element of surprise," David whispered.

David checked the spare clips in his back pocket and his knife on his right hip. Nervous, Phil checked his coat for his spare clips, then tapped David on the shoulder. They descended the stairs.

The basement had four doors spaced along a long, narrow hallway. Voices came from the door at the end of the corridor. David pointed to the door at the bottom of the stairs and then the second door.

Phil knew what he wanted; he was to open the first door at the same time David opened his. With guns in hand, they stood by their doors. David nodded and swung the door open. Phil's door led to the furnace and laundry room. He stepped back into the hallway. David's room was also empty except for mattresses on the floor. They moved to the next door. There was no light coming from under it. Phil stood to David's right as he opened the door. This room had four desks, four file cabinets and a safe. David closed the door. They positioned themselves at the last door where the source of the voices came from.

David kicked the door open and stepped into the room. Phil stepped in behind him and moved to David's left. Four men sat at old wooden desks. They all wore glasses and three of them had cigarettes that hung out of their mouths. The men all froze.

"Good morning gents," David said. The smallest of the men stood up and reached behind his desk. David pulled his trigger twice. The silencer helped, but the two pops of the bullets, when they left the chamber, still echoed through the house. The man fell backwards on the floor, dead.

"Any other heroes?" Phil asked.

The other men placed their hands on their heads.

"Okay, you guys must know the routine. One at a time, starting with you." David pointed to the short, stout man. "On the floor and spread out, please. As you move, please tell me your name and what your skill is."

The first man fell to the floor and crawled closer to David to give the others room to lie beside him. "Armen, forger."

The second man lay on the floor beside him with his arms spread out. "Vahe, handwriting specialist."

Then the third. "Aron, forger."

Phil searched them for weapons. He found nothing threatening and, checking the fourth man's neck, confirmed he was dead. Phil looked to see what he had reached for, a baseball bat.

"Okay, one at a time, slowly sit up. Cross your legs and your hands go on your head." The men followed the instructions. "Who wants to talk? We need to know what is going on in this house."

"Are you police? Are you government men?"

"Far from it," said Phil.

Vahe said, "I will answer any questions you have if you spare my life."

"How about this? I won't kill you first," David said.

Vahe said, "We live, well, are prisoners in this house with twelve other men. We are all from Armenia and specialists in our fields. The others have their jobs to do, too. Some men visit grow houses to make sure the Marijuana plants are healthy and growing. Others watch the women that are kidnapped and brought to Canada to work the streets. Others travel farther away from the house to distribute fake ID's and sell drugs. I don't know where. We stay in the house to create fake credit cards and identifications. The other day we heard they are preparing to start a large check kiting operation in Toronto. There are other groups living in Montreal, Edmonton, and Vancouver. Occasionally, they meet with people from the States."

David walked to Vahe's desk and rummaged through the items as Vahe continued. "We are known as the best at what we do throughout the other groups."

Looking through their desks, the workmanship astonished David and skills they had. He held up IDs, credit cards, and government passports from many countries. What he held in his hand was better than any of John's top people.

Phil rifled through the other pieces. He couldn't believe what he was seeing, one-hundred-dollar bills that had all the water marks precisely placed.

"These IDs are very good."

"It's because they are real. We have a connection at the factory where the IDs and credit cards are made. I have seen where our guards get them. So has Armen. It is the only time we get outside."

"Do you know where the place is?" asked Phil.

"If you have a map and can show us where we are on the map, I can show you, yes," said Vahe.

"Okay, are you men happy with your lives here?" David asked.

"We're forced to do this. This is not why we came to Canada, leaving our families," Armen said.

"We can help you. Where are your controllers?" asked David.

"They are out on business or at a bar they own," said Armen.

"So, why are you left here alone? Are they not afraid you will run away?" Phil asked.

"The guy you killed, his name is Maxim. He was watching or guarding us," said Vahe.

"Isn't that a Russian name?"

"Yes, Russians brought us here. They promised us a new life. Lies, as you can see. Most people are from the old Soviet Union. But the guys that are overseeing everyone are all Russian."

"Okay, we're going to take you guys away. We are going to bring you to our shop for safe keeping. How does that sound?" said David.

"Are you John? Or maybe, what was the name, James?" Vahe asked.

"Vahe, they are too young. John is older, in his sixties, and James would be old enough to be their father," said Armen.

"Who are you talking about?" David said.

"I don't know for sure. I keep hearing their names when the Russian men come to the house. It seems those two men really upset, or enrage is the word, the Russians when they come to pick up IDs or drugs. I think it's funny."

"Right. I need you guys to gather up all your tools and personal stuff. We need to go," said Phil.

"I'm not going anywhere," said Aron.

"Suit yourself," said David. "We can tie you up and leave you down here. What about you two?"

"If you don't kill me, I will go. Anywhere is better than here. It is a house full of mattresses. There is nothing else. I assume you have seen that. We are not allowed outside."

"Yes, we have. We don't want to kill you. We need you for your skills," David said.

"I am going with you two," said Vahe.

"I want in too," said Armen. "Can we get up and pack up our tools?"

"One at a time. We will also tie you up to travel."

"Whatever it takes, they lock us in our rooms to sleep, anyway. Aron, come. Why stay here? You know it won't end in your favor."

"No, I would rather take my chances here," said Aron.

David took Vahe upstairs to gather his personal items, a few pieces of clothes, and a photo of his parents. While they were upstairs packing, Armen packed up his desk under the careful watch of Phil. A few things from Aron's desk made it into Armen's bag while Aron loudly protested at him in Armenian. Phil pointed his gun at Aron and told him to shut up.

When David returned with Vahe, he had rope. Phil took Armen upstairs. With his hands forced behind his back, they tied Aron up. Vahe looted any items of value before they went back to the main floor.

They turned the lights off to the room with Aron tied and gagged in it. David followed Vahe up the stairs and met Phil and Armen at the front door. They walked out the door and to the car with Vahe and Armen both smiling. "I don't know if we will live for another twenty-four hours, Vahe, but I think the abuse is behind us."

"No talking," said David. He tied their hands and put them in the back of the car. "I am going to go back in and give Aron one last chance to come with us."

He looked at Phil. "Be right back."

David entered the room in the basement and flipped on the light. Aron pushed himself under a desk, kicking at David as he approached. David reached for him and pulled Aron to the center of the room. David rolled him onto his belly. With his knee pressing Aron to the ground, he pulled out his knife. His left hand lifted Aron's head and his right hand slowly slid under Aron's neck.

"You should have come with us," David said. In one rapid motion, his blade sliced across Aron's neck. Warm blood covered David's hand and knife as Aron's body shuddered. He stood up, shook the blood off his hand, and left the room. Before leaving the house, he washed his hands and cleaned his knife.

David started the car. "Where is Aron?" asked Vahe.

"Still in the basement. Stubborn that one," said David.

On the road back to Guelph, David said. "You know how you mentioned John and James at the house?"

"Yes," said Armen.

"They are our fathers. We will take care of you two and pay you for your services. Welcome to the real Canada. We might even try to help reunite you with your family back home."

Both men cried.

•　　•　　•

David and Phil met John and James in the office. Vahe and Armen sat at the conference table with a map of Toronto and the surrounding cities. The next step was to talk to the person with the inside information on getting the cards. The work to free the Armenians would be for nothing if they couldn't turn the inside person.

Vahe studied the map. He traced the roads they took to pick up the cards. The few times he went with one of his Armenian handlers, they picked the items up outside a pizza takeout from an Italian man. Armen located the house where he met the card lady and a few Italians.

James asked questions about the lady, her background, how much they paid her and her schedule. Any information to help turn her. John followed up with more questions about the Italian men they saw. With the questions asked, and most not fully answered, the boys were on the road again. This time to a strip mall in Mississauga by the airport. A small eight-unit plaza, it had a pizza joint, a real estate office and a karate dojo. The other five units held one of the most secure factories in Canada. What looked like vacant units held the biggest credit card and government identification card maker in Canada. From the outside, the units looked abandoned. No staff cars parked in front of the units. The windows and doors were blacked out.

They drove past the strip mall and headed to Eleanor McHale's house.

At 5 p.m., after a long day at work, she returned home. David sat in the kitchen with his knife on the table. Walking into the kitchen, Eleanor jumped from the shock of seeing a man in her house. She turned to run, but David chased her and placed his hand firmly on her shoulder before she left the kitchen. Directing her by the shoulder, he forced her to sit at the table.

Across the table from her, he picked up his knife and placed it back in its scabbard under his hoody.

Her first question didn't surprise David. "Are you from the government?"

"No, not the government, and I am not a cop. I met a couple of Armenian men that talked about you. So, I will ask the questions. Your job is to answer all of mine, honestly. I have all night, and many ways to get the answers from you. So, let's start from the beginning."

She told him about the history of her family and how they lived in poverty. Her parents worked hard, but they never got a break. She put herself through college, a security and justice course, and got the job with the card company straight out of college. Her dad had ties with Italian men in Toronto and he made money with them. Soon after that, her brother was also working for them. David knew exactly who she referred to.

"One day, my brother mentioned to these mobsters where I worked. Then the fool brought the men to my house. I was so mad at him for doing that. The last thing I need is mobsters knowing where I live." She smiled at David. "One afternoon they were waiting for me, like you were today. They asked me to steal cards for them, IDs, and credit card blanks. I refused. That night, they beat my brother up pretty good. When I woke the next morning, he was on my couch and a large gentleman asked me to reconsider."

"Was your brother okay?"

"Yes, it was pretty superficial from what I could see. They offered me a lot of money to get the cards. So, we spent the day discussing the building, the security, and my role as a manager. Being a graduate of a security program helped me understand the systems in place. I spent a week investigating ways to get the cards out. There was no way I could hide them in my clothes or on my body. We have a security team that runs us through all kinds of random checks as we enter and leave the building. I found a small opening in the bathroom by the toilet paper dispenser. It was big enough that I could slide up to fifteen cards into the hole."

"That's interesting."

"So once we figured out where it was located on the outside, they sent a mason over to remove a brick. The new brick looked like it belonged, but they hollowed it out so it could slide in and out of its opening."

"What about cameras?"

"Nope, blind spot. Part of the security of the building is not to have any visual external security. It just looks like empty units. No cameras, no nothing from the outside. There are cameras that look out the windows but they have blind spots. We enter through the fake real estate unit. But inside, the place is covered with cameras."

"Huh, that's pretty smart, actually."

"Yeah, I know. So, the management washrooms back against the pizza place. My contacts bought the pizzeria. They have delivery trucks in and out of the place daily. What they do is back their van up to unload, walk close to the wall and grab the cards outside of any cameras, because of the blind spots. I get my order on a Monday night and I have it ready for Thursday night. I pay my floor supervisor well to miscount the output of the presses. We almost got caught twice, but he skillfully explained the missing inventory. One of the bean counters wanted to see if we could eliminate waste. The boys almost eliminated him. But that allowed us to find the threshold of how many items could go missing in a day."

"So, how does he do that? I would think they are pretty tight with the numbers."

"Yes, they are, but the *'they'* in that equation, is me. I have final sign off on defective cards and startup of the presses. We have three machines that stamp out the cards. They are fed from sheets of plastic. There is always an assumed waste when we do maintenance on the press. They sharpen the cutters daily, after every 1230 sheets. I am always there when they are changed. And Craig, my supervisor, is the one who does the sharpening. We have a system where we palm the extra cards and slide them up our sleeves. Then we go back to my office to sign off on the preventive maintenance we just completed. My boss loves paperwork. I hide the cards in a fake bottom of the pot of my fern. During lunch, when the Directors and others leave to eat, I hit the washroom and make the delivery."

David was shocked how she was so free to pass on this information.

"I think that covers it. No wait, I get paid very well for it too. I pick the money up at my local grocery store on Saturdays."

"Who pays you?"

"The same guys since I started this a few years ago."

"Okay, so where do you hide your money? You obviously know enough to not live above your paycheck."

"I tucked that away for my early retirement. I don't think you need anymore information than that. Listen David, why don't you bring Phil in? I'll make you guys sausages and then we can all go to the store."

"What? How do you know my name? I don't know a Phil."

"Yes, you do. He is your handler. David, I know you took the Armenians last night. My guys know it was you. They said you would pick me up at some point and talk to me. I was told to tell you everything. Angelo isn't worried. He told me to say to you." She cleared her throat and in her best bad seventies mob movie voice said, "You fuckin' boys and your demand to run everything. Fuck you, share the wealth."

David laughed at her attempt. "So, Angelo wants to see me? Is that what you're trying to say?"

"You and Phil. He told me; all is good. He knew shit was going to go down when some jackass sold your sister a fake piece. He's just glad you can have the meeting peacefully. Go get Phil, I'll make pasta to go with the sausages."

• • •

Phil, David, and Eleanor entered the grocery store. She stopped by the potatoes and spoke to the produce manager. After she introduced David and Phil, she walked the boys through the stockroom and into an office where Angelo was counting out fifty-dollar bills. Two other men stood beside him.

"David, you piece of shit. How are you doing? It has been a while. Phil, I bet you weren't expecting this," Angelo said. He got up and hugged both boys.

"Of course we were. This had your greasy hands all over it. Marcio, how are you? And who is this?"

"This is George. He is Eleanor's contact. And a butcher, he is good with all kinds of meats, if you know what I mean. He owns the store with his brother, the produce guy out front."

"Nice to meet you. You could do better than these clowns," said Phil.

"Whatever," said Angelo.

"Okay, so what's the deal? This has been a lot of fun playing mobsters, but let's get real. Angelo, Marcio, you know I'm not a negotiator. I come in after the discussions break down. This is Phil's department. But you sold my little sister a fake ID."

"Whoa, no not me David. I'm not taking the blame for this. We have dealt with the goof and his family that sold Amy the ID, and I understand your dads had a conversation with our biker friends. So, David, I assume you're just here to see how civilized people run a business then? No need for violence, eh?" said Marcio.

"Not yet," David said with a smile.

"When you're wandering our streets, it makes us all nervous. Where is the knife? You have it hidden well," said Marcio.

"Okay, sorry to break up the reunion, but I have a store to run," said George. He turned and walked out of his office.

"Why don't we set up a proper sit down in Guelph. We can work out all the details," said Phil.

"Yeah, yeah, are we all good?"

"All good here. You two need to relax. When have I—never mind." David laughed as the other three stood in silence.

"Okay, but we do have a slight problem. Maybe we need to consider it before we all sit down."

"Okay, give us some background before we leave."

"So, boys, my family used to run this entire operation, right? But about a month ago, these Russians came in, took out four of our men and took ownership of the team in the house you were at yesterday. They took everything from that operation we had in Scarborough. None of us were happy, and we tried to take it all back. They killed eight more of us. They are ruthless."

"Yeah, so I have heard. You know what happened to me a few months ago?"

"Yeah, Anthony was in Guelph to see John about a delivery. He told him. Sorry about that, brother," said Marcio.

"And this leads to the question we should all be thinking about. Do we, or should we, look at combining our families to fight these Russian fucks? They don't give a shit how much damage or death they cause. They have no respect for the old boundary lines we all abide by. Please think about it. We can talk later."

"Angelo, I think you are right. Problem is, we, our family, have so many sticks in the fire right now. I don't know if we can take on another battle, even though I believe we are already fighting a common enemy."

"I understand. Just bring it up at the next meeting at home. We can talk in a few weeks to see what you decide," said Marcio.

"As for the incident with Amy and the fallout? Are there any further actions required for it? The way I see it, you guys will do our work from now on. Good?" Angelo asked. "Can we agree on that? We can still do the pickups from Eleanor and deliver to you guys. Honestly Phil, we don't give a fuck who does the work if the price is reasonable. We just want those two Armenians doing the majority of our work. They do fucking beautiful work."

"I don't see that being an issue," said Phil. "I'll get Dad to call your uncle. We can have a meal, work through the details. Who would have thought this was all because Amy bought a fake ID from a kid in school? Funny how life is at times."

"Okay, well, keep your ears to the ground. If you hear anything about the Russians moving into more of our territories, we will give the shop a call," said Angelo.

"We will do the same thing," said Phil.

"Phil, our other shipment, still coming next week?" Angelo asked while he pointed a finger pistol at Phil.

"Yes, I haven't heard differently."

"Okay lads, we will see you soon."

David and Phil headed home. They were pleased they could get the deal done with no violence. They now were sure the Russians were closing in on their territory.

CHAPTER FOURTEEN

With the new knowledge of the Russian Mob, Rodstvo, moving into southern Ontario, and the lack of time for updates and meetings, the family sat down and met. They spent the afternoon together and had an inner circle meeting. Amy worked hard for them in the office but was not invited to the meeting, even though she asked to attend.

They gathered around the table. Amy sat by John's desk, hoping not to be noticed.

"Amy, Luv. You need to leave," said James. "I explained the inner circle meetings to you and with you not being initiated, you can't stay. You need to go upstairs. Frank will find some work for you."

"I know, dad. Is there no way I could just stay this once? I have one question, if I have to leave. When is mom coming home?"

"Good question. We will call you back when we have that talk. But for now, go see Frank."

She packed up her papers and left the office.

David began the meeting. "It seems this new group, the Rodstvo, is in Canada and growing by the day. They are pushing their way into Toronto. From other conversations I have had, it seems they are focused on Miami and Southern California right now. So that is a big problem." John wrote a note on his pad of paper. "Where is Igor? Has there been any communication from our contacts about him?"

"It has been quiet, David. Igor is doing his thing, I guess, or he could be dead. It seems that the Rodstvo has taken out many people in Russia. Let's table Igor and the Rodstvo for now. I need to spend some time on it. There is so much happening at once."

"Any word on our issues in house, Dad?" asked Phil.

"Yes, and no. I have a couple of people I am watching. We are all too close to the staff. I reached out to Angelo yesterday. They, as we know, have their own problems. But he has a guy that runs a couple of warehouses in Brampton. Once things quiet down, hopefully in the next couple of weeks, he will send him up to us. We can use him as a new employee to work undercover for us. Until then, we keep things quiet around here."

"That makes sense to me," said Phil.

"I have spent some time with our Armenian forgers. That is going very well. Eleanor is getting us blanks, and these guys are knocking them out. I have them doing passports and medical notes. Angelo is now prescribing pills for his customers." James laughed at the last few words.

"I had a meeting in Richmond, Virginia, with Peter last week. He has a list of people that are working together. As he confirms them, David, you will get your page."

"All right. The *cut the credit card* page. I still chuckle every time I see that on my pager. Funniest code for a hit ever," said David.

"Scott has a few large shipments coming up. He is worried about warehouse space and wants to buy a couple more to store our inventory. I will look at that with him when I am back home," said James.

John reviewed the sales and deliveries of their inventory. He shared a document with the group about how the legitimate businesses were doing on laundering their money and how he was negotiating with three large factories in Buffalo to move money through.

"We have one other issue to discuss. It's funny actually. Remember the mobster from Chicago we hid away four years ago?" said Phil.

"Gino, or sorry, his new name was Walter. Now what?" asked James.

"Well, he was at a baseball game two weeks ago. And guess who made it on the stadium screen and national television," said Phil.

"Fuck off. I am done with this guy. We have moved him three times. Don't take his calls. If the wrong people saw him, that is on him. I am done," said John.

"Okay, so we stop sending him payments? Do you want me to release his identity too, huh? Who are we hiding him from? We have so many now," said Phil.

"Yes, stop the payments. Don't release his name. He will expose himself through time. If he hasn't already," said John.

David ran upstairs to get Frank and Amy. When they were all seated around the table, John called Scott. With many of the known threats under control or manageable, John wanted to know if it was time to return the families.

"I am enjoying the break from Elizabeth and her complaining," said James. He pointed to Amy and then David. "Never repeat that to your mother or..." He slid his thumb across his neck. All those around the table laughed.

"I can't argue with that, dad," said Amy. "It has been nice not hearing you two fight. But we can't just leave them down there."

"We could try," said David.

"Scott, do you have any objections to bringing your family home?"

"No, I know my brother is just joking about his wife. James, you miss her."

"Frank, can you make the arrangements to get everyone home, please? I guess James and his kids can have a day or two of freedom before they are back under Queen Elizabeth's rule."

The meeting wrapped up. Scott hung up and those in Guelph locked up the shop and headed out for supper.

With all the traveling, it wasn't just gatherings around the office table they had missed; they hadn't had a meal together in over a week. They invited Amy, but she had a date with a boy from church. David joked with her that they would do a background check and surveillance on him and his family to be sure he was up to their standard.

In La Fontana's restaurant, wanting to have a section of the restaurant to themselves, John paid the tab for a couple of young lovers and a young family to move.

David's pager chirped as they finished the main course. He unclipped it from his belt and read the text, *'need some credit cards cut'*.

"John, I have more cards to cut up. Let me call them and see what they need and the timing. I might need to delay my trip to see Scott."

"Aye, we always play second fiddle these days. Eh, John," James said, winking at David.

David went to the pay phone outside the front door. He dialed a twelve-digit number. "Hello," said Peter.

"Peter, it's David."

"David, I will have a package dropped at the shop in the morning. I need this wrapped up by the end of the week."

David hung up and returned to the table.

"Looks like we're traveling Phil. We can fly out in a couple of days. The package will arrive in the morning," David said as he checked his watch. "I was thinking, why don't we have a private jet? The money we're making on the Armenians alone would cover the maintenance costs. If we are worried about being tailed and our security, why not? We help that small airline on Toronto Island. We could use their hangar in Waterloo and their team could maintain it. I'm just saying, why are we risking being followed on commercial flights when we can do things a little classier? Think about it. I'm getting sick of layovers and timing flights. A small aircraft for even flights in North America would be beneficial. I am just putting it on the table."

"It isn't a bad one either. This last year we have expanded our territory and our sales. We can discuss it later. For now, let's order dessert and enjoy an evening together," said John.

"Sounds good," said Phil.

• • •

The following morning, the team waited at the shop for the package to arrive.

David entered John's office with coffees in his hands. "Morning everyone. Sorry I am a little late. I stopped for coffees."

"Good morning, David," said James.

"I booked the flights and a hotel for you guys. You will be there a few days, I suspect. It looks to be a kill and clean job. You will need to hit a hardware store once you arrive. I ordered you a white cargo van as well. It can be the service call from hell. Peter believes this is his mole, an operations manager on the west coast. He believes this guy is the one that has been feeding Igor and others information on us. Remember Tom Elliott? The FBI agent you did in a few years ago?"

"Tom, Tom. Yeah, Grand Island job." David hesitated. "Amazing chicken, yeah, I remember."

"Yes, that guy," said James.

"How is this connected?"

"Well, I guess they grew up together and when Tom died, this guy," John flipped a few pages over, "Keith, Keith is his name. He did a bit of investigating of his buddy's death. He has a high clearance so he could get into the CIA's databases and archives. Peter has proof he is out to get us and the CIA for the hit. He is, or was, Peter's right-hand guy for South America and the West Coast. He has fed people and organizations the details of our jobs, the ones that we do for the American government. I assume if he has done his homework, he knows a lot more about us than just his agency's requests. Peter says Keith asked him a question about us last week, which made him put a tail on Keith. So, it seems Peter did his job and found the rat. Now we need to dispose of him."

"Okay. Well, that will be tricky. I'll think of something. This is good news, one less item to worry about, I guess."

CHAPTER FIFTEEN

"The weather is always so nice in California. We should spend more time here," said Phil to David as they drove the white cargo van to the hotel.

"We will have a few days here; I want some time at the beach once we plan out this job."

"Agreed," said Phil. "It seems the last few jobs we have been on have been in extreme heat or extreme wet. I could use an afternoon on the beach. We can swing by the target's house. It isn't too far from the hotel, anyway."

In a white full size rental van, they drove past Keith's house. In the subdivision of the medium-high-income households, they saw no security or signs of a dog.

They checked into the hotel, unpacked, and discussed the plans for the job. The one thing they both noticed while in the subdivision was the amount of service vehicles that were around. Their white van fit in perfectly. Using that as an advantage, they played the role of contractors. The next morning, they headed to the local hardware store and purchased tools, parts, and drop sheets. With the tools and equipment purchased for the job, they loaded the van. They reviewed their plans for the night and headed to the beach to relax.

•   •   •

David sat in the car six houses down from his target. He checked the street before stepping out of the car. The only house with lights on was five houses away. The television flickered and glowed through the front window.

David stood at the end of Keith's driveway. Dressed in black, he put on his gloves and pulled down his balaclava. He walked beside two Fords parked in the carport. The job had to happen in the house and the request was to keep it clean, even if it meant the wife had to die.

David tried the door at the side of the house. It was locked. He went to the rear of the house; the sliding door was locked. He gently wiggled the sliding door, side to side, then up and down. Finally, the lock loosened. With one big lift, the sliding door broke free from the latch, and he slowly slid it open.

David was never a fan of house invasions, especially in older houses. The floors announced when someone entered a room. He walked the perimeter of the rooms to avoid any loud noises from the floor as it settled. The stairs were always tricky, but these were carpeted, which always helped to muffle the sound of wood settling. Finally, he stood at the doorway to the target's bedroom. He gently and carefully entered the room. The carpeted floor still had wood underneath and sang its song of loose nails and dried wood as he walked to the foot of the bed. Both husband and wife lay topless under a bedsheet. The ceiling fan hummed. *The bearings are going, as are these two,* David mused.

He had one chance at this. Two for one deal without a mess. David walked to the right of the bed. His plan was to take out the target, then deal with the wife.

Looking over the couple, David noticed two medicine bottles on the night table beside Keith's wife. He assumed they were sleeping pills. Her snoring proved she was in a deep sleep.

Out of his chest pocket, David pulled a syringe. He removed the safety cap and looked down at his target. On the floor, beside the bed, lay a couple of thick pillows. David picked one up and placed it over Keith's face. He leaned over him and with his left hand, he pressed down hard. With his right hand, he thrust the needle into Keith's thigh. He pressed the plunger, the contents, medical grade fentanyl, flowed into Keith's leg.

After a few seconds, Keith clawed at the pillow with his hands. Forcing the pillow down harder on his victim's face, David felt Keith's nose break. Like a fish out of water, Keith kicked and flopped on his back, struggling. David mounted him, straddling his torso. The struggle on the bed woke his wife. Her eyes opened to a black shadow over her husband. She froze with fear. David pressed even harder on the face and throat of Keith. He stopped moving. Unconscious but not dead, David had to leave Keith and deal with his wife.

Groggy from her pills, she slowly sat up and let out a scream as David pounced on her. They both rolled off the bed and landed awkwardly on the floor. Grabbing her from behind, his right arm wrapped around her neck, his left hand grabbed her hair down by her scalp. He smashed her head on the floor. Then a second time. "Keith, help me. Keith, help…" she cried out to her husband.

David dragged her to the bedside table and drove her head against it. She went limp. Her skin opened on her forehead, and she bled. David grabbed the sheet from the bed and wrapped her head to stop the bleeding. She was not dead, but immobilized.

He went back to Keith. His body was still. The fentanyl was working, taking over his body. David stood over him and waited.

Reaching for Keith's neck, he checked for a pulse and then a breath. Target one was static.

David walked to the right side of the bed. There, lying on the floor, was the job he still had to finish. She lay motionless. David acted quickly; he didn't mind his targets suffering, especially traitors to their country, but bystanders should not have to suffer. He grabbed her by her hair and dragged her to the bathroom. She woke when David placed her in the stand-up shower. Not even in her scariest dreams did she ever imagine this nightmare. With her kneeling and facing the shower wall, David moved her head backwards. She opened her eyes and looked at the dark figure standing over her. David whispered, "Sorry." His knife slid across her throat.

●　　●　　●

Phil pulled into the driveway at 8:15 a.m. He went to the side of the van and took out his small toolbox, and knocked on the side door. David let him in with a coffee in his hand.

"Morning, I understand you need some—"

"I need cream for my sun burn, is what I need right now. You want a coffee?"

"How did things go for you last night? Routine job?" Phil asked, as David handed him a cup of coffee.

"Yes, a little excitement. Nothing to worry about. They are still upstairs. They are both in the ensuite. We can set up there. I have done the laundry to wash the blood out of the bedsheets. They need switched to the dryer. And I moved the one car to the mall parking lot. We can grab that on the way out too," said David.

"Yeah, okay. You have been busy. Coffee is surprisingly good. Any cookies or something to go with it?" Phil searched for cookies. Not finding any, he took a banana.

"Well, let's get going. See if we can be out of here by lunch. You bring the tools in, and I can set up. Leave the two by fours beside the van. That should help explain the saws and noise. Lean the sheet of plywood against the house."

Phil headed out to the van and brought in the tools and drop sheets. David hung plastic sheets around the bathroom to protect the walls, ceiling, and floors from what was to come.

Phil brought in the chop saw and reciprocating saw and plugged them in. Over the next few hours, they cut up Keith and his wife. They piled the body parts in the tub, the bit of blood left in the chunks of meat found its way to the drain. Once they made smaller, manageable pieces, they filled garbage bags with the body parts and brought them to the kitchen. They took their time to clean the bedroom and bathroom. David put the pillow with blood on it in a garbage bag. They flipped the mattress to hide the blood stain from Keith's broken nose. David cleaned the blood and skin off the bedside table. Phil put multiple bottles of bleach down the drains, then cleaned the bathroom. They found a couple of suitcases and filled them with their victims' clothes.

With all the garbage bags in the kitchen, they did one last review of the upstairs. David made the bed with the same tucking and folding as the two beds in the other bedrooms. Satisfied, they moved the bags into the van and cleaned the kitchen.

"Hey, looks like we might have more work in the area," said Phil. He handed David a piece of paper. "It was under the wiper."

"Call me. I need some work done in my kitchen, looking for a price." David read the note out loud. "Good to know. We can either retire here and do renovations, or if this clown can identify us, we now have his home number. Win, win."

"Yep, maybe by *needing his kitchen done,* he means he wants rid of his wife," said Phil.

"Are we loaded up? I guess we have a boat to get to."

They stopped at the mall and David jumped in Keith's car. When he moved the car earlier, he left Keith's ball cap and sunglasses on the front seat. He put on the ball cap and the sunglasses to disguise himself. The highway was busy and, in some areas, almost at a standstill as David followed Phil and the van. With the sun dropping low in the sky, and four hours of driving behind them, they pulled down a remote road and opened a privacy gate. A mile down the laneway was a new Chevy truck and a boat, a lot nicer than they expected. The boat, a thirty-four-foot cruiser, had a small kitchen, with an empty fridge and a sleeping area with beds that had no sheets. David turned over the engine, and the boat came alive.

"I have an idea," David said. "It's getting dark, so let's stay on the boat tonight. I'll stay here and load the boat while you shoot back to that small town we drove through. Call your dad and tell him we're okay. Then grab some food, sleeping bags and fishing poles and see how many days we can have the boat for. I wouldn't mind just crashing here for a week."

Phil took the pickup and headed to the small town they passed through. Using coded words, he told his dad they were both fine and would finish the job in the morning. "There is one extra vehicle to remove. We left the scene as if Keith and his wife ran. We took clothes and left the house orderly." Phil told his dad.

After he grabbed the items on his list, he headed back to the boat. The bags were loaded on the deck of the boat and David was sitting in the pilot's chair napping. Phil honked the horn twice, causing David to jump.

"I'm starving. What did you bring back to eat?"

"Plenty, here, take this." He handed David a bag and a cup. "Eat your burger while I talk. Dad said the Asian guys paid up, so we don't need to visit them. He called the owner of the boat. We can use it for as long as we want. I told him we would stay for three nights. He'll have the van and car removed from here once we leave in the morning. So, once we finish eating, if you want to help load some groceries, we can unpack and get some sleep."

"Is your dad calling Peter?"

"Yes, if you would read the reports we receive, you would know the full plan. Peter will send a team to investigate his missing staff member. It will be revealed he skipped town all the way to Russia."

"Nice, I guess maybe that was the issue anyway, he was a double agent."

• • •

"I have never slept so well. I love the gentle rock of the boat," said David as they sat on the deck of the boat.

"Oh, I know. Your snoring was like a series of explosions all night. I'm going to go back to bed while you get us out to a fishing spot. The map has a couple of areas circled," said Phil.

David woke Phil when they arrived at the location on the map marked with five stars. There were no other boats in the area, and David confirmed he had seen no boats for the last fifteen minutes of the trip.

"Okay, if we toss a couple of pieces in, do you think we can attract some sharks?" asked David.

"Don't know. We can only try," said Phil. "It all has to go at some point."

They tossed the wife's thighs into the water and waited. After several minutes, a ripple on the surface of the water appeared. As it grew, David thumped Phil on the arm.

"Holy shit, it's a great white. I have never seen anything like this. Look, see it there?"

A shark six feet long broke the surface of the water; it took the thigh and dove. Another shark appeared and took the other thigh.

"Quick, throw in more parts. Keep feeding them. There might be more wanting fed. This is a lot more entertaining than the pig farm at home. Look at the size of that one. Phil, this is amazing."

The sharks continued to surface around the boat. David studied them, how they moved, how they slowly approached their targets, then, in a flash, they hit it hard. It amazed David at the power of the majestic creatures. What a new, exciting, and entertaining way to dispose of a couple of bodies.

CHAPTER SIXTEEN

John cut the few days of vacation short for David and Phil. From California they flew to Northern Ireland. With Scott, David did a hit in Berlin, met with a client in Paris, and dropped another in Prague. Phil organized shipments of weapons to Africa, Vietnam, and Australia.

When David and Phil arrived at Waterloo Airport, John and Amy met them. David had information for John, but with Amy in the back seat, he didn't want to discuss it.

"John, are we telling these guys now or waiting?" Amy asked.

"Let me grab some coffees. Are you guys tired? Do you want to go straight home, or can we talk?"

"John, this sounds serious," David said.

John parked the van at Riverside Park. They drank their coffees and John told them how Frank had found multiple recording devices in the shop and around the offices.

David looked at Phil. "John, this is what I wanted to tell you too. An MI6 agent that was at Scott's shop said he overheard a couple of phone conversations on a few men he was following. He said, the one call came from our shop, in Guelph. Someone made it to the Russian group he was tailing. The information referred to a shipment Phil and I are scheduled to do in a week."

"He didn't hear any names, but the information was confidential. He said the voice was very recognizable, like Darth Vader. If we can't identify the person, he will come to the shop and walk around. He said if he met the person, he would recognize the voice," said Phil.

"Then there was the information from Aleksi. Remember, before I killed him, he said we had a rat in our shop too. I think we know we have an issue."

"Well then, that helps with what we discovered. Amy looks like it's your turn to talk."

"David, we have a real problem," she said.

The group sat quietly in the van as Amy spoke. "You guys might all have been too close to see what I found. Fresh set of eyes, as they say."

"Amy cracked this? Nicely done, sis," David said. He put his hand up for a high five. Amy gave him the look only sisters can give to an older brother and get away with.

"With everything going on and the wives out of town, I have been helping more around the office. Glenn is on vacation, so Frank told me to use and maybe even clean up the office. After school, I would go to the office and help with the invoices and inventory ordering from the day. I didn't realize how nice and smart Frank was. I love that guy."

"I hope, don't think the story is about Frank, is it?" asked David.

"NO! Thankfully," said John.

"I must say, listening to you and Dad talk at meals and around the house about plumbing jobs helped me understand what some parts were and what they were for. I think I would like an apprenticeship once I'm out of school. But we can talk about that later. I was in Glenn's office. When I had the stuff Frank wanted done, I thought I would get into the file cabinet and boxes Glenn had jammed with paper. So much junk. I worked through the cabinets and drawers. The one drawer was especially a mess. There was a bank book stuffed in the back. At first, I didn't look at it, but then I looked again and noticed it was for a bank in the Bahamas. I opened it and saw large deposit numbers. I thought it was part of the business, so I gave it to John. John looked at it and next thing you know, we're tearing apart Glenn's office. John told me to look for anything that looked out of place. Well, with the other businesses you guys do, everything looked out of place."

"Glenn was never organized. I told you that many times, John. Dad too," said David.

"You know how many times your dad, Frank or I told him to clean it?" said John.

"So, I dug through some boxes and found some listening devices and telegrams from Russia and the Middle East. I also found a Russian name on multiple notes with addresses in Burlington, Oakville, and Hamilton. John sent the name over to a contact in CSIS. We did further digging into the office and found another three listening devices. There was another bank account Frank found. It was a German one. I kept going through the office while John and Frank swept the building and basement for other devices."

She looked at John, who picked up the story.

"Boys, we swept the building. We found devices both inside and outside the building. They were all tied to the electrical system, and some were unknown technologies. I made some calls and had Craig from MI6 look at the devices. They are less than a year old. Russian and exceptionally good devices."

David shook his head in disbelief.

Phil looked at Amy. "Where is Glenn?"

"He is on vacation till Monday," said Amy.

John started the van. "We have some time to plan this one out. But I think—"

"We are going to kill this fucker," she blurted out.

Surprised by what he heard; David spit his last mouthful of coffee over the dashboard.

John stopped the van. "We *are* going to kill this fucker. Thank you, Amy."

They all laughed uncontrollably. John put the van in park. He couldn't drive until he caught his breath.

• • •

David was at the shop early to meet Glenn the day he returned from his vacation. Glenn was an old family friend and a groomsman at James' wedding. James helped him moved to Guelph in 1983 after an incident where Glenn's car broke down in a Catholic area in Londonderry. With his pregnant wife stranded in the car, he went for help. He approached a couple of men walking. They offered to look at his car. When they returned to his car, they beat him in front of his wife. Kenton and Scott found those involved and dealt harshly with the men and their families.

David met Glenn at the counter and asked how his vacation to British Columbia with his family went. After a glowing review of the spots they visited, Glenn asked how the shop was while he was gone. David reviewed a few highlights of plumbing jobs they secured and how the new plumbers were doing. The conversation ended when David told Glenn that Amy had used his office and apologized if anything seemed out of place. Glenn headed to his office and David headed to the loading dock to pack his van with pipe and fittings.

Looking over his shoulder, Glenn opened his office door and entered it. At his desk, he looked around to see what they had moved. Wanting to open his filing cabinet, he checked his day timer and looked at the work for the week. Two other plumbers arrived and loaded their vans with copper, toilets and sinks to complete a new house build. While David talked with them, he surreptitiously watched Glenn through the office window, but noticed nothing out of the ordinary. John arrived; David left. They wanted to make the activities at the shop look as normal as possible. Phil arrived with Frank. They opened the warehouse and waited for the first customer of the day.

Glenn met with John, then Frank to catch up on what he missed. The day was busy for Glenn at the warehouse.

John called James, who was in Singapore, to review all the items they found in Glenn's office. Knowing James and Glenn were close, he wanted to discuss what to do with Glenn. The partners discussed their business for a couple of hours.

David arrived back to the shop later in the afternoon with coffees for everyone at the shop.

Phil followed David to John's office, where Amy sat at the conference table, focused on inventory files. Files that were not plumbing related.

The phone rang, and Phil answered it. "Thanks Frank," Phil returned the receiver to its cradle. "Glenn just left. I'll head upstairs and see what he has touched today. Amy, I could use your help."

Frank had a line of last-minute customers at the counter. With help from Phil, they quickly served them and met Amy in Glenn's office. They dusted the high touch areas for fingerprints, and found Glenn had opened every drawer, all his boxes and cabinets. With the dust wiped away, they locked up the office and returned to the counter. After they locked the warehouse doors, they headed back down to John's office. John and David had traced and listened to the recordings of Glenn's phone calls. One message David heard mentioned an additional threat.

"Amy, I think you need to leave," said David.

"David, what does mom say, in for a penny in for a pound? I think I'm at that point with all this."

"Yes, I suppose," David said.

"Amy, if it wasn't for you, we would never have known. She can stay," said John.

"Well, are we sticking to the original plan and taking him out tomorrow, or did Dad want some time with this?"

"No, he was upset, but like we are all aware, it is part of the business. Continue on as planned."

"Okay."

"I just got an address on the Russian he called in Burlington," said John.

"Well, I guess I have a date with that person now too," said David.

• • •

David was at the shop early the next morning with a coffee on the counter, waiting for Glenn to arrive. When Glenn arrived, he refused to take the coffee, citing he had one on the way to the shop. But when David insisted, he sipped it as they stood and chatted about a new subdivision job and who should run it. After six weeks of waiting, they were awarded an apartment complex from a company with tight deadlines. Glenn had concerns about the apartment job and was vocalizing them to David when he coughed. He leaned against the counter and coughed again. He looked at David. Coughing again, Glenn asked. "What have you done, David?" He dropped to his knees.

"Glenn, what the fuck have *you* done?"

"You poisoned me? You bastard, you poisoned me."

"Glenn, you poisoned yourself."

"David, please, save me. I don't want to die. David. Please."

Glenn collapsed to the floor. David walked around the counter and stood over him and watched. Glenn's breaths were quick and shallow. His face darkened to a blueish hue. David smiled as Glenn's cheeks expanded, then his eyelids close.

Struggling to speak Glenn said, "David, you." He struggled to take a breath. "You and your family are all evil, and the evil needs to end." He clutched at his throat as he rolled on the floor. Saliva dripped from his lips as his tongue, swollen and blue, protruded from his mouth.

"You crossed the line Glenn, and you know it too. You see what you did? You could have had us all killed. Why? Glenn, why? Dad loved you. You betrayed The Family that protected you."

Glenn lay still on the floor. Blood seeped from the scratch marks on his neck.

David kicked Glenn's lifeless torso in the ribs. He went to his van, where he left a body bag. From behind the counter, David dragged Glenn's body to the loading dock. He opened the back doors to his van. This time, David would not be loading any plumbing material.

CHAPTER SEVENTEEN

David returned to the shop without Glenn. Tommy, The Family butcher, had Glenn hanging in a hidden freezer. Once Tommy ground up the body, it would be spread around ditches and forests for wild animals to feast on.

Upset about what happened earlier, David went downstairs and showered. After cleaning up, he entered John's office, hoping for more information on the Russian to whom Glenn had revealed The Family's secrets to.

John tossed a yellow envelope to David. "Here you go, hot off the press."

Once they confirmed Glenn as the shop mole and who his associate was, John called his contact at CSIS, Arthur, to see what information his department had on the Russian. Arthur knew exactly who John referred to. His team had followed him for years, but they lost him and believed he had returned to Russia. The information John passed to Arthur confirmed what CSIS had feared, the Russian, Sasha, was still in Canada and working for the new Russian government.

The next day, Arthur called the shop. "John, I have permission to have Sasha dealt with. The history we have on him and now the knowledge of him still being in Canada, the upper brass want him gone. Can you send the documents you found in your shop? Can your team handle it?"

"Of course, we can, and will take great pleasure in it."

"I want the body found. Make it look like a mugging gone wrong."

"Sounds good. I'll have my guys do some recon on him, then send in the boys."

"Take care John."

•   •   •

Burlington's waterfront had paved trails designed for runners and cyclist along the edge of Lake Ontario. David and Phil had biked these trails before. The last time was when they prepared for a race.

A week after the phone call, David parked the van on the street by the trail, parallel parking to get it in the tight spot. A skill he mastered for his driver's license test and then quickly forgot, like most people. They walked part of the trail and thought about how to do the job. Searching for areas off the path and hidden from view, David walked into the bush area while Phil checked the angles to see if he could see David. They picked three locations that would work for the job. Satisfied, the boys headed back to Guelph.

The next day, David reviewed the notes from his team and burned the target's image into his mind. Sasha was a six-foot tall, thirty-four-year-old Russian who spoke full English without an accent. He rented a basement apartment in Burlington. His schedule started at 8 a.m. with a five-kilometer run along the lakeshore trail. Once home, he showered and ate. By eleven in the morning, he was on the train into Toronto, spending the day in an office on Yonge Street just north of Front Street. He took the 7 p.m. train back to Burlington. On the weekend, he would do his run, but not until 9 a.m., before heading to Mississauga to meet with a Russian family at a mall. Once again, he returned by 7 p.m. to his apartment.

The boys headed out for the job at 4 a.m. They both brought their bikes, backpacks and David had his knife.

They parked closer to the QEW, the main highway to head back to Guelph, and wove their way through residential streets to the waterfront. On a park bench, they drank coffees and admired the sun as it rose over Lake Ontario. With the job reviewed and prepared, David talked to Phil about how he missed his grandfather. With their coffees finished, they took off on their bikes, heading down to the lift bridge.

"Okay, Phil, show time. Our boy should be putting on his shoes right now. Let's get back to our first choice for the hit."

They turned around and pedaled back to the trail closer to town. At the designated spot, David stopped his bike and moved off the trail while Phil continued down the trail to locate the target. The morning that had started out with a beautiful sunrise had clouded over and raindrops were falling. David took off his front wheel and took out some tools from his knapsack. He placed his knife on the ground beside the wheel and covered it with a rag. Carefully, he put on his latex gloves.

A cyclist approached David and stopped. "Flat tire, eh," he said. "Do you need a hand?"

"No, I have it, but thanks for the offer," said David.

"Okay, have a great day," the cyclist said and pedaled off.

David played with the wheel and watched for Phil to return. After twenty minutes, Phil rode by and nodded. David glanced up the path. His target was close. Right on time, Sasha approached in a blue hoody, baggy green shorts and running shoes. He slowed a bit as he approached David.

"Excuse me, I could really use a third hand for a minute. Would you mind? I'm sorry to break your pace, but I need to get to work," said David.

"Sure, what do you need?" asked Sasha.

David checked the pathway for any witnesses. Except for a squirrel rushing to a tree, the trail was empty.

"If you could just hold the rim here and here," David pointed to two parts of the rim. It caused Sasha to lean right into David's reach. "I need to just pop off the tire." David reached for one of the plastic tire levers with his left hand. His right hand reached for the knife. The rain came down harder. David's hands moved in time with each other like an orchestra leader leading a movement of Beethoven. With his left hand, he grabbed the target's right side of the head. In one lightning quick movement, his right hand lifted the rag and his knife. He forced the knife into the left side of Sasha's neck. David felt and heard the blade of the knife scrape against a bone in the neck. Sasha looked up at his killer in shock and yelled something in Russian as David's right hand twisted the knife clockwise. Falling forward, Sasha landed on the wheel lying on the ground. Blood jetted from the wound onto the dirt and grass beside the trail. David jumped to his feet, pulled the knife out of Sasha's neck, and grabbed the rag draping over the wound to prevent blood from collecting too close to the path or running out to it. Sasha was dead.

David rolled Sasha off the wheel and onto the ground. He whistled for Phil to return. Blood ran under the bush and into a secluded location beside the path. With another look at the pathway, he saw no witnesses except for Phil, who was riding towards him. Phil leaned his bike against a tree and put on his gloves. The rain continually got harder and puddled on the dirt while they moved the body further off, away from the trail. To imitate a mugging and fight, David took his knife and poked a hole in the now dead Sasha's stomach and sliced his arm. Picking up the Walkman that had fallen out of Sasha's pocket, Phil packed it in his backpack. Stepping back out to the trail, Phil watched for any curious runners or cyclists. David opened the pockets of Sasha's jacket. He found a twenty-dollar bill and took it. Another pocket had car and house keys; he took them.

Through the trees, David heard Phil talking to someone on the trail. Phil explained they were fine and just had a flat tire. Packing his gloves, knife, and all of Sasha's belongings into his bag, David waited for Phil's all clear signal. The runner left and Phil whistled. David stepped out from behind the bushes as another cyclist passed by and asked if they needed help.

"No, we are fine. We fixed the wheel. We just have to clean up and head out," David said.

"Okay, have a good day."

"You, too."

The rain continued to fall, and one puddle showed some blood. With his tire irons, David scraped a small trail through the dirt to the bushes. The puddle drained. Phil inflated and installed David's wheel while David looked at the scene to be sure there was no sign of them being there, except for a hidden body.

They biked to a pay phone at a garage in Burlington. David called John and got the answering machine. His message was to the point. "Credit card has been deactivated."

The boys, soaked and cold, headed to the van. After they loaded the bikes, they headed for home.

David chuckled, "If you think about it, never stop and help someone with a flat tire. This is what, the fifth or sixth job I've done with either my bike or car. People fall for it every time."

"Yeah, maybe it's time to change up your routine. You know how word travels; you won't always get the target that way."

"I wonder when they'll find the body. It could be a couple of days."

Amy met David and Phil at the door when they returned to the shop. She wanted to have a talk about where they were all day and what happened to Glenn. Frank walked around the corner and heard Amy's question to her brother. He smiled at David and asked Amy if she could help him grab parts for some plumbers.

With Amy distracted, David and Phil hurried to the office downstairs to debrief with John and James.

•   •   •

Two days later, everyone was in the office watching Global News. Once the newsman finished with the international news, he turned his attention to local news and the body that was found hidden on a trail in Burlington. Police believed someone mugged the victim on the trail. He fought back but was killed. The reporter reminded his listeners to always be aware of their surroundings and, when out exercising, take precautions, tell people your route, and when to expect you back. The identity of the victim was unknown, and it concerned the police. It had been a couple of days, and no one had reported a missing person in the area. The Family, Arthur, and some people in Russia and Southern Ontario knew his identity. Igor knew it was no accidental mugging, but a professional hit.

CHAPTER EIGHTEEN

The world was back to normal after the quick and powerful Gulf War. Those that abided by the law of man and those that did not, found their routines in life, again.

David, the only one available, took the assignment in Afghanistan. Originally scheduled for Phil, the plans changed when authorities at the Mexico City Airport stopped him for questioning. Someone tracked him from a weapons delivery location outside Toluca back to the airport, where they detained him. John had to call Peter for some diplomatic help. Reminding Peter that he requested the job and there was a good chance his leak caused Phil's detainment. He needed to help release Phil.

American lawyers spent several hours with the Mexican authorities before they discharged Phil. Neither John nor Peter wanted to risk Phil traveling internationally so soon after his issues in Mexico.

Through a contact of The Family in Pakistan, a meeting was scheduled with a young Saudi, Yazid. His father was the head of an oil company and a millionaire many, many times over. Yazid wanted to buy weapons and other pieces of military equipment to continue to build a group of freedom fighters inside Afghanistan and Pakistan and throughout Europe where many political and religious issues he believed could only be solved by spilling blood. In the seventies and eighties, Kenton and John, with the blessing from the Pentagon, supplied and shipped him equipment to fight the Russians in Afghanistan. With that war over, the Americans had abandoned him. He needed to rebuild his relationship with The Family and their supply chain to fight a new enemy.

David met with his driver and translator in Pakistan. They spent a day there before taking the dirty, rough roads to meet Yazid. Not prepared for the negotiations or a sales pitch, David spent the trip studying the notes John wrote for him; what they could offer and the prices. David would also offer his specialty service to the client.

When David arrived at the meeting location, he found the area abandoned. It was a small compound with a large airplane hangar, many small warehouses, and two locations where Yazid and his group lived. It looked like they had all left in a hurry. Upset, David climbed back into the vehicle and instructed the driver to take him back to Pakistan.

The interpreter, Omran, apologized. They left the compound, taking the same road they arrived on.

"David, I am so sorry to waste your time. I was here two weeks ago. I stayed in the compound. That was when Yazid asked me to reach out to Kenton. When I explained Kenton had passed, he asked for John. I don't know what went wrong. I am embarrassed about this and very sorry."

"Omran, it's okay. It is for the best. This isn't what I do, anyway. If there is another meeting, hopefully we can send Phil to meet him."

"Yes, When I saw it was you, I thought we were doing another kill. Like your last trip."

David turned and looked out the window at the colorless landscape.

•   •   •

While David was on the road, Peter called John. He needed a quick hit on a second employee he believed to be compromised. "Sorry Peter, David is in Pakistan. James is in Vietnam and as you know, Phil can not travel right now. I have no one for at least a week," said John.

"John, this is the problem. I can keep you busy. So, I don't know why you do these other jobs."

"David would be available if your rat hadn't tipped off the authorities in Mexico about Phil. You need to get your house in order, Peter. And remember, you are a client, not a business partner." John hung up the phone.

•   •   •

Omran broke the silence and asked Hanif, the driver, to pull over. David, sitting in the back seat, put his hand on Omran's shoulder. "No funny stuff. I am not in the mood."

"David, we are not fools. I have another reason to stop. I have another meeting for you. Would you be interested?" asked Omran.

Guarded about a new "out of the blue" meeting, David decided he still wanted to attend the meeting. He had worked with Omran and Hanif before and had a thin veil of trust for them. Before they took him to a new meeting, he would need to check-in with John.

•   •   •

When they pulled into the small town, David noticed the damaged and abandoned buildings on both sides of the street. Bullet holes and explosions had left holes in walls and on roofs. "I wonder if this is how the allies felt driving into cities at the end of World War Two," he said.

The other two shrugged their shoulders.

"There is no way there is a working phone around here," David said. "This place looks abandoned."

The vehicle stopped in front of a store. They walked towards the building. David noticed wires from the streetlights ran into the building. David opened the door. Inside was a modern store with food, guns, clothes and, on the counter, an old rotary phone.

"Does it work?" David asked. He picked up the receiver. After a few seconds of clicks and noises, a lady spoke in Pashto. David handed the phone to Omran so he could speak to the operator. A few minutes later, he handed back the phone. An English-speaking operator asked for the number. David passed the number to her and heard the phone ring and then John answer.

"Hello?" answered John.

"Sir, this is Anne, operator at Bell. Will you accept a collect call from David?"

"Yes," said John.

"Thank you for using Bell. You may talk David."

"Hi John. Everything is fine. The bird wasn't in his nest. But our friend has a new nest for me."

There was a pause and David heard John shuffle papers. "Where are you?"

"I have no clue. We left the nest and are about forty miles from it, mostly west. I am in a small town no bigger than Aberfoyle."

He shuffled more papers. "Okay, I see it on the map. If you feel safe, take the meeting. If not, head home."

"Roger that John."

"How far away is this meeting?" David asked Hanif.

"Twenty miles, then two miles down a road." Said Hanif.

"John—"

"I heard him. I see where you are going. Looks like an abandoned Russian military base."

"Okay, I'll take the meeting and call you back in twelve hours."

"I'll turn on the short-wave and scan the channels in case there are no phones. Eyes open David. Eyes open."

"Hold on John. Omran wants to make some calls about what happened. I'll call you shortly before we leave."

"Bye."

Omran made his calls. During the second call, the conversation got heated. The store owner pulled a pistol out and waved for David to leave. David put his hands in the air and walked to the door.

"No, David. It is okay. Stay. You can call John, then we will leave," said Hanif.

"What am I telling John?" David asked.

"David, Yazid got cold feet. He took all his people, and they went to the caves to hide from you. An American told him you were in Afghanistan to kill him. They packed up and left five hours before we arrived. I tried to tell him it was not true, but he is an extremely nervous person. He has had many attempts on his life and will not meet with you. I'm sorry."

David called John and told him the news. They agreed David would have this meeting, then come home.

David, Omran, and Hanif headed for the next meeting.

•   •   •

Omran wanted David blindfolded to protect the camp where his contact was. David refused the blindfold and called the meeting off. Using the CB in the vehicle, Hanif radioed the camp to confirm David could arrive without a blindfold.

The Jeep stopped in front of a group of tents. From behind mounds of sand and rock, six men approached the vehicle. Each man was in a Russian officer's uniform and carried Russian automatic rifles.

David jumped out of the vehicle while the men ran at him. With their guns pointed at David's chest, they yelled in broken

English for him to raise his hands. He put his hands above his head, as did Hanif and Omran. The men patted down and removed their pistols and David's knife. David turned to elbow the man who took his knife.

"Stop. Stop. These are our guests. Give back their weapons." An older gentleman, tall with white hair and wearing high-ranking epaulets on his uniform, said as he exited a tent. They stopped the pat down and returned the pistols and, more importantly for the one soldier's life, David's knife.

"Is this him? Welcome. Put your guns away. He is our guest," said Michale.

"Who are you? And what do you want from me?" David asked, his knife in hand.

"I am Michale. You are David, James' boy, no?"

"Yes, I am. How do you know me?"

"I don't know you, but your friend here told me he worked for The Family. I asked the next time he accompanied you on one of your jobs to bring you here. Honestly, I was hoping for John or Phil, but you will do. Come to my tent, please. I have food prepared."

"What's this about? And I take offense that you would rather have John or Phil," David said with a smile.

David entered the large tent. Inside, a large table with linens, plates, and silver utensils was in front of three desks and a series of cabinets. There were more men lined up by rank, waiting to shake David's hand.

With the introductions completed, David sat at a table with six high-ranking officers. The back of the tent opened and men with food trays entered.

"Michale, please tell me why I'm here. It wasn't for a home cooked meal."

"David, you killed one of my friends. I am thankful you did; his death would have been terrible if not for you."

"Aleksi?" David asked. "Your name was on the list he gave me."

"The very man. He gave you a piece of paper with names on it."

"Yes, John researched the names. He found they were all dead."

"This is true except for me; I faked my death during a battle. The writing was on the wall, so to speak. The war was lost, and my men were dying for nothing. We staged a battle. Some men didn't want to go along with the plan. They died. The rest of us?" He raised his arms and looked around the tent. "We are now in business with the Western world."

"I don't understand. What are you selling?"

"I have an entire fleet of planes, tanks, small ships, medium ships, and anything else you can imagine. All for sale. When the war ended, my country just walked away and left the equipment. We have gathered it and serviced it. Good as new. We also scoured bases, airfields, and factories. With the confusion in the old Soviet Union, we now have a better inventory than the government. I, we, all of us, would like your family as a customer. We have a few small customers, but we are ready to expand. We can get you helicopters, bombs, even people. Whatever you need."

"How did you find out about us?"

"Igor Volkov told me about your family years ago," Michale said.

"Igor? Do you know where he is? Maybe you can help me meet him?"

"Sorry David, I haven't talked to Igor in many years. Maybe a decade ago. I had forgotten about him until recently, when one of my South American customers brought up his name. I assume he has upset you?"

"That is one way to put it. If you ever find out where he is, you need to call me immediately. He owes me a couple of favors."

Looking around the tent at his men, Michale said, "Did you all hear that? If anyone finds any information on Igor, it goes straight to David. David would like to talk to him."

"So where is this treasure chest of equipment?"

"We can see it right after we eat. I have sent your driver and interpreter away. We can get you home. They left your belongings outside."

"Do you have a phone or a short-wave radio?" David asked.

"No to both, David, not here. I can get you to a phone in about six hours. But please, eat."

"I'm starved. John will have to wait," said David. He loaded his plate with food.

• • •

From the air, David could see lines of tanks, helicopters, cargo planes and jets. There were nine hangars at the airfield they circled over. The plane, an Antonov An-12, landed on a rough but useable runway. David gathered with the team who flew in a cargo plane, and the ones that walked out of the hangar.

"How was that for a ride, David? The plane and the pilot are for sale. It is all for sale," said Michale.

"Where are we? And what is this place? Plus, I need a phone."

"Oh yes, you need to check-in. Very good, smart. You have an exceptionally good team protecting you. Follow me. David, you can use my office. It might be the only phone not bugged on this base. We are in the Ukraine. Why don't we leave it at that for now?"

David followed Michale through the hangar and into the offices. There were offices, a small meeting room, and washrooms. They passed them and walked to the end of the hallway. David expected someone to jump out from behind a door and inject him or knock him out. They entered an office. It had photos on the wall of Michale in combat. His medals hung behind his desk. On his desk was an old photo of a group of men.

"Here, David, call Phil or John whoever you need. I'll be outside enjoying this beautiful day with the others. Please come out when you're done."

David sat at the desk and dialed the office. With a tone of concern in his voice, John answered the phone. He told David that Omran, the interpreter, had called to say David was alone with a group of Russians. Reassuring John, he was safe, David reviewed his time since he called John in the small town.

After David ended the call, he checked the office for a gun. A loaded pistol was in the top drawer. He took it and hid it in his waist band, pulling his shirt over it and putting the extra clips in his bag.

In the hangar, David found the men looking at two helicopters and one corporate jet. David spent four hours on a tour of the airfield. Each building had an inventory sheet describing equipment once owned by the Soviet military. Before the tour ended, David rode in tanks, helicopters, and a MIG jet out over the Black Sea. The personal movers and anti-mine vehicles were ugly, but effective. With the tour done and a promise to fulfill any orders in the future from The Family, Michale offered David a flight to anywhere he needed to go.

After calling John, they decided he should take a flight to Northern Ireland. The ground crew fueled and prepared the Lear jet. David thanked everyone for their hospitality and reminded them he wanted to meet Igor. An hour later, David was in the air alone with the pilots. He had a handful of business cards, photos, phone numbers and the promise of quick, accurate orders and deliveries within days of a request.

In Northern Ireland, David met with Scott, then hopped on a flight home.

· · ·

The Family sat in John's office and listened to David's story. While David had been with Michale, John researched Michale and his operation. The whole situation seemed to be perfectly legitimate. John, through his contacts in Russia's government, had found out that Russia, and the old Soviet countries, were in poor shape. The military was not paying staff and had broken apart. The entire system was bankrupt. Even the nuclear plants were only maintained because so many of the staff had families within the blast zone of a reactor. They confirmed that the new Russian Mafia, the Rodstvo, had grown out of the old military ranks.

"Do we have anything new from Peter on his rats? It sounds like he has an infestation on his hands. Michale and his group promised if they hear anything about Igor, they will call me right away," said David.

"Peter is buried with work right now. He wasn't happy about us doing work that he wasn't aware of. But he will get over it. He knows we are dependable. He called because he has identified another person," said John.

"Dad, did you tell me he had a few men down in Mexico? I wonder if it was one of them who tipped off the authorities?" asked Phil.

"Yeah, they said it was an American that spooked my contact in Afghanistan, too. I don't envy Peter right now," said David.

"One last thing and we can grab some food," said John. "I had a request from Juan in Columbia. He has an extensive list of equipment. Does anyone object to giving the order to Michale and his team? It will be an excellent test of his equipment and we can see if he is as good as he claims."

No one objected to the order or to who they were getting the equipment from.

David wanted the jet they flew him to Northern Ireland in added to the shipment for The Family to use. John and James said no. "David, right now we can't be bringing any unwanted attention to ourselves. I understand your point about a private jet, but not right now," said John.

James nodded in agreement. The meeting ended, and they went out for a meal. Frank and Amy joined them. James and David enjoyed the extra time they spent with Amy.

CHAPTER NINETEEN

Things had become manageable for The Family and the plumbing shops. Peter was still working on his internal problems, the Rodstvo had a setback in Canada with the RCMP, thanks to a phone call from John, and they were quietly regrouping.

John, Scott, and James decided they needed a nice long vacation with their wives and left on a three-week getaway to celebrate John's twenty-fifth wedding anniversary.

David and Phil stayed home to help run the plumbing shop, complete three shipments of weapons, and babysit the other businesses with Amy and Frank. This was the longest span of time David stayed at home since he recovered from his injuries.

Sitting in the office, David reached out to contacts to see if there was any word about Igor's location. Igor and his men had become quiet. They continued their shipments of drugs, people and weapons around the world but avoided crossing paths with The Family. Rumor was, the Rodstvo left Igor with a tiny piece of the pie. Just like what Igor said about The Family, he was now vulnerable, too. One of David's contacts revealed Igor was playing tour guide to the Rodstvo. He was introducing them to many of his contacts and handing over his business to them.

The contact figured that once they had all of Igor's clients under their umbrella, they would kill Igor.

The note that David left in Aleksi's pocket likely had something to do with Igor's unfortunate loss of business.

Frank went to get lunch for the group, and David took over the counter. A steady stream of plumbers entered the wholesalers. They picked up parts, asked questions about old faucets and scheduled deliveries to job sites. There were other plumbing wholesalers in Guelph, but John had grown a successful business by having the best customer service and a knowledgeable staff at the counter. John stressed to Phil and David. "Customer service, the most important part of any business, whether it is hiding a body properly or getting plumbing parts that are hard to find. Always exceed expectations."

Frank was the only person who worked in the warehouse without a plumbing license. John believed in hiring licensed plumbers who had used up their bodies in the trade to work behind the counter or on the delivery trucks.

Fred Walker, the owner of Fred's Plumbing, came to the counter. He needed a few fittings and a ball cock for a special European toilet. Fred and David, at one time, attended youth group at the same church. Married with a couple of kids, all before twenty-five, Fred still attended church and was happy to have a traditional life with a million-dollar family.

David searched the shelves for anything that would help him out. He found an old British unit that would get the toilet working. With a hit shortly in Italy, David knew he could get Fred the right ball cock. "I'll get one on order. It will take a few weeks to arrive," said David.

When Fred left, David went down an aisle to continue pulling orders. Fred returned and came behind the counter and down the aisle David was in. He tapped David on the shoulder. David spun, swept Fred's feet, and knocked him to the floor.

"Fred, sorry, I'm a little jumpy. Are you okay? Fred, I'm so sorry. Here, let me help you." David reached out his hand and pulled Fred up to his feet.

He smiled at him. "Wow David, that was fast. I didn't see that coming at all. All your training in martial arts when you were younger paid off. I'm fine. Don't worry. I rarely see you working at the counter. Is everything okay?"

"Oh, yeah. Everything is fine, Fred. I just want to mix things up. Dad is away and I'm helping. This is much cleaner than pulling condoms and tampons out of someone's sewer line."

"Yes, I just got done doing one this morning. The people had three inches of sewage in their basement. They just moved in and were at the bottom of a hill in a new subdivision, all brand-new houses. Well, it seems the contractor forgot to tie the main sewer for the street into the city main. So, twelve house's worth of sewage collected into this person's basement. I had over one hundred feet of snake down the line. Popped the sewer outside and saw it was full. What a mess. The builder was there in thousand-dollar shoes wading through the waste. Too funny, at least for me, not for them, obviously."

"Oh man, that sucks. I assume they had most of their belongings down there too?"

"Yes, boxes of clothes, furniture, you name it. Terrible, I can't imagine." He paused. "Hey, there is something I want to ask. I didn't think anyone was here so—"

"Yeah Fred, I always say, only ask if you really want the answer."

"Okay. Well, okay, David, why don't you come to church anymore. You and Phil used to attend. You know God still loves you and wants to be with you. Your mom and Amy come. I like the guy she is dating. Amy, not your mom. He is a super kid. Wants to be a minister."

"Yes, I like him, and I'm happy for Amy, too. She has someone stable in her life."

"That's the other thing, your life. People talk, and I feel I can talk to you. God loves you and forgives everyone who asks of their sins. No matter how bad. Even killing."

"What? No, I just don't go because we're busy with the business and except for you and Roger, Phil and I never felt welcomed."

"No, David you were. You guys just kept to yourselves. Okay, so I think you answered my question without answering it. So that leads me to my next issue. Can we go somewhere else to talk? I'm worried people might hear us. Kenny is at the counter waiting. I really need to talk about church," Fred said. He winked at David.

Confused by the conversation, David agreed to hear Fred out. He served Kenny, then a steady stream of customers continued to enter. David told Fred to come back at five, they could get supper. The conversation with Fred weighed on David all afternoon. He couldn't think what else he wanted to discuss.

Five o'clock came and went, and Fred never returned.

"Another day in the books, David. Thanks for your help today. Are you around tomorrow?" asked Frank.

"I think so. I forgot how much fun the counter was. Like I told Fred earlier, beats being elbow deep in somebody's shit. Oh, that reminds me, Fred said he was coming back for a talk. He is late, but I assume he is stuck on a job. I'll lock up. You head home."

"Okay, do you want me to stay?"

"No, Fred is not a threat. I think he wants me to come back to church. Started with the God loves you talk."

David pulled orders for the next day while he waited.

"David, are you here, David?" Fred called from the contractor's door.

"Fred, back here. I'm in the ABS fitting aisle."

Fred slowly walked down the aisle to David. David could see he was nervous; he was pale and shaking.

"Where can we talk?"

David brought him down to the office. "Wow, I heard about this place but to see it. Unreal. Sorry David, I'm so nervous, as you can tell."

"Do you want some water, a pop, anything?"

"No, I'm fine. But you might not be."

"What?"

"Okay, David, there have been rumors about you and your family since you came to Canada. I was always too scared to ask and still am. But I was on a job today and saw some stuff. I prayed about it, over and over. I believe God needs you to know this. You, your family, and extended family are all in trouble. This building and your trucks, everything David, everything you know."

"Okay Fred, start from the beginning."

• • •

Fred's Plumbing and Heating had a contract with a rundown, by the hour, day or week, motel on Woodlawn Road. A quiet motel on the edge of Guelph it was across from the city graveyard. An old lady, Joyce, who had seen most of her sunsets, cleaned the units daily. She smoked three packs a day and drank nightly.

Smoking her cigarette, she knocked on the door. Once she took the last drag off the cigarette, she entered. She blew the last bit of smoke out of her lungs as she walked into the unit. Unit six had checked out, and the unit needed a full cleaning. The salesman had left early that morning, but the hooker he had the night before was still in the bed.

"Housecleaning. Hon, you need to get up and leave. The man who paid for the room checked out," said Joyce.

The lady on the bed, naked, did not move. Joyce went to her and shook her. The needle on the bedstand was enough for

Joyce to understand she wasn't moving anytime soon. She checked for a pulse and felt one.

Well, at least this one has a pulse, not like last week, she thought.

She started her usual routine, cleaning the kitchenette and bathroom. Noticing the kitchen sink plugged; she tried her plunger on it. She left the room to find Garth, the owner, and reported two issues with the unit; a lady was half dead, strung out on something from a needle, and the kitchen sink was plugged.

The owner called Fred about the plumbing and headed to the unit to remove the "dirty girl," as he called them.

Fred arrived an hour later. He checked in with Garth, and they entered the room together. There was some small talk about the findings that morning in the room with the plugged sink.

Fred snaked the drain through the trap's cleanout. The snake head didn't drop into the stack. It crossed over to the adjacent unit. After a few attempts, he cursed the code book for allowing double Ty's in drains and pulled his snake out. He needed into the unit on the other side.

The unit Fred wanted access to was rented out for three days. Garth didn't like to disturb his customers, especially those who paid extra for their privacy. When the client checked in, he stressed to Garth that they did not want or need the room cleaned during his stay.

Frank knocked and waited. With no reply, he slowly opened the door.

Joyce placed a note on the door. *Emergency service. Please see front desk before entering.* Fred moved his equipment to the second unit with help from Joyce. Joyce stayed with Fred to clean up any mess he might make from the greasy water.

She had a habit, not always a good thing, of looking at more than the sheets on the bed and the bathroom floor when she was in a room.

"Fred, look at this," she said. She had opened the bedside table drawer. There was a Glock and a magnum gun in the drawer. She closed the drawer. She went to the desk. "Fred, hey Fred, you have to look at this. I know this guy."

Fred stopped the snake and went to Joyce, his knees buckled. "So do I, what is this?"

They carefully moved the papers. Fred read the few notes, which were written in English. There were photos of The Family, Amy, the shop, and their houses. The notepad had addresses, times, and locations of where they had been over the last three days. There was a folder on the small stove. He opened the folder. Flipping through pages and photos, he found one diagram that showed where to place explosives. Under it were drawings of the shop and David's house.

Fred went back to the sink and pulled out his snake. "I think we should leave, Joyce. Put everything back the way it was. I don't think we want to be in here when the person returns."

"Look, there's a plane ticket for Friday, three days from now. Someone, or multiple someones, are going to die before this guy leaves. I just feel it," Joyce said.

"Hold on," Fred said. Fred ran out to his van and grabbed a camera. He had it for jobs he priced. He had three photos left on the film. Trying to get as many pieces of evidence in the photo as possible, he snapped photos of the guns, the documents on the table and one where Joyce was pointing to the notes about explosives.

"We have to call the police," said Joyce.

"No, I know him and his family. They do not call the police, believe me."

"Okay, but—"

"We need to leave. Make sure you put everything back."

Joyce grabbed her cleaning cart and left. With his tools in his hands, Fred followed Joyce out. Two units away, Joyce had lit a cigarette and was leaning on her cart. "Take the note off the door Fred, before he returns."

Fred grabbed the note and headed back into the first unit. The sink still needed fixed. Joyce took the note from Fred to the office and told Garth not to tell the customer they were in there. Once she explained why, he was in full agreement.

Fred went to his van. After clearing the drain to get parts to put the drain back together. A car pulled in beside him. A stout man pulled himself out of the car and headed into his unit. The unit.

Fred went back to the room he had been in. The fire barrier between the units was movable, so he removed the loose material. He could hear the man on the phone. He had a thick accent that Fred couldn't identify. Fred had traveled little and didn't watch television. When he had free time, he spent it with his family or studying the Bible.

"Yes, my flight is booked—yes, they seem relaxed here. Their guard is down—no, I'm picking up the explosives tonight in Toronto—don't worry, consider it done."

Fred bumped his head on the bottom of the counter. Joyce had come back into the unit. She whispered through her cigarette smoke, "He's back."

Fred packed up his tools and loaded the van. He pulled out while the man looked through his window at all the activity outside.

•　　•　　•

"With that, I came straight here to see you at lunch. Should I be worried David? He knows my business name; my office is at home. David, will my family be safe? What about Joyce? She is a crazy old lady, but I really like her," said Fred.

"Okay, thank you for this information. You might have just saved mine and my family's lives."

"David, so this is all true, all the rumors, the whispers at church, all real? You're a killer too?" Fred stood up and walked around the room. He rubbed his hands together. "Let me get my camera David, you will need to process the film."

"No problem. I will make a few phone calls. Knock before you come back into the office."

David called Phil and told him they were under attack. He needed to grab Amy and come to the shop. He tried to reach his dad at the resort, he left a message with the front desk. "Please leave a note, for James Grant only. I would like it to say. David's tree house is about to fall down. But we are trying to fix it."

David called Frank and told him about the situation. He needed Frank to get their photographer to process the film right away.

Outside the office, Fred waited until David let him back in. He tossed David the film. I need the photos back, though. I have photos of a septic for a customer in Milton.

"Fred, of course, I won't even charge you for the eight by tens."

"David, how can you joke right now?"

"Bud, if you only knew, but believe me, you don't want to. Here's what I need you to do. Give me the manager's name and number. I need to contact them. I'll find Joyce too."

"You aren't going to, you know?" he ran his hand across his throat.

"No, no, not at all. I want to make sure they are safe, no don't worry. Now as for you," David chuckled.

"What?"

"Seriously, you and your family, I need you guys to disappear."

"WHAT!"

"Relax. Just for a while, Fred. But I need you to listen to me."

"Oh, and I am not sure, but Joyce was sure the man has a Russian accent."

"Of course he does." Phil entered the office without Amy. "Where is she?" David asked.

"I don't know. She's not at the house. I was hoping you knew."

"Who are you talking about, Amy? She's at our house for teen and twenties Bible study. It just started. I should be there too. Actually, can I call my wife?"

David motioned to the phone. Fred called his wife and explained he was on a job that was not going well. He asked if everyone had shown up to Bible study and confirmed Amy was there too and hung up.

"She's at my place, David."

"Okay, what time does it end usually?"

"Around eight thirty."

"Phil, go watch his house, then grab her and her boyfriend. We don't know how much this guy knows about us. Fred, once Bible study is over, you'll go home, get your wife and kids and leave. I don't know how you'll do it, but get out. There will be a hotel room for you at the Holiday Inn. Get me a list and schedule of your work for the next couple of weeks and forward your business phone to the shop. I'll have my plumbers do your calls. Tomorrow, I'll have you moved up to a cottage or shipped south for a vacation. I need you out of the town. You tell me where and I will make it happen, all expenses paid for, of course."

"No, you don't have to do that for me. How do I explain this to Cheryl? She isn't going to just pack up and leave."

"Fred, you need to make her. I don't have enough people to protect the hotel, the shop, and your family. Whoever this is knows we run plumbing companies. He might be very suspicious of a plumber working in a unit beside him. He probably knew the sink was plugged, which is good. But please, until this ends, I need you out of Guelph. Phil will drive you home. Leave your van in the yard. Get to the Holiday Inn before ten. Phil will make all the arrangements. Just keep in contact with him. Anywhere, you name it, all expenses paid. We will run your business while you're away, and of course, you will get the money from the jobs."

"Anywhere David? I can't have you do that."

"Anywhere Fred, just not here. By here I mean Southern Ontario. And no mention of this to Cheryl. I don't know how you will do it, but I need you to leave. I have more calls to make, ones you don't want to know about. Thank you, Fred. Honestly, thank you. When this blows over, we will talk more."

"Okay, will you be all right?"

"I will now, thanks to you. But keep us in your prayers, please." He hugged Fred and walked him to the door.

CHAPTER TWENTY

David had Frank head to the graveyard to set up a watch for their new target.

Phil brought Amy back to the shop into the office. "David, what is going on? Why am I here?"

David told her about Fred's adventure, the issues at the motel, and how she would not be safe at home alone.

"I want in on the action, David. You will need help on this one. Dad and John are away. We can't trust anyone. Let me help, please? Phil, tell him."

"Amy, I have Russians hunting me. You would think that should scare me, but it doesn't. What scares me is telling Mom you helped on a job, or worse yet telling Mom you were hurt on a job where assassins are trying to kill me. Mom scares me, not trained assassins."

"Oh, David, don't be so dramatic. Mom will understand."

"Amy, I don't think she will," said Phil. "David is right, your mom scares me too."

"Look you babies. I am in. What do you need me to do?"

"Fine, we do need the help. You will do nothing tonight. You are right. We will need you to take a shift to watch the motel tomorrow. Tonight, I will take you to our hotel. You will not leave there until one of us, and I mean only Phil or myself, pick you up tomorrow morning. We will have a plan for you then."

"To help?"

"Yes, to help. But tonight, you will go to the hotel. You need to set an alarm for every four hours and call here. Good?"

"Thank you, David, Phil. Whatever I can do to help you guys stay alive."

"Okay, let's go. We can stop at the house and get you some clothes," said David.

When David entered the hotel with Amy, Fred and his family were at the counter. They had just checked in.

David headed back to the shop where the photos waited for him. The bit of information he could see from the photos was they had done their homework. He needed to talk to the manager, Garth.

$$\bullet \qquad \bullet \qquad \bullet$$

David woke Garth. His wife rolled over and screamed before Phil could get his hand over her mouth. David turned on the nightstand light. Garth reached for the drawer.

"Garth, relax. We're not here to hurt you. Is there a gun in the drawer?"

Garth nodded.

"Okay, both of you get up. Keep the lights off and get dressed. We're going for a walk. Does Joyce live here too?"

"No," Garth said. "She lives with her son and daughter-in-law. Close to downtown."

"Okay, Garth, all the excitement that happened yesterday is about me. I want to get you guys to safety, okay? So, I want you to walk with me and my partner."

"Can't we just talk here?"

"I just don't want to be identified, for reasons you are well aware of. I don't know if your place is being watched. If we walk to the car and anything happens drop to the ground and stay down. We will protect you. I still don't know if he suspects anything from the plumbing issue this morning."

Garth and his wife dressed. They left by the back-office door, and walked towards the cigarette factory, where David had parked.

At the car David said, "I am David. This is Phil. It may not seem like it, but we are here to keep you safe."

"How?" asked Garth.

"Tomorrow we will move you out. Does four in the afternoon seem good? Have some clothes packed but not in suitcases. We can buy you whatever you need. So, pack light. Joyce needs to do the same. I need you two and Joyce to act like it's a normal day. Once your chores are over, we will pull you out."

"Four would be good. Joyce goes home at three and I usually stop around four."

"Okay. During the day, monitor the Russians and call with any updates, anything at all. Do you understand?"

"Yes. David, two more Russians moved in today. They are two units down and sharing the room," said Garth.

"You will need to tell Joyce this and keep her safe," said Phil. "If we are done here, David will walk you back to your motel."

David walked them back to their motel. Then David and Phil headed back to the shop.

"Okay Phil, we need to do this tomorrow. Fuck me, there are three of them to kill. We have to do it in their rooms. This will be tricky. What about this? We get Amy and have her watch these guys when the sun comes up. We will need to be on the offensive and Frank must be part of the team. He will need to get some sleep."

Once the sun rose, they went to the hotel and woke Amy. She always wanted some action. Well, come hell or high water, she was going to get involved. David would deal with his mom later.

Amy parked a car across the street from the motel in the graveyard. She sat in the car and took notes. The only action she noted was Joyce cleaning. To Amy, it looked like Joyce's job was to smoke, with a little cleaning on the side.

David spoke with Garth to see what rooms his customers occupied around the Russians. Garth checked his ledger. The room to the left of the first man and a room in between the two Russians rooms currently had customers. David requested to have those people moved to rooms further away. While the Russians were away from the motel, Garth moved his customers, as David requested. The long-term guests protested, but once Garth explained there was a potential for an electrical fire due to worn wires, they packed and moved to the side wing of the motel. He also handed out vouchers for the diner down the street. Amy documented it all and had her notes ready for David.

Around four in the afternoon, Frank arrived rested and ready for a night of activities. David had him check on Amy and bring the owners back to the shop. Once Garth and his wife arrived, David revealed his plan to them. The hotel needed to be shutdown for a week. Like Fred and his family, David offered the couple a trip anywhere they wanted to go. Hesitant at first, David offered them cash and a promising future under the umbrella of The Family's businesses. Their concern was the police would arrest them for their involvement or investigate their motel for other matters that had happened on the property.

With all their concerns quieted, Phil brought them to the Holiday Inn and booked them a room. After settling them into a suite, Phil headed to the graveyard to see Amy. Bored, she complained that this was not being part of the action. She noted more men had shown up and delivered three boxes to unit five. The men she watched had spent the afternoon in unit five and recently left.

Phil returned with his report and the notes from Amy.

David was in the back room. He had five Colt Mustangs and Glock 19's on the counter, cleaned for use that night.

David made a few calls and tried his dad and John again. *Where are they? They must be having a good time if they're not returning my calls,* he thought. He called the Guelph police and spoke to an inspector who was on John's books. Wanting to be sure no police patrolled the Woodlawn Road–Highway Six area, he loosely explained the plans for the night. If there were any calls, he did not need any emergency services responding. He contacted the family butcher and told him to prepare for a delivery early in the morning. Once done with the delivery, Tommy, the butcher, would need to send the ground meat to the pig farm by Owen Sound. Finally, he called a business associate who owned a furniture store. As a gesture of goodwill to Garth and their new business agreement, David placed a large order of new beds and furniture for the rooms. With the last items checked on his to-do list, he took a few minutes to himself. It had been a busy couple of days, and it wasn't over yet.

•　　•　　•

David had Amy stay at the shop in case their dad called. At 1 a.m. David and Phil pulled into the parking lot of Canadian Tire. They walked to where Frank parked at the sub shop.

Everyone checked their weapons, put on their gloves, and pulled down their balaclavas. The foggy night helped to hide them as they walked to the motel. David stood in front of unit five and Phil stood behind Frank by unit nine's door, guns in hand. They watched David put his key in the door, Frank copied

David. They nodded, turned the keys, and opened the doors. David stepped into the unit of the man that was there to kill him. The room had two double beds to the right of the door. Along the left wall was a set of drawers with a television chained to a loop fastened to the wall. Beyond that was the kitchen and bathroom.

The target was on the bed towards the back of the unit. David took three long steps and jumped on the bed and his target. His left hand grabbed the spare pillow while his right hand lowered the gun onto the pillow. The Russian struggled and kicked as David pulled his trigger three times. The gun's silencer muffled the sound. Only three quiet "pops" were heard. The target went still. Climbing off his victim, David removed the blood-soaked pillow. He pulled out his knife and slit his victim's throat. He looked closer at the face. "Ruslan? You little shit," he whispered.

He left his room, careful not to slam the door. Entering the second unit, he saw Phil sitting on the bed. Pale and shaking, he looked at David. Frank stood in front of Phil in a full belly laugh.

David closed the door. "What happened here? Phil, are you okay?"

Frank tried to catch his breath while he controlled his laughter. "I don't know why we bring this guy David, comic relief, I guess. I entered the room and took the back bed, as we discussed. Phil entered behind me. He jumped on his target's bed and slipped right off. He landed hard on the floor in between the two beds. Of course, that woke his target. Mine already had three bullets in his head. Phil's target sat up and reached for his gun on the nightstand. Luckily for Phil, he lay there, so I could get a couple shots off. I then stepped on Phil as I jumped to the front bed and Phil's target. I put three more bullets into him and there he lies. We all know why you're the paper guy, Phil. I'm just glad you stayed down."

"Phil, will you ever do one of these jobs, right? At least you know to stay out of the way when things happen," David said.

"I just don't have it in me. You might have been better off bringing Amy," Phil said.

David walked to both men on the beds and slit their throats. Phil looked at him questionably.

"For the photos, we will send to Russia and Igor. They need to see my signature. Are you all right?"

Phil sat on the edge of the bed. "Yeah, but I can't do this. I was all pumped up, so pumped I—fuck it. Laugh it up Frank. We need to go."

David laughed, "Phil, we have known since we were kids what our roles would be. I think this just confirms it. Can you show me how you did it?"

"Look, the bedspread is slippery, okay? I misjudged it. I slid right off," Phil laughed with Frank and David.

"Okay, Phil, grab the van. Frank, can you call our cleaners? They can start in an hour. Actually, you guys need to come see something or someone. Before you go."

Walking to the beds, David looked closely at the two men, those men he didn't recognize. Phil and Frank followed behind David to his unit.

"See this tub of lard? This was my babysitter on the boat. This guy was Ruslan. I can't believe he's here. We now know that Igor paid for this hit. He told me Ruslan was one of his top guys. I just wonder why he didn't send the other guy. I can't remember his name. He introduced him as his top assassin."

Phil went to get the van while David gathered all the paperwork and photos. He called the police. "All done here. Just the clean up left."

Frank loaded the bodies and drove them to the butcher to be ground up and fed to pigs. Phil and David returned to the shop to clean up and review the documents they had taken from the rooms.

When they entered the office, Amy was in John's chair.

"Hello," David said.

"It's about time you got back here. I've been worried the whole time you were away."

"Amy, calm down. We're fine. Don't turn into Mom, please. I don't need you panicking when you know we're out on jobs. You're sounding like Mom."

"Don't call me that."

"We're all safe. Well, not the guys we visited, but the job went well. You did good today, too. Did Dad call?"

Before she could answer, the phone rang.

"Who is calling—" David said.

Phil picked up the phone, "Hello—well, well, well, do you know what time it is? Yes, fine—hold on."

He put the speaker on. "What's wrong, boys?" said John.

"Are you guys okay?" James asked.

"Everything is fine. Are you guys okay? I was worrying since you hadn't checked in," said David.

"We're fine. We took a sailboat out for a few days to travel through the islands. Never mind about us. What happened? What is going on?"

"Dad, everything is fine. We had visitors from overseas. We showed them a good time, and we even had a big surprise to end their visit. But they have left. Amy was a tremendous help. We are going to clean up and take her out for breakfast."

"Okay, we will be home next week. Take care."

"Love you, dad." David put the phone back in the cradle.

"Dude, you are getting good at the cryptic messages. Another skill you can put on your resume," said Phil.

They cleaned up and headed to their favorite breakfast restaurant.

Garth, his wife, and Joyce enjoyed their three-week vacation. When they returned to the motel, they could not believe the work David had done for them. The motel was like new. The deal Garth made with David looked to have paid off. Unfortunately, a week after they returned, Joyce, with a cigarette in hand, had a massive brain aneurysm and died in her favorite chair, watching Jeopardy. David paid for her funeral.

Fred returned with his family from their trip to Scotland. He met David at the shop. David said, "When times are slow, Fred, I promise you will have enough business to support your family." They went through the list of jobs David had completed for Fred. David handed him a thick envelope of money before he left.

Knowing they would never be friends, Fred told David. "I will pray for your safety and forgiveness, nightly."

He sent photos of the three Russians to Igor through a mutual contact John had. Included were fun photos David took with Ruslan.

PART THREE

CHAPTER TWENTY-ONE

In Cuba, Igor received the photos of his three men. He had many emotions looking at the photos, one that he did not have was pity. They had screwed up and deserved to die.

Igor knew he now had additional problems. Ruslan, a man he trusted, just extended an unwanted war with The Family. There were problems at home with the Rodstvo. With the KGB quietly supporting them, they were expanding into the western countries with their drugs, weapons, and human trafficking. Counterfeit money was being used to purchase properties and businesses. In Miami, there was a shootout with police and the Italian Mob. Twenty-three officers and civilians were killed. As was the Italian Mob's rule in the southern region of Florida.

Igor was trying to keep himself alive and in business. He was meeting with the Rodstvo, introducing them to his clients, then losing those clients. Now the Rodstvo was asking him for more information on The Family.

After Kenton's death the rumors were, The Family was weak and confused. They had lost their way. Igor knew it wasn't true. Kenton had prepared his sons and grandson for such an event. Igor was the one who was weak without direction. His own men, or dead men, were doing things without his knowledge. The

Rodstvo had pushed him into a corner and taken most of his business away, leaving him some small weapons deals and the ability to import small, approved amounts of drugs into Russia, but their cut was unreasonable. He wondered how many more of his team flipped to the other organizations.

He sat in his office; the rain tapped against his window. He had orders to fill for new buyers in the Middle East, a potential new area for him to grow in, if he could hide it from his new bosses. With his elbows on his desk and his head in his hands, he decided he needed to call John. This war between him and The Family needed to end before David found him. His last conversation with John was rough, years ago. He needed the next one to sound sincere and concerning.

• • •

John was in the office with James. David's next job needed to be reviewed: find and kill Igor and all his merry men. They had taken enough losses with the business and all these issues were, they believed, at the hands of Igor. The phone rang on John's desk.

John answered, "Hello."

"John, please listen."

"Igor?"

"I'm sorry about what has happened to us. John, I had a few guys go out on their own. I am so happy to hear David took care of them and your group is safe."

"Igor, what the fuck? You are calling me now?"

"John, John, yes, it is Igor. Stop and listen, please. Those guys David killed were my top men. The Rodstvo knows about your family and Kenton. Those three went rogue, backed by the Rodstvo. They were on a job in Mexico for me. We had to deal with a couple of Mexican officials. I guess you turned it down? John, I did not order this hit. Honest. We have had our differences lately, but John, I would never go this far. John, I am not sure how we got here, but it needs to stop. John, John, are you still there?"

"You kidnapped David. What could you possibly be thinking right now? That was an act of war against us, Igor. Listen, we haven't worked together since the early eighties, but we all stayed out of each other's ways. Yes, Sergio was a big-ticket item, but you could have walked away when he got away from us all. But you fucking took David. You think this phone call and your pathetic apology are going to make everything okay? Kidnapping Kenton's grandson a year after his death seems to be a statement to me. Plus, you beat the shit out of him. Now you come to our town and try to take us out! Seems the old gentleman's agreements are gone, Igor. None of us would ever go to the others' house to do a hit. I thought even we had rules."

"John, John, listen. I loved Kenton. I love you and James. John, please let's talk about this. Let's get right with each other. My hands are clean. The David thing John, that was me trying to survive. The new mob is cutting me out. They have their own people. They don't need me. I thought if I brought them David, I would show I was an ally and committed to the new ways. I am sorry John. This was a mistake."

"Igor, you're telling me this is all a misunderstanding? Then say you took David to have him killed by your new bosses. Your English isn't perfect, but I hope you said that wrong."

"I did not, sorry, John. I am trying to survive. I swear I had nothing to do with Kenton's hit, either. If I find out who did, I will bring them right to your office myself. You know that John."

"Let me talk to the family. I can't guarantee anything, but to start, you owe me money and shipments. I can at least present that to them. You have cost us a lot lately."

"Again John, it wasn't me. They are pushing me out. Trying to make these things look like I did them. I had nothing to do with anything that affected your shipments. John, I will send you tanks, helicopters, and cash. John, you name it. This needs to end. I wish I had known of their plans. I bet once they were done with you guys, they were coming to take me out. So, thank you for stopping it."

"Igor, I have to go. I need a detailed list of the gifts from you by morning to show me you're willing to make this right. Transfer the money into our old account in Austria today. Neither one of us is benefiting from this war, Igor. It needs to stop, and it looks like the ball is in your court now. So, send me the details and don't insult me with the money, either."

"John, thank you. Yes, I'll put a package together. Thank you, John. Is David there, John? I would like to speak to him."

"Oh, you will get your chance to chat, Igor. Just not right now."

●   ●   ●

Igor sat in his office in Havana. He looked at Alek and Dmitry. "You heard him. What do you men think?"

Alek replied, "Igor, we need to leave. He seems to want to end this. Get back to business. Make money, that is why we are all here. But I think he would prefer if we were not here anymore."

"You are right. We need to be packing up. He knows where this office is and where we live. Those three assholes screwed up. I never ordered the hit. I knew I should have kept Ruslan here. He wanted to kill David. I should have known. We are fucked. No one is going to believe I didn't order that hit. I only wish David had spent more time killing that great ape. We need to pack up and head to Poland, where we can hide. All our phone call did was buy us a few days, maybe three or four. Just enough to pack and run. I was hoping he would have said where David was. I don't like how he said David will be chatting with me."

"Igor, I agree. No matter what we do or say, it will not change what John and James think of us right now," said Alek.

"I think so too. He is a talented actor, but we're not in that business. We're in the business of making money, filling orders for our clients and now our most important job, staying alive. I want everyone ready to move by morning. In the meantime, call the Rodstvo gang in Toronto and get eyes on David. If John sends anyone, it will be him."

"Igor, they will kill you. I think now is the time to tell them about The Family. Not start another war we can't finish."

"What? Have you flipped to them too? Do I not have anyone left?"

"Igor, of course not. But if we are to survive, we need to work with them."

"Yes, I know." Igor snapped back. "Dmitry, you stay here and help me make a peace offering. What do we have available? If he wants it shipped to Scott, maybe we can place some gifts inside some of the equipment."

•　　•　　•

After John put down the handset, he looked at James. They knew Igor made the whole apology up, but something, a gut feeling, made John think Igor wasn't the only one involved with the attempted attack on the shop.

"Well, all I can say is, if he bought it, we might get to him before he leaves his current location," said James.

Within twenty-four hours, they would know if Igor was sincere by the money deposit and list of items they would receive. But no matter what Igor sent as a peace offering, David needed to get to Igor.

John had already upgraded the security systems at the shop, farm, and all their houses. If, like Igor said, "it wasn't him," then the rules had changed. They needed to be ready.

Amy was John and James' biggest concern. She wanted to be involved with them, but this was not the time to train anyone.

Frank entered the office. "Hey guys, the call came from Cuba, Havana, to be exact. I guess he is in his office there. But I doubt for long."

"Thanks Frank," said John.

"Well, let's get the boys down there today if possible. They might just catch him at the airport."

John called to book the flights while David and Phil sat at the conference table with James.

"The next flight out is tomorrow at ten."

Frustrated by the delays, David complained. "This is why we need our own plane. We all know he won't be there when we arrive. He will be looking for us. We will be the targets again."

"David, we will look into it. You are right. We need to be better prepared for immediate international travel. But the delay also prevents us from running into a situation without planning and taking time to think about the consequences."

David and Phil left, disheartened. Knowing they would likely miss Igor and their chance to take him and his remaining team down.

• • •

Once off the plane, David and Phil checked in with John. He confirmed they had missed Igor by twelve hours. Phil grabbed their luggage, and they headed to a resort with a planeload of tourists from Toronto. With hats and sunglasses on, they tried to hide their identity in case Igor had someone at the arrivals level of the airport. They settled into the suite at the resort, the only room available at the last minute.

"I wouldn't mind settling in here for a few months. But let's face it, we are going to be filling up our passports with many stamps," said David. He collapsed on the couch. "Tomorrow we can take the tour into Havana. Then head to Igor's office and see what we can dig up."

They headed to the restaurant and loaded up their plates with food, then relaxed by the pool for the evening. The urgency of the trip was gone. Phil found people who were ready to party. David, not the sociable person Phil was, headed to his room. Reluctantly, Phil followed him, knowing they were in Cuba to work.

•   •   •

They were the first to get on the transport for a day of sightseeing and touring Havana. David arranged with the driver to include tickets for them at all the attractions and stops he planned to visit with the two other families. David paid for everyone's day out in exchange for the promise that if asked, David and Phil were with them the entire day.

The driver dropped them off downtown, close to Igor's office and apartment. David and Phil headed to Igor's apartment first. They walked around the building and found an unlocked back door into the complex. They took the broken, at least by North American standards, unsafe stairs to the third floor.

David said, "Well, hopefully that's as close to any danger as we get today, getting up those stairs."

"Yeah, that was more of an obstacle course than a stairway. I can't believe Igor lives in this shit hole."

"Wait till you see his place. I've seen photos. I believe they keep the exterior like this to prevent anyone from breaking in. Make it look like another poor apartment building. These places are some of the nicest ones on the island."

They stood in front of Igor's door. David knocked with authority. No one opened the door, and he could not hear any commotion on the other side of it. From his backpack, he pulled out a small kit to pick the lock. He worked at it for almost two minutes while Phil watched the hallway. Finally, the pins released their hold, and the door swung open. Stepping from the dark, dirty, moldy hallway, they entered a room with bright paint on the walls only hidden by large pieces of artwork. The furniture was all European, and the floor was a rare wood Circassian walnut only found in parts of Russia and Eastern Europe. They closed the door.

"You take the bedrooms and bathroom. I'll hit the office and the other rooms."

"What are we even looking for, David?"

"Anything that can help us. I don't care if it is a piece of paper proving he didn't kill Granda. We all need answers about him, any answers."

Phil opened and closed drawers and closets, all mostly empty. He found a compartment inside the box spring of what he assumed was Igor's bed. It contained a couple of pistols and seven clips. Not a bad little spot to keep weapons for any issues during the night.

David had better luck. At Igor's desk, he found two documents. One had dates of deliveries Scott had made over the last few months. The other listed addresses in Africa, Poland, Singapore, and two in Russia.

David continued to search for more documents. He looked behind the artwork on the wall for hidden safes. He lay on his back and pulled himself under the desk. There, he found what he was looking for. A button on the right corner of the desk. He held the button in and heard a spring release. Inside the bottom drawer, a false bottom had revealed itself. Reaching in, David moved the Browning gun and lifted the paperwork and business cards. He didn't stop to read them, instead he placed the papers in his satchel and continued to search the rooms. When he met Phil in the kitchen, he had a pastrami sandwich and a pop in hand. He had taken the time to make them a morning snack with food from Igor's fridge. They relaxed on the balcony and ate their sandwiches. "I don't know Phil. This seemed too easy, like he wanted us to find these documents. Maybe I am just overthinking this, but all these documents we found are in English. Like he had them interpreted for us."

"Dude, who knows anymore. We have had a crazy year, and what I thought was impossible seems to be possible. We'll see what we find in his office. Maybe you are right."

They cleaned up, always polite guests, they headed out. Their next stop was the office.

• • •

The office building was more secure than the apartment, and the boys noticed that no one entered it dressed as beach bums. They decided they would need to pick up suits and proper clothes before they entered the building. Walking the streets of Havana, they found a tailor. He had a few suits on the rack. They fit with a little customizing. While they waited, David found a luggage store and purchased two new leather satchels. With the new suits fitted and on, Phil took the lead and headed to the main door of the office building. Security stopped him, but after a quick conversation and the exchange of American currency, they were let in.

David and Phil headed to the eleventh floor. They checked the directory for the door to Igor's office. It was down the hallway near the end. David expected to have to pick another lock. When he tried the door, it opened to a reception area where a lovely looking receptionist welcomed them. David looked at Phil. Shocked at the size of the reception area, they stood in the doorway, speechless.

The receptionist looked up from her desk. "Can I help you?"

David answered first. "Yes, well, no. I think we entered the wrong office. Sorry."

"No problem. Who are you looking for?"

"Well, you," said Phil. "You are the woman of my dreams."

She smiled at him.

"No, no, hear me out. I've dreamed about you. You're perfect in my eyes. Tell me you're single, not even a boyfriend. What's your name?"

"Okay, I have work to do. What can I help you with?"

"You can give back my heart," Phil said as he approached her and leaned on her desk. "The fact that we opened the wrong door was destiny, you and me together."

"You know what? I think you are right. I get off work at five. My bosses are on another business trip and I'm the only one here. What about your friend? I can make a couple of calls and bring a friend along. She loves Canadians. She isn't as pretty as me, but in your eyes, who is? My name is Maria, by the way."

"I'm Bret, and my buddy here is Cam. It's almost lunch, and I saw a little cafe outside. Why don't we grab a coffee and talk some more?"

"It is almost my lunch break, but I usually just read. I don't know. I never do this. This is crazy." She laughed and twirled her hair. "Yes, I don't know if it's because you are cute, or the suit, or a smooth talker, but sure, let's go have lunch."

"It doesn't look like I'm invited to this gathering, so I guess I'll do the work we're paid to do. Try to make the plane in two days, partner."

"It's only lunch, partner."

She grabbed her shawl and walked to the door. David held it for her and Phil. As he closed the door, he slid one of the business cards he found at Igor's house against the latch. She turned and locked the handle. Walking to the next office, David watched Phil escort his date to the elevator.

David entered the next office and did his wrong office routine again. Phil and his date entered the elevator as David stepped back into the hallway.

David re-entered Igor's office. He stood and laughed to himself; the little innocent boy trick still worked for Phil. He opened office doors and searched through the desks and filing cabinets. David searched Igor's office. He found documents in English and Cyrillic. Some about The Family that went back to the mid-seventies. Taking his time, David reviewed the documents and notes he thought were important. He found evidence of Russian meddling in American politics back in the sixties. Another folder disclosed proof that Igor sold drugs in Russia while he moved weapons, missiles, military vehicles, tanks, and heavy machinery to Peru and Venezuela. It shocked David to see Igor had sold three jets to a cartel in Ecuador. Surprised by the variety of items Igor moved into Russia, David found evidence of drugs, jeans, albums, electronics, and many other American products, imported for Russian and Polish teens during the 70s and 80s.

Unlike Igor's house, David snapped photos of the documents and notes and tried to put the papers back in the locations they were found. With three rolls of film full of photos, he headed for the elevator. Once outside, he stood by the statue of Castro knowing Phil would look for him.

He could not see Phil, but knew he was around and not back at her apartment, taking one for the team. After a few minutes, David spotted Phil walking towards him.

"Where is the little lady?" David asked.

"She had to powder her nose. So, I gave her a phone number and told her I would pick her up after work. She believes we're here trying to buy cigars in bulk. That was the story I used when she said you went into the office where they export cigars."

"I think she knows exactly who we are. She called us Canadians and greeted us in English. Igor told her we were coming."

"Huh, good catch. So, you're saying my smooth talking and good looks were not the reason I was out for lunch? You're just jealous," Phil said.

"So, are we heading back to the resort, or are you still interested in her?" asked David.

"Oh, I am extremely interested. But we're here for business, not pleasure. I assume there will be some documents to review?"

"Yes, we can stay, if you want. Nothing is time sensitive anymore. I doubt she is the type that would take us out and hide our bodies."

"Nah, let's go before she comes back. Last thing we need right now is me having a relationship with our competition's secretary."

"Good point."

They wandered around Havana and met up with the cabdriver at three in the afternoon to head back to the resort.

Maria looked for Phil and David. When she didn't see them, she headed back to the office and called Igor's office in Poland. He didn't pick up, so she left a message for him, "Like clockwork, they were here, Igor. You didn't tell me how cute Phil was. I can't be sure if David was in our office and reception. I know I locked the door and your office door. If he got in, I don't see any evidence he took anything. Call me tomorrow when you arrive."

After another buffet supper, the boys reviewed the documents they had collected. They both found information that concerned them. They packed and prepared to fly home early the next morning. The evidence on those papers and film had the potential to change the future of all their lives.

•　　•　　•

The boys arrived back at the shop in the afternoon. James and John dug right into the documents from Igor's house. Later in the day, the photos had been processed, and the documents written in Cyrillic had been translated to English. They found notes on The Family from the seventies where Igor had skimmed money off the top of jobs he did with James, John, and Kenton. Some documents revealed communications with a CIA agent called Gregory. He had worked as a double agent throughout most of his career. Igor was his liaison to the KGB. He gave the Soviets information about the Americans. There were receipts for weapons sales to groups in Vietnam and Japan.

The one piece of paper that had everyone's attention was a telegram, buried in a folder full of notes. Sent to Igor just after Kenton's death, from a Dermot in Dublin. It informed Igor, the hit on the Grants was only one quarter successful. "We killed Papa. The other three survived." James stared at the paper for minutes. He couldn't believe Igor funded that job. And it was originally for all of them, not just his dad. Another document showed Nigel, the man who identified James years ago on a job in Belfast, was the one to place the bomb under the Range Rover that night. James hugged David.

"Looks like I have another one to add to my list of people we need to kill," said David. "If and when we get a chance to corner Igor, we can't kill him. We need to bring him back here or to the shop in Portadown. I have so many questions for him about the past and our futures."

"Agreed. We need some answers from him before we put him down," said John.

They continued to review the documents. They found details of Igor's drug and weapon exchanges and his relationship with Castro. There was the handwritten letter from a top KGB minister. It explained how Igor could live and make money, but the Rodstvo would take a large cut of his business. They restricted his sales to a limited variety of weapons and drugs. If he stepped outside his bounds, there would be harsh consequences. He was to escort leaders of the Rodstvo to meet his customers, their new customers. In the file folder was Igor's carbon copy of his response. He questioned why he was set up to look like he was the one interfering with The Family's weapon deliveries and jobs.

Once they had all reviewed the documents and discussed the many surprises they found, James and John were ready to listen to David and Phil on their thoughts about how to move forward. Some papers proved they were behind in several aspects of the underworld they worked in. David now had the names of the people associated with the death of his grandfather and The Family discovered was there was more than one CIA rat for them to deal with.

CHAPTER TWENTY-TWO

John received a call from Peter with a couple of items to review. Peter was very apologetic and saddened by all the stress his team had caused The Family. He believed the last of his rotten apples were in Columbia. With them out of the way, they could get back to normal. He also had information that Igor could be in Columbia, too. His gift to The Family for the problems his team was causing.

He said to John, "Igor and his new partners had stepped up their sales, and on top of selling small arms and some vehicles, there was evidence he shipped anti-aircraft weapons to cartels in Asia and South America."

John had done the same. He had moved pieces of equipment to smaller countries in Africa and Asia to counter the communist push in those regions.

Peter wanted David and James in Columbia to take out the bad agents and, if possible, kill Igor. The operation needed to be done right away. The United States government wanted their agents taken care of before they released any secrets, like Sergio continued to do. Peter had a flight scheduled for David, James, and Phil. A plane would be at Trenton AFB ready to go within fourth-eight hours. Their pilot would have the latest details on the team and Igor.

"Peter, before we hang up. I have some information for you. Last week, the boys were in Cuba. Igor was there. We missed him by less than a day. David got into his office and took a bunch of files and documents. Some interesting stuff and a few things you should know about."

"Oh? In Igor's desk? Well, that's interesting. Send them to me. I would like to review them too. Was I mentioned in any of them? I don't mean me, but the CIA?"

"Yes, there were notes on a Gregory and Sergio and... Well, it's best if I send it all to you. We don't know whose phones or offices are bugged. I need to go, Peter. Take care. I'll get the docs sent to you this week."

John hung up.

•   •   •

David and Phil arrived with Scott, in Canada from Northern Ireland. Phil had worked on a shipment with Scott while David took out three IRA supporters wanted for the death of six police officers in Belfast.

John had a car pick them up and deliver them to the shop. They arrived at the office, shocked to see Amy at the table.

"Amy?" David said before he greeted anyone else in the room. "Amy, really Dad? Mom must be dead. What happened to her? Did we finally do her in?"

Amy laughed as James said. "No, your mother is still healthy and alive. She thinks Amy is heading to Mexico with friends and their parents."

"Dad, she can't come on this trip. Seriously, this is too big of an—"

James shook his head. "No, she is staying with John. We're taking Frank with us. John will need help with some administration and running the shop."

"Okay, that makes more sense."

Everyone sat around the table as John broke down what the Americans wanted from them. The need for this to be successful in solidifying their relationship with the United States was of utmost importance.

The team went out for supper and then headed home. At 6 a.m. they were to meet at the shop to drive to Trenton for their flight.

• • •

The plane landed on a little known grassy airfield in Columbia, about fifty miles east of Neiva. CIA ops and The Family's planes used the airfield many times to transport weapons. They unloaded their supplies, vehicles, fuel, food, and weapons for the next leg of the trip. The latest information was a team of Igor's and possibly Igor himself was held up in a grow operation about one hundred miles West of Neiva. The wanted CIA members, hid in Tulua. Peter believed some had turned to work with Igor. The plan was to be done and back on the plane within five days. He gave a new piece of equipment to James. A satellite phone, to call for the plane when the team had completed their mission.

Driving on the dusty back roads in a defensive formation, James drove one vehicle and Frank took the other one. With large caliber weapons on their laps, David and Scott looked for anything of concern.

Their first stop would be a house in Neiva. From there, they would split up. James and Frank would head to Tulua to locate the CIA men while David, Scott and Phil would head to the location of Igor and his men. When they arrived in Neiva, it was obvious the contact they were to meet was not around. They found a ransacked apartment and a dead lady and child. With the image of the young girl in their minds, the team headed to a gas station where they loaded their tanks and spare jerry cans and headed out on their missions. It would not be safe for them to be in the city.

David and his team headed east while James and Frank took the roadway to Tulua. James noticed a pickup following them. With their vehicle pulled off to the side of the road and automatic rifles laying flat on their laps, James and Frank watched the vehicle pass. As the pickup passed, the three men inside glared at James and Frank. James put the vehicle in gear and followed them. The pickup slowed down and allowed James to catch up to them. Pulling up behind the pickup, a muzzle of a gun poked out the rear side window. James pounded the brakes, throwing them forward as the vehicle skidded to a stop on the roadway. The pickup stopped in front of them, and the three men exited the vehicle. A car passed James in the lane to his left and another one approached. James cranked the wheel to the left and pulled away as bullets hit the back of the vehicle.

"Did you get a look at them Frank," James asked.

"Yes, I think we are both thinking the same thing. Those guys were not Columbian. If they were any paler, they would be ghosts."

"Exactly, fucking Russians, Igor's Russians. How the hell did they know we were here and would be on this road?"

"John needs to know this; he could be in danger. The only time we discussed our mission was on the phone with Peter and when John reviewed the job when we all met. Someone's tapped a phone or office," said James.

"Well, let's see how this cellular phone works," said Frank. He pulled the phone out of his bag, extended the antenna, and dialed the office. After a few strange noises and delays, Frank heard a phone ring.

"Hello," John said. His voice was clear, like he was standing beside Frank.

"John? I have never heard you so clear on a phone. John, run the office again. We have bugs. Be careful John. They might know you are there alone. If it isn't our shop, it must be on Peter's end."

"How do you know?"

"We were just shot at on the road. Our contact in Neiva is missing, and his family was raped and killed. We're still running the operation."

"Okay," said John.

"We will call again in twenty-four hours," said Frank.

Frank pushed a couple of buttons on the phone until he figured out the red one ended the call. James pulled the vehicle around and headed back to the road they originally traveled. He watched the front window while Frank surveyed the surrounding road.

After a nine-hour drive, they arrived in Tulua. It was dark, and the streets were full of people. There was a celebration happening, and it distracted and concerned James. They pulled into a gas station and Frank filled the fuel tank while James purchased a map of the city. "What is with all the street parties?" James asked, handing a twenty to the cashier.

"Just another Friday night in the city. People feel blessed to be alive and the work week, for most, is over." He handed back change. "There seems to be a lot of gringos around this week. I wonder where they are all coming from?"

James shrugged his shoulders and left.

They found the address of the house where the agents were and drove by.

James found a hotel in town. He took the first watch. The parking lot and hotel were quiet. Several people passed out in the gutter in front of the hotel. Frank took the second watch at 3 a.m., he watched a robbery of three women and a prostitute work her trade in a car beside theirs. As the sun rose, Frank woke James, and they headed back to the house and the field agents.

James knocked on the door. There was no answer. He knocked harder. It was early and from what he could see, the people of this town were not early risers. Still no answer. Frank checked the back of the house. He found the back door was ajar. He cautiously entered the house. As he stood in the kitchen, he saw blood on the floor. He drew his gun and stepped back outside and circled the house.

"James, there's blood on the floor in the kitchen. It looks fresh," said Frank.

"Okay, you go back around and enter the back again. Where are the stairs to the second floor?"

"When you go in, they're to your right in the front room."

"Okay, I'll take the second floor, you secure the first floor."

James gave Frank a minute to enter from the back again. He entered the house and proceeded to the stairs. He could smell blood, the rusty metal smell he had become too familiar with. His gun leading him, he carefully climbed the stairs. At the top of the stairs, he saw his first victim. With three holes in his back, he lay face down in a pool of dried blood.

"Fuck," James said out loud. He looked into the rooms. "Frank, I am clear."

"Clear here too, but I've got an issue," said Frank.

"I have four issues, Frank. Something bad happened here."

"Oh, okay. I'm coming up."

Standing in the bedroom doorway, James and Frank saw a man in his bed. His white sheets stained with blood. On the floor beside the bed was a body and a puddle of blood seeping from the torso. James walked into the other bedroom with Frank. "I think I saw his chest move, James."

"What?"

James walked over to the man on the floor. He placed his finger under the nose. Then felt his neck. "Frank, get the bag. There is a faint pulse, and he's breathing. I guess I'm too used to finding dead people."

"Do we kill him or try to get some answers from him first?" asked Frank.

"I think we need some answers," said James.

Frank nodded. "I will get my medical bag." He headed downstairs with his gun in his hand.

James rolled the man onto his side. He had a bullet entry hole in his lower back and one in his leg. He groaned as James moved him, and he lifted his head. The puddle of congealed blood that surrounded him looked like a large bloody spider web as it clung to the floor and the victim's shirt. A bullet shell encased in dried blood lay under his chest and under his stomach was a gun.

"Hello, hello. Can you speak English? Mate, I got you. Hello," said James.

"Huh," he said. His head dropped, and he went limp.

"Mate, hello, come on. We are here to help. Come on. Wake up. Focus on my voice."

Frank entered the room. He pulled a needle of adrenaline out of his bag. James lay the person down on his back.

Frank looked at James. "No, this won't work. Smelling salts?" he asked as he pulled a package from the side pocket of the bag.

"Might as well. What other options do we have?"

Frank waved the stick under the victim's nose. He coughed, opened his eyes, and went limp. They both watched as Frank waved it under his nose again. The man twitched and shook. His eyes opened, then closed, his legs jumped, then he lay still. He took a deep breath and exhaled. Finally, his eyes sprung open and stared at the ceiling. He tried to get up, but James pushed him down onto his back.

"Hello, do you speak English?"

"Y'all saved me, I think. What happened?"

"Just lay there. We still need to clean you up. You have two bullet holes in you," said James.

"I do? I feel fine."

"That would be the smelling salts. It won't last. Lie still. I don't know where the bullet in your lower back is."

"Who are you?" James asked.

"Tom Winter. Who are you?"

"I am James. This is Frank. I guess you could say we were here to meet you. Your boss, Peter, sent us."

"Peter caused this. He sent them after us. No, not dead, until now, I guess. Kill me quick, please. I know who you are. You are the clean-up crew."

"What? Peter caused this? How? No. Save your energy. We have time to talk. Let's sort you out first. We need to roll you over and bandage you up before we leave."

They rolled him over, and Frank inspected the holes. He could not get the bullets out. He could manage the blood, but Tom needed a hospital.

"There were supposed to be three agents here. We have found five people, six, including you. I assume three are not part of your team?" asked Frank.

"I guess." Tom looked up and out the door. "I killed him. He wasn't one of us. They broke into the house early this morning. Are you guys Americans? What agency?"

"No agency, we are Canadians, and we do freelance work, I guess. Peter sent us on this job," said James. "We are here to—"

"Okay, we need to get you out of here. I think you can walk with us supporting you. You can lie on the backseat of the car, and we'll get you to a hospital. Can you identify the men as we leave?" asked Frank.

"I guess so. I assume I am the only survivor?"

"Yes, that we have seen. I didn't even think you were one. Frank saw your chest move."

Tom smiled at Frank. "Thank you."

They helped Tom up and walked him through the hallway, down the stairs, and then out through the kitchen. As he passed the three assailants and his two partners, he identified each man. When they rolled the man in the hallway over, James recognized him as the man who drove the pickup they met on the road.

With Tom in the back seat of the car, they drove to the hospital. Luckily, or maybe not, but with all the festivities from the night before, there were multiple shootings. Bringing Tom into the building, the staff received him as just another victim from the celebrations the night before. The doctors in the hospital rushed him into surgery. After two hours, the two bullets were removed and placed in a cup with twelve other bullets from the previous night. The staff found a location in a hallway for Tom to rest and recover. Frank stayed in the hospital to protect Tom while James drove out of town to call John.

The deaths and knowledge of everyone's locations concerned John. They both agreed James and Frank would have been targets in the house if the Russians had survived. But most troubling to John was the statement, "Peter caused this."

"I know we are here to kill the agents, as Peter requested, but I think we need to keep this one. But no one should know. None of this adds up and my fear is there is innovative technology that Peter isn't aware of monitoring his office. If you can have a face-to-face with him, I think he needs to have his office checked again and possibly move to a new one," said James. "How rotten is that department he runs?"

"I will get hold of him. You might be right. Like us, he has been in the game for a long time. We are all falling behind."

"Okay. I better get back into town. I'll call you tomorrow. Hopefully, the others are having a better time of it."

"Take care, James." The sun disappeared behind the mountains and James went back to the house and recovered the two Americans. He took photos and fingers of the three men believed to be Russians. He checked the bodies and found no ID, just a tattoo of an eight-sided star. With the two American victims in the vehicle's trunk, James headed back to the hospital.

Frank was outside. He just lit his cigarette. The lack of air conditioning, the smell of an over packed hospital and an empty stomach were getting to him. He wanted James to go back into the hospital, he would sit in the vehicle.

James entered the hospital and located Tom. "Tommy, we need to go. Which means I need you to get up and walk. Can you do that? Or at least get in a wheelchair so I can roll you out. I know you just had serious surgery, but we need to get on the road. Do you understand?"

Tom nodded his head. They had just topped up his pain meds through an IV and he felt fine. James motioned to the nurse that Tom needed a cigarette. She handed James a pack and a lighter. *Wow, you don't get this service in a Canadian hospital,* he thought.

James motioned to her for a wheelchair. She pointed to a room behind him where he located one. With the help of the nurse, they loaded Tom into the wheelchair. Once she clipped the IV bag to the chair, she smiled at James. Pushing the old chair, James walked out the door to the vehicle.

Carefully, they lay Tom down in the back seat. Frank removed Tom's IV and made him as comfortable as possible. "Tom, the ride is going to suck. In a couple of hours, I'll bump you up with morphine from my bag," said Frank.

"Cool, are you a doctor?" asked Tom.

"No, I manage a plumbing warehouse and service company," Frank said.

James put the car in gear, and they headed for Neiva.

• • •

David, Scott, and Phil were on a dirt road to La Pena as James and Frank were being shot at on the road to Tulua. The only disruption to the beautiful scenery was when six Soviet era military personnel trucks passed them. With a map open on his lap, David raised his hand, showing all five fingers. "Five miles out," he said.

The last update they received at the airfield revealed that Igor and his team were there to meet with cartel captains.

Bouncing along the rough, exposed road, they slowed and pulled over to move their guns and ammo onto their laps. David noticed a plane flying low in front of them. The plane circled the compound. Then, in a flash of fire, it disappeared. They shot the plane from the sky.

"Did you guys see that?" asked David.

"Yes. That plane was just shot down by a missile. It came from the compound.

Slowing the vehicle, they watched the plane fall from the sky in three large pieces.

"Well, fuck me. It must be nice to have enough money not only to buy anti-aircraft missiles but to sacrifice a plane and a pilot to test it. I don't think John is charging enough," said David.

"David, Scott, what is that dust cloud coming towards us. I think they have identified us. Are we staying to fight?" Phil asked. He bolted his gun.

"No, no. David, get the truck turned. We need to get out of here. They're coming fast," said Scott.

David had the vehicle turned around and moving. "Phil, keep looking out the back window. Let me know if they are getting closer. The problem is, they know these roads better than I do."

David wrestled the old truck while Scott called out the turns as best he could between the map and what he could see out the window.

They sped through a couple of small towns. "Should we stop and try to hide in the next town or keep going?" David asked.

"As much as I would like to see who is following us, I don't think it's a good idea."

"They are getting closer. We need to decide what to do, and quickly."

"Okay, we keep going and hope we can make it to Neiva. We can hide in that city."

David continued to steer and skid on the dirt road. Cars approached the group and as each vehicle approached, Scott located the driver in his gun sites. The sun set before they finally merged onto a main road full of slow traffic.

David wove his way through the traffic while Phil continued to watch the rear, looking for any cars to pull onto the road from where they came. "David, I see them. They have stopped, and it looks like they, yes, they are turning around."

David settled into the traffic and headed to Neiva. Once they arrived, they secured a hotel room and, like James and Frank, each man took watch. The next day they spent in town and waited to hear from James. They decided not to make another attempt at the compound, assuming whoever chased them would be on high alert. Poor judgment of approaching a secure area was to blame. They knew better.

• • •

The next day, Phil went to the meeting location and waited for James and Frank.

"Where is everyone else?" James asked.

"In a hotel. Things didn't go well. We were spotted. We can give you all the details once we're together. Do you want to follow me? We have reserved five rooms, so we have plenty of space until our pickup in two days."

"Aye, I'll follow you. Problem is, we have two decaying bodies in the back."

Phil looked at James. "Ours?"

"Yes ours. Bring them home. Always."

"Always."

Phil drove back to the hotel, with James following behind him. David had picked up food from a street market. The team reunited with one additional member.

James sat in David's room and ate. "I need to call John," said James. "This is messed up. I will get that new phone from Frank and chat about our next steps."

"Dad, maybe find a pay phone. Something is up. Peter is compromised. Someone is listening in on all his calls and maybe on that phone, too."

"Aye, you are right, son. And no mention of Tom to anyone. We were here to kill these guys. Peter had his reasons."

James left and found a pay phone. He reviewed the missions and their complications with John. "I think you need to tell Peter we couldn't find Tom or his body. Let him know we searched the area around the house and in the town."

"I agree. We need to hide him from everyone until we find out what happened. Peter wants the bodies dropped off in Florida. Two bodies only," said John. "I'll get you a plane as soon as possible. Call back in the morning and I will confirm the flight. Stay alert, James."

"We will talk in the morning. I have this covered, John. Just get us home."

They hung up, and James returned to his team.

•   •   •

The next morning, James called the shop. John confirmed their pickup would be at noon local time. There was one additional issue that needed to be taken care of before they could come home. It was a last-minute request from Peter. James confirmed the request and hung up.

With a pistol in hand, James knocked on the hotel door that Frank and Tom shared. He entered the room and looked at Tom laying on the bed.

Frank had just changed the bandages. "Frank, I need you to head out when you're cleaned up. Grab David and get us all some food. I don't know about you, but I'm starving," said James.

"Yes James, I could eat. Just need to give Tom his pills and I will be on my way."

James shook his head and motioned to the door. Frank dried his hands and left. "Tom, I hear there are a few loose ends I need to deal with before I head home."

"Loose ends? Not any I can think of."

"Well, maybe you need to think harder. Really search your mind," James said and placed the pistol on the TV stand.

"Umm, right. Well, there is one item they assigned me to, right here in Neiva. I just never had the balls to do it. But I guess you do."

"Tom, you are floating between life and death. Can I help you with this?"

"No, I know what you're meaning. He is a good kid, gave me a lot of information, he gave us a lot of information. But I suspect he is giving others just as much."

"Where is he, Tom?"

"You can find him at the auto shop behind the market David went to last night. This breaks my heart. Can we—"

James shook his head. "I know I hate these orders too, but they have to be done. The phone call I just had was not good at all."

James left the room and stopped in Scott's room. With Scott, James left to take out the fourteen-year-old boy. He had given the Americans information on drug cartels and activity within the city. But he had done the same for the cartels and others.

James entered the auto shop with Scott. They moved the mechanics, secretary, and two customers into the lunchroom, where Scott watched them. He lined them up against the wall and moved his gun from person to person.

James took Manuel to the parts room. He said nothing. James pushed the boy to the ground, he landed on his stomach. Manuel struggled to get away, but James pressed his knee into Manual's shoulder blades. With a handful of hair in one hand and his knife in the other one, he thrust the tip and shank into the base of the boy's neck. Manuel's body locked, then relaxed. James then rolled him over and ran his blade across the boy's neck.

Locating Scott, he nodded. They left through the back door of the shop in silence. James did not feel any remorse, but did not feel any joy, either.

•   •   •

The team arrived at the airstrip an hour before the plane. On the backseat of David's vehicle, Tom rested. In the other vehicle, James sat quietly alone.

The plane approached and Scott and Phil waved their arms to show all was clear and safe to land.

Frank and David removed the bodies from the trunk. "Boy, in this heat, it doesn't take long for the bodies to smell. I hope they brought body bags, or else these two are going into the cargo area."

"Yes. There is nothing worse than being able to taste the smell. You know?"

"I know, Frank, I know all about it."

They lifted the second body out of the vehicle and placed it beside the first one. Frank straightened up, holding his lower back. "I'm not getting any younger," said Frank. "Can you get the pilot to help David? I want to stabilize Tom before we move him onto the plane."

"Of course, old man."

"I can still kick your ass," Frank said, and motioned at David with his fists.

While the team watched Tom at the front of the plane, James sat at the back, alone. David looked back but could tell his dad wanted to be alone. David informed Tom he was now under The Family's witness protection program. Peter believed Tom was killed and they did not find his body. Recently divorced, Tom was delighted to have someone, or an organization, take care of him and let him start his life over. Once Phil explained who The Family were, Tom offered to move to Britain and help Scott with his work if they wanted.

When the plane landed in Florida to refuel, David and Phil got off. James and Scott joined them. An unmarked truck pulled up and removed the two bodies, to be returned to their families for a proper funeral.

At the Waterloo airport, John and Amy picked up the weary men and their additional cargo. The ride to the shop was quiet. Tom slept. John reserved a room and a doctor at the hospital. A new identity was being prepared for Tom. Once he told his story and answered all The Family's questions, they would move him.

CHAPTER TWENTY-THREE

John met with James and David in the office. They sat down, John poured himself and James a small glass of rum. David grabbed a pop. Phil and Scott were in Canada for three hours, after the last job, before they traveled to Northern Ireland to prepare a large shipment of military equipment to send to Yemen.

John called Scott's office. Both phones were on speaker, which created eerie feedback. They hung up and tried again. With a better line the second time, David gave an update on Tom. If he kept progressing at the rate he was, the doctor would release Tom within the next couple of days. They had all agreed to let Tom have his time to recover in the hospital. Once released from the hospital, they would interrogate him before hiding him away in protective custody.

The first topic John needed to review was the Russian General. He had been one of their best suppliers since the meeting with David.

"He told me that the shipment you and Phil just received and are preparing to send out will be our last one from him," said John.

"John, you're joking. We have never had such excellent service," said Scott.

"I know. He is not happy about losing us, either. But the Rodstvo has shut him down. They will be his only customer going forward. He tried to push back, but they appeared at the hangar in the Ukraine and killed two of his men."

"I feel they are slowly making their way to us," said David. "Better to be on the offensive for this one, I think."

"David, let's just stay on topic right now. He told me these guys are ruthless. They don't fear death and have no respect for anyone. No wonder Igor wanted to please them. He said they asked about us, too."

"All right, I guess we need to pressure our old suppliers to get us the quality and quantity we were getting from him," said John.

"Dad, I'll start making some calls from here," said Phil.

"Okay. I convinced him to ship us one last enormous order. Not to add more to your plates, but you will need to find somewhere to hide it all. We will need to spread it out through Canada and the States."

"I am on it," said Phil.

"Now, for some good news. Peter called and told me they found Igor outside of Russia, and he is all ours. He is on a boat docked in Saudi Arabia. I have a flight booked for James and David that leaves in four hours."

"Serious John? Peter pulled through for us. Nice!" said David. "Maybe I can tie him up in the ship's hold."

"You two will need to be careful. He is with a few Rodstvo leaders."

"Okay, let's get going Dad. I am not missing that flight."

After a quick discussion of how well the Armenians were doing, they ended the meeting.

A day later, James and David arrived in Khafaji. They took a cab to the port and drove past the one-hundred-foot yacht Igor was staying on. It was an average size compared to the other boats in the harbor.

A hotel overlooked the port where John had made reservations for them there. David watched the boat while James checked in. In the room, he set up a camera and binoculars. When James flashed the flash of their camera out the window twice, David headed to their room to finish the setup of surveillance equipment.

David took watch for the night. At one in the morning, the party on the boat ended and everyone went to bed.

James took over at seven and waited. Finally, the door slid open to the deck and James picked out Igor. He was with an entourage of seven heavily armed men.

"David, there he is. He just came onto the deck of the boat."

David put down his coffee and looked out the window. "Wow, they protected him for this trip. I assume those guys are his new bosses. They aren't shy about carrying their weapons. How do we get around that much security?"

"I wonder if they would be just as happy to get rid of Igor as we are. Maybe if we can plan something, they will take care of him for us."

"Maybe Dad. Well, let's see if this fancy microphone the government gave us actually works." David pointed the directional microphone at the boat. He picked up, mumbling. Then Igor turned towards the hotel. David heard each word like Igor was standing beside him. He hit record and listened. They spoke Russian, a language David did not understand. The man with Igor had an interpreter. They spoke for half an hour. The expression on the interpreter's face showed there were some parts of the conversation he didn't like.

"Dad, if we had the right rifle, we could take him out from here. It wouldn't be a hard shot."

"I know, but remember where you are. They believe an eye for an eye. We get caught well—I don't believe we would be leaving."

"Right, and a shot from here would bring too much attention. Like Granda always said, guns are impersonal, and that's why we use knives."

"Exactly. Okay, why don't you get some sleep. You watched the boat all night. You will need to do the same tonight. He'll be leaving tomorrow and that is when we get him."

James continued to record the microphone conversation and the footage the camera captured. David slept on the bed, but he didn't sleep deep. He was ready for his father to call him for action.

• • •

James was up early the next morning. Their notes showed Igor was scheduled to leave later that morning. They needed to be at the small private airport before him. James checked out while David hailed a cab. At the airport, they walked the perimeter until they found a spot to cut open the fence. David pulled out a small set of bolt cutters and, hidden behind a hangar, he opened the fence.

"See, Dad, we wouldn't have to sneak in if we had our own private plane like Igor," David said, then winked. He carried the camera equipment while James had a backpack on and a pistol in his hand.

"Maybe one day, David. But not yet. You know it would bring too much attention to us. And we seem to have plenty right now."

"I know, I was just joking. I think maybe in a year it might be worth it. Like I keep saying, the world is changing."

They walked to the hangars and checked three before they found the one with Igor's plane. Through the open hangar doors, they watched the pilot walk around the plane doing pre-flight checks. James saw a fuel truck approach and flagged it down. Without speaking, he used the international language of a pistol and pointed it at the driver. The driver knew immediately what he needed to do. He stepped out of the truck. David found some rope and an extension cord behind the seat. Once they gagged and tied the man, they walked him to the back of the hangar and tied his feet. James sat him down and pointed the gun. He pressed his finger to his lips. The man nodded.

David drove the truck back to the hangar while James hung onto the back. The pilot had just used the pull cart to move the plane out of the hangar. Hanging from the cockpit window, he flashed four, five, then zero with his fingers. David waved and wrote 450 on the notepaper. He showed it to the pilot, who gave a thumbs up.

David looked at his dad. "Okay, fill them up with four hundred and fifty gallons of fuel."

"If only I knew how," he said. They both laughed.

They parked the truck behind the wing, and James pulled a hose off the truck. Entering the plane, David found the pilot and co-pilot flipping switches in the cockpit. He coughed to get their attention. They turned and looked at the gun.

"Do you speak English?"

The pilot shook his head. The co-pilot answered. "A little."

"Okay, you two are going to get up one at a time and head to the back of the plane. Tell your friend I want to see his hands at all times."

The pilot put his check sheet and clip board down. David stepped to the door. "All clear," he yelled outside. James ran up the stairs and entered the plane with his gun in his hand.

"Okay, him first," David said. He pointed the gun at the pilot. "Tell him to stand and walk to the rear of the plane. NOW!"

The co-pilot said something in Russian. The pilot looked at David, then James.

"MOVE," said James.

Slowly, the pilot stood and walked towards James. Followed by James and his gun, the pilot walked to the back of the plane. From his backpack, James pulled out a rope and rag. He tied and gagged the pilot, then placed him in the washroom. David followed James with the co-pilot, who received the same treatment.

Back outside, James moved hoses around. He opened a door that was tagged, fuel.

David sat in the pilot's seat and closed the door. A black car approached, with two other cars following. Igor got out of the first car. From the other vehicles, six men got out. Igor walked to each driver and shook their hands, then walked up the stairs to his plane, followed by three men. He knocked on the cockpit door and in Russian yelled, "Why aren't the fucking engines started? Why are we only getting fuel now? I told you to be ready for eleven sharp."

David didn't answer and had no clue how to start an engine. They brought the luggage on the plane, followed by James. He knocked on the cockpit door. David stepped out, and they both turned to their passengers.

"Hello, gentlemen, please raise your hands. This is your pilot speaking."

Each man looked up to see they were now hostages. "Ah, David, James. I didn't think things were so bad you had to take jobs at an airport. And the guns? Please. Your father was so much more sophisticated."

"Igor, come up here. The rest of you, hands on the seats in front of you. Let's go, Igor. Out the door."

"No problem, James. I am so glad to see you."

The others remained seated as instructed.

Igor stood and strolled to the front of the plane. "Let's get off the plane and talk. Maybe we can work something out. I know I have something you want even more than me. But what can you give me in return? Huh? That is the question for today, gents." Igor pushed past David and James and walked out the door.

James looked at David, then followed Igor off the plane. "Sure is hot here, James. I think this is my sixth shirt since I arrived. I am not used to sweating this much, but David has heard my complaints before. How are you doing? Sorry about your father. Terrible thing. He was a good man. Do you want me in the truck? If so, I hope it has air conditioning."

"Shut up, Igor. Fuck, you talk too much. I'm sure I've told you that before," said James.

"Many times, James, many times." The humor in his voice was gone. They entered the hangar. "James, I wasn't leaving on the plane. See those men in there. Let them go or they will kill you. They plan to kill me soon, or so they think. Where did you hide the pilot?"

"We stuffed them in the back of the plane."

"Okay, let me back on the plane. I'll tell them who you are. They know of you. Be ready. They might want you two dead, as well as me. Funny thing is, James, I was never leaving on that flight. I was just seeing them off. I have a meeting in the hangar shortly."

"Well, I guess we will attend your meeting too, Igor."

"James, listen, the pilot is an old friend of mine. Tell David to release them. He will fly away with the others on board and then we can talk safely."

James looked at him. He could see the stress on Igor's face. "Okay Igor, but if this goes bad—"

"I know you will kill me yourself. Honestly, it's you or them." He pointed to the plane. "I just think I can negotiate with you. They never learned that word."

James walked Igor back up the stairs to the plane. Igor entered and spoke in Russian. Stepping out of the plane, James motioned at David to do the same. Igor returned to James and they walked back into the hangar. David ran around the building and released the fueler and showed him how much fuel the plane needed. The fueler nodded and started his routine of filling the plane. With the truck backed away, the pilot started the engines. David watched the plane taxi to the runway. Each man had a window and stared at David as they passed him.

"James, I have another meeting in an hour. I have never met him, only talked over the phone and telegram. He is taking me in. Says he will put me into protective custody. I have made my last deal. In an hour I will be officially retired, moving to somewhere in Utah. He told me he'll protect me as long as I walk away from this life and never speak of the life I lived."

"Who is this contact?"

"What, no small talk? James, we haven't seen each other in years, and this is our last time together. Forget the business. Let's chat as old friends. I can ask if he can hide you, too. I know David's answer already."

"Who are you meeting?"

David entered the hangar with his gun pointed at Igor.

"Ah David, you look good. How are you doing? Please put the gun down, we are all friends here."

David looked at James. James nodded his head. "But Dad, I want—"

"David, he has a meeting shortly. We will let him have it. We need to take whoever he is meeting with us, too. Then we will fly the two of them back to Portadown. But we need to see who he is meeting."

"David, your grandfather would be so disappointed in you if he were here. You of all people would shoot me? David, please, if I am to die in your hands, I want the proper treatment. Where is the knife? I would like to see it. I was going to keep it when I had you on the boat. But well, I do have a sentimental side to me."

"Igor, shut the fuck up. I've never met someone who talks as much shit as you do. Dad, what's going on?"

"Okay Igor, you will have your meeting. We are going to hide in here. You will not leave with him. Understand? We'll be interrupting your meeting. I'm very curious to see who this contact is."

"James, I would leave right now if you and John would hide me. Let's face it, you guys are much better at it than any government."

"Dad, I see a car coming up the road."

"Ah, he is early."

"Igor, no funny stuff. Play it straight. If we see you point to our location, I'll shoot you."

James and David moved behind a toolbox as Igor walked to the large hangar door. The car stopped by Igor. A man in a baseball cap and sunglasses stepped out of the car on the opposite side to the hangar. Neither David nor James could see his face. As Igor approached him with his hand stretched out, James moved along the wall to get a better look at Igor's savior. Igor stopped and turned. Three shots echoed outside the hangar. The bullets hit Igor in the back, causing him to fall forward. His body bounced off the ground as two more bullets penetrated his back. Kneeling beside Igor, the stranger placed the gun on the back of Igor's head and pulled the trigger one last time. He stood up and walked back to his car, got in, and drove off. James and David ran to Igor. His blood ran to the grates at the front of the hangar.

"What the hell? I guess Igor didn't see that coming."

"Dad, we need to call John right now. Let's find a phone. I want John to call Peter right now. We need to find out what is going on. I think—"

"We need to get out of here, David. Saudi Arabia is not the country for a couple of Canadians to be found standing over a body," said James.

"Let's get back to the airport and get a flight to anywhere."

"Agreed."

They headed for the hole in the fence. A mile from town, they found a cab driver who took them to the airport.

•   •   •

Sitting in Scott's office in Northern Ireland fourteen hours after Igor's death, James and David revealed to Scott, John and Phil what they encountered in Saudi Arabia.

David finished the story and wanted John to call Peter. "John, we know it was an American Igor was to meet. One with enough pull to offer him a new life in Utah and someone he had worked with enough to trust. I want to know where Peter was when the hit happened. He needs to check travel or flight plans with his staff and maybe expand it out to other agencies. Someone from the American government killed Igor. I want to know why and who."

"David, I completely agree. I will call him."

CHAPTER TWENTY-FOUR

It had been a week since Igor passed away. Peter continued his internal investigations, and he was stressed. The leaks and issues had reached congress and within the next month he would sit in a Congressional hearing. Before that meeting, he needed all his internal issues resolved. He had one last person for David to visit. The information James and David gave him about Igor's killer sealed the deal. Peter knew who the last man in this nightmare of insubordination within the ranks was. The man who he believed killed Igor. He tasked David with the job to take down an Army Major, Casey Clarke. He worked in the Defense Intelligence Agency and collaborated with Peter on counter-intelligence jobs, the ones they didn't need David for. Peter's report stated Casey was selling technological secrets to militaries, people in power, and governments. He had the drawings of the top-secret B-2 stealth bomber and stealth fighter, both unknown technologies, until the Gulf War. The report stated Casey had names and operational histories of agents, active and retired. Selling their names and the operations they were associated with, to the enemy, would jeopardize their lives and the lives of those around them.

According to Peter's report, Casey was in Australia. He was there to sell those items to Iraqi government officials. Peter's report noted that he was armed and could have protection around him.

Tom's recovery wasn't as quick as everyone had hoped. David wanted to interrogate him, but he had slipped into a coma. The information in Tom's head would stay there for a while longer.

• • •

James sat with David in the living room while Elizabeth prepared supper. David was to leave for Australia once he finished dinner. The plan was for him to pick up Phil and drive to Waterloo, take a plane to Buffalo, then hop on a couple of different military cargo planes to arrive in Perth. They would discuss none of his travel plans at the family supper.

Elizabeth called James, David, and Amy to the table to eat. Ham and scallop potatoes fresh from a box were on the menu for the family, with a side dish of angry Elizabeth. Until that morning, she had been in the dark about Amy's knowledge and participation in parts of the family business.

That morning, Elizabeth was out for coffee with Brenda, John's wife, and ladies from the church. Before the others arrived, Brenda brought up how she had seen Amy at the shop a few times and had been told about how Amy picked up a rental car by mistake. Amused, she related the story of Amy buying a fake ID and how that purchase had caused changes to the business for the better. She wasn't sure if Elizabeth was aware of the new recruitment.

When Elizabeth got home, Amy was in her room. She was in the middle of a Tom Clancy novel, Patriot Games. She questioned Amy, and just like when David was a young boy, Amy denied any involvement with operations and claimed she only worked in the office on the plumbing business. But like with David, she knew Amy had lied to her.

"James, David, Amy, my family. The ones I love and trust. The ones I do so much for with no expectation of anything in return," Elizabeth said. "Dinner is ready."

David looked at James, then at Amy as they walked to the dining room. He knew what was coming.

"James, David, remember when we all agreed Amy would never know about—"

"Elizabeth, not now," James said.

"Mom, I can explain. Let me explain. This had nothing to do with them. Be mad at me," Amy said.

"So, it is true. They looped you into their boys' club. Amy, how could you? We talked about this. What about your future? Our talks had nothing to do with these guys. Now I have no one here for me at all. Who will take care of me? What about your boyfriend?"

"Mom, you isolate yourself from us. You take the benefits of my hard work. You have your fancy vacations, summer, and winter homes and all the other benefits, yet still look down on us. Honestly, Mom, get with the program. I'm done supporting you," said David.

"David, I get nothing from your work."

"Dad, really, are we going to sit here and listen to this? Amy, tell her the truth. Can we put an end to this, please?"

"Mom, just listen. After Granda died, I had a lot of questions, a lot of them. Maybe if my whole life wasn't based on lies, it wouldn't have been so hard for me. But you lied to me all these years."

"Oh, here we go again. I'm the reason this house is so messed up, eh? Your father and brother are trained killers, traveling the world, but I'm the problem. Oh, I see it now," Elizabeth cried and buried her face in her hands.

Amy stood and hugged her. "Mom, no one is blaming anyone. But you did lie to me. Nannie was the one who spilled the beans at the funeral. All the time she spends in Canada, and I had no clue. Mom, stop crying and listen. It's okay. I'm happy, very happy."

"How many people have you killed, Amy? How many people have died in your arms?"

David and James laughed at her comment.

"Elizabeth, honestly, we don't keep a count," James said, laughing.

"What? Amy, no."

"Mom, he is just joking. Amy hasn't killed anyone. At least that I know. Sis, are you taking work from me? Is John slipping you jobs behind my back?"

Amy smiled, and James and David laughed. Elizabeth did not see the humor in any of this conversation. She was so confused by this.

"Seriously, Mom, this band of brothers needs a sister, too. Aunt Sarah helps over home."

"Don't remind me."

"I have done a few jobs here and there with David and Phil, watching people, moving things. I thought I knew everything. David had me watch—"

David shook his head to have her stop talking.

"Sorry," said Amy

"No, continue. David what?"

"He had me watch some Russians while you were on vacation. I also drove for him on a job where he roughed a few guys up when Phil was away."

"James, when are you cutting her finger off?"

"There will be no ceremony for her, Elizabeth. Just stop. You could have been helping too when you were younger. You chose to separate yourself," said James.

"Mom, you knew this day was coming," David said. He filled the kettle and made tea, and Amy cleared off the dishes.

"Okay. So, Amy is now involved. I have to worry about her now, too. You guys get to go out and play the A-Team while I sit at home and worry. How is this fair? Amy, what about school and marrying someone?"

"I know Mom, stop. I'm not planning on doing what David, Dad or the others do. But I will say the money is good for the work I do," she said with a smile. "I enjoy it. Mom, I spent my whole life with you. I never really got to know my real dad or brother. Even John and Phil, they are closer than family. Please, Mom, don't be mad. I want to help. It's the nineties, not the fifties. Girls can do this shit. Oops, I mean stuff."

David poked himself with his fork on his lip and spilled the apple pie back onto his plate when she swore. Between the word and his mother's facial reaction, he figured he would never see anything as comical again in his life.

"James, David, promise me you will not put her anywhere close to harm."

"Mom, she doesn't have the training. No way will she ever be in a compromising position. No one will do that and if they do, they will have a chat with me. What about me? You don't seem to be worried if I am, though. Amy mostly just works in the shop, doing admin work and helping to pull orders."

"David, you are your father's son. I love you but must compartmentalize you and your father, or I would be dead with worry. As long as she stays in the shop."

"I might be a plumber too, Mom. I'm learning a lot in the shop and the one thing the plumbers say is if they could hire a female plumber, she would be worth double any man. Especially the guys who do institutional service work."

"Dad, any issue if I bring her on my next trip? Mom seems okay with it now," said David.

"I never said anything of the sort, David. No, I am not okay with any of this—this—shit. I just have no fight left in me. James, can I go home for a few weeks to visit my mother and clear my head?"

"No, hon, you can't, sorry."

"Not a chance, Mom. Then we would have to worry. I can bring her home with me next week. Would that work?" asked David.

"Where's my nerve tablets?" Elizabeth went into the kitchen and opened a cabinet where she kept her pills. "Why can't I travel."

"Elizabeth, we have a bit of a situation and travel is restricted right now."

"Russians," said Amy, with confidence.

"Russians," James said, nodding.

"Then why can she travel?"

"Because she is with David and Phil."

"Mom, I am heading out on a job. I should only be away a few days and it will clean up a few loose ends. When I get back, I will fly you over home. I can keep an eye on you, and we can take a few days to hit some of the tourist areas I never seem to get to when I am there to work."

"Okay, son. But no one dies when we are there. Aye?"

"Aye."

The rest of the evening was more relaxed. Finally, Elizabeth allowed work to be part of the conversation. She didn't enjoy hearing about the business side of her family and knew she was getting the 'G' rated version. Her "nerve tablets" kicked in and it hid away her anxiety for the evening.

• • • •

David, Amy, and Phil arrived in Australia at a base north of Perth. Casey, the last leak Peter could identify, was located in a small apartment close to downtown Perth.

Phil called the office to check-in before they headed to the hotel. He was on the phone longer than David liked. When he hung up, he walked to David.

"Plans have changed. Casey has a meeting with two of Saddam Hussein's men and now also a Russian Eight Chief Directorate, one of the top communication men from the old KGB."

"How well timed was this? Our luck might be changing," said David.

"Intel says he arrives shortly. The Iraqis are here already. Dad and Peter are not sure if it's a bidding war or if each group will get the same items. At this point, all that matters is no one gets anything except train tickets to hell. I'll wait here and follow the Russian. Amy, you will have eyes on Casey if that is okay, David."

"Amy, this is not why we brought you."

"David, I will be fine. Honestly."

"David, you need to take down the Iraqis at the same time. They are the priority, not the Russian. The meeting is around dinner time. So, we have a bit of work to do before then."

"Okay, I'll get a rental. Then get Amy set up outside of Casey's place and head to the hotel."

"Okay, if I don't see you before you head in, remember, there are two missions. First you need to takeout, the Iraqis, and this Russian. Confirmation is required."

"Wow, that is a lot to plan for. Good thing we have Nancy Drew with us, for this one," said David. Amy punched him in the arm. With a few last confirmations and a passing of weapons, Phil waited at the arrivals door. David and Amy picked up a rental and headed into town.

David luckily found a parking spot in front of Casey's apartment. "Are you ready for this, Amy? Do you remember what our target looks like? What about his guests?"

"Yes, David, I do. It will be fine."

"You need to listen and be alert. I have a gun for you but, this will not be easy, and you're not to use it unless your life is in danger. This is the same one Dad has been training you on, a Browning, at the farm," said her brother. He had concern in his voice and doubt in his heart. He was seeing why his mother always said she worried about him. "Actually, I will stay here with you. I will sit in the back and prepare. There is no way I could relax if I leave you here alone."

"David, I don't want to cause any trouble. Go."

"No, Amy, it's fine."

David climbed into the backseat of the car. He napped, then changed. He was ready to work.

• • •

Walking around the building, David found a service door propped open. He assumed the electrician that owned the bright red van with the even brighter yellow electrical bolt across the side of the van did it.

David walked through the basement corridor. Looking for a stairwell or elevator. A door opened behind him. Turning, David expected to see the electrician leaving. Instead, a man was running at him with a knife in his hand. The man, dressed in black with a balaclava over his face, swung his knife at David. Sidestepping the attacker, David pulled out his own knife.

Skidding to a stop, the assailant spun around and faced David. David dropped his backpack on the ground. He switched his grip on the knife to an overhand grip.

"Who are you?" David asked. He backed towards the door he had used to enter the building.

"Stop, do not take another step, David." The man said with a Russian accent. "We end this here in this walkway."

"*We* don't end anything, friend. I will end it. You will just be an unlucky participant." David stepped forward. "Take your mask off and let's do this. I am going to be late for my appointment upstairs. But I guess that is your intention."

The man pulled off his mask.

"Alek?" David said.

Alek took his mask and threw it at David. He followed it with a leap and three steps. His shoulder drove into David's chest. Falling against the wall, both men dropped their knives. Hooking David's leg with his own and with a push, Alek fell on top of David. Rolling with the momentum of falling, David lay beside Alek. With his free hand, David jammed his finger deep into Alek's eye socket.

Screaming, Alek clawed at David's face. He gripped David's hand and David pushed even harder into the eye. Blood leaked around the eyeball and Alek released his grip on David. Jumping to his feet, David dropped his knee down onto Alek's chest. The sound of bones cracking rang through the empty corridor. David searched for his knife. Reaching over Alek's head, he picked up his knife with his left hand. Alek pulled David tight to his body and tried to head-butt him. With his arms trapped in Alek's bear hug, David swung his head at Alek. His forehead connected with the bridge of Alek's nose. Blood exploded from it, causing him to release his grip. David swung his knife and plunged it into Alek's kidney. His body stiffened with the shock of the injury. David jumped to his feet and stood over Alek.

"Don't move," David said.

"David, I couldn't if I tried. Igor was right about you and your training."

"Well, I guess this makes things easier for me to get to Casey."

"Casey? Who is Casey?"

"What?" David looked down at Alek, confused. His internal clock was sending out an alarm. He had spent too much time in the basement. With the swing of his boot, he knocked Alek out. He picked Alek up onto his shoulders and cautiously carried him to the garbage bins located outside the service door.

Placing Alek in the bin, he slit his throat and buried him under the bags of garbage. He took three black garbage bags back to the hallway.

David picked up Alek's knife, a souvenir, and placed it in his backpack. He placed the garbage bags over the puddle of blood and David headed to the elevator.

CHAPTER TWENTY-FIVE

With his balaclava pulled over his face and blood drying on his knife, David entered Casey's apartment. The living room was full of computers and screens. To David, it looked like a scene out of the movie *War Games*.

Casey was lying on the couch watching Aussie Rules Football. The television volume was loud, too loud to hear David enter the suite. The job request was to leave the scene looking like a suicide. David had a bottle of pills and a note to leave behind. If he was closer to home, John would have sent in a staging crew to finish the job. This time, David was on his own. David walked to the bedroom and took a pillow from the bed. He returned to Casey.

Jumping over the couch, he landed on a surprised Casey. He forced the pillow over his face and kneed him in the gut. Pulling back his leg, David kneed him a second time.

Casey exhausted most of the air in his lungs. Struggling to get air, David kneed him in the groin, then once again in the stomach. Casey reached between the pillows on the couch.

Seeing Casey pull a gun out from under the couch cushion, David released the pillow he held and seized Casey's arm. David forced Casey's arm away from him. They rolled onto the floor;

the impact caused Casey to drop his gun. Wrapping his arms around Casey's neck, David squeezed. Casey twisted, breaking free of David's grip. Spotting the gun, David stretched and wrapped his hand around the barrel. He pulled it back and pointed it at Casey. Winded, Casey raised his hands. David stood up and motioned for Casey to sit on the couch. They were both winded. A deafening silence filled the room while they both caught their breaths.

"Whoa, Whoa, sunshine. Who the fuck are you?" Casey asked. "Are you assigned to kill me?"

"Shut the fuck up. Do not move from the couch. Who the fuck am I? Well, I'm not in Australia to sell secrets to our enemies and yes, I'm here to kill you, you fuckin' traitor."

"Sell secrets? No, NO! Never! I'm a major in the United States Army Intelligence. I have planned and reviewed this operation for months with my teams in the DIA and CIA. I'm not here to sell anything; well, I am, but not secrets. It's part of a plan to get viruses and trackers into computer mainframes in Russia and Iraq. We were hoping for Iran too, but they backed out. I'm fourth generation military. Son, I am not turning my back on my country. I'm doing my job."

"Isn't that what someone would say when their killer is standing in front of them?"

"Son, listen to me. I can show you what I'm talking about, but I have two Iraqis coming to see me in about a half an hour. You just missed a Russian by minutes."

"Who do you work with in the CIA? I can get a clearance within minutes."

"Son, Peter Thompson is my contact. I have reported to and worked with him for years."

"Peter? Peter is your boss. Fuck me, of course he is. You have to be kidding me. Who is your contact in the DIA?"

"That's classified."

"Well, declassify it, I am still holding the gun."

"Fine, Trenton Freeman. He is my DIA contact. One of the most dedicated officers I have ever met."

"Okay, sit there."

David backed over to the kitchen and picked up the phone. He called John and passed on the information he just received. John needed time to research David's intel. He hung up, intending to call back after the Iraqis left.

"Did you ever work with a Keith? Sorry, I forgot his last name." David said. Thinking of the first mole, Peter sent him to kill. "Or Tom Winters or Sergio Garcia?"

"Yes, to all three. They've all gone missing. Peter says Sergio defected and Keith and his wife are in Russia, living it up, that piece of shit commie. They killed Tom with two of the best agents I know in South America. The report showed the cartel killed them. We never recovered Tom's body. Terrible thing, it destroyed the morale of Peter's group. I have worked closely with all of them during my career. We were all Peter's. He worked a very blurred line for most of his career. Well, let's just say, we all walked that line with Peter. Peter maybe leaned a little too far to the other side. But we all tried to pull him back."

David lowered the gun. "Sit there and don't move." David ran his hand over his head.

"Sir, you and I are both fucked."

•   •   •

"Okay, we don't have much time. I believe your story. I hate to say it, but you're the last team member to die. Tom is alive, he is safe. He is in a coma right now. We are protecting him."

"What? How is that possible? Who are you? Are you—holy shit—it is, David, right?"

David nodded and smiled. "The one and only."

"You're here to kill me. What an honor."

David looked at him.

"Well, you know what I mean. So, Peter sent you to kill me? Well, that explains my last few communications with him."

"As for your bodyguard downstairs, he is in a garbage bin outside. I met him on the ship with Igor. How did you hook up with him? Was he a double agent or something?"

"I have no clue what you just said. What goon downstairs? I didn't know you were coming. If I knew our best hitman was coming to my apartment—"

"So, how did? No—no. NO! It all makes sense now. How could we..." said David. He shook his head. "I can't believe this. How could we be so blind? Of course, it was him all along. He was the one—"

"What?"

"We can talk later. We will talk later. What's on those disks you're selling?"

"Okay, this is where it gets weird, very weird, but with you here now, maybe not so strange. Wow, David in the flesh. Cool."

"Do we have time? Do you need to get ready?"

"We have a few minutes. We have been working on this operation for about a year. I have been deep undercover working with about six different countries and their spy agencies and military. In case you don't know, computers are the future. There will be a communication system called the world wide web. We designed a virus for their mainframes, a backdoor, is the terminology. I have been working with those countries to convince them I have secret documents on military equipment and government secrets. We can discuss the details later. Last week Peter gave me the disks. I ran them on a computer to make sure we got the programming right. Guess what?"

David shook his head.

"It *was* government secrets, David. It was a lot of secrets. I called Trent, my DIA contact, and told him everything. He had the right programming, viruses, and disks hand delivered to me yesterday. I believe you and two others were on the same military flight."

"I wish we had more time," said David. "Do you have any other weapons in the apartment?"

"No."

"All right, we have about fifteen minutes, so let me give you my quick rundown of well, I don't know what it is anymore. Sit down and have a drink. You will need it after this."

Casey stood up and opened a bottle of the vodka, a gift from the Russian. He poured himself and David a glass, then returned to the couch. David refused it. Casey held both in his hands.

"Ready? This is going to go quick we can get into details later. Peter told me you guys were all dirty. He gave me a list of people on his staff to take out. Your partner and friend Keith, I killed him and his wife, fed them to sharks off the coast of California. I am sorry. Tom, my team found in Columbia barely alive. Russians had taken down the rest of the team. We were lucky to find him. My partner saw his chest move. Now I can see that Peter revealed their operation to the Russians. I'm here to kill you by order of Peter Thompson, the same man who signed the contract on Keith, Tom, and many others, I think. I now think Alek, the guy I killed downstairs, was told by Peter to kill me, and I believe Peter gave him my location. There are so many other instances that were just too perfect now that I can look back. The information you just gave me and with what I believe is really on those disks, I believe Peter is the one who needs to disappear, not you. My team believes Sergio is in Iran. Oh shit, it was Peter who killed Igor! He said it was you." David rubbed his forehead with his left hand, the gun moving aimlessly still locked in his right hand. He sat on a chair and stared at the floor.

Casey drank the vodka and placed the glass on the floor. He paused and drank the second one. "You're the guy Peter uses to do our dirty work, crazy. I didn't think you were actually real. It is an honor to meet you. Really, I'm blown away."

"Okay, you make the transfer and no funny business. I'm being paid to kill you and them. Right now, I don't plan on that. Don't give me a reason to change my mind."

"Hide in the bedroom, David. Hell, pack my overnight bag while you are in there. Wherever you're going, I'm going too."

"So, you're sure there is nothing top secret on those disks?" asked David.

"Nothing, they have the virus, they have nothing on them that would benefit anyone, except us."

"Silly question, we don't have time now, but why do you keep saying virus?"

"There's too much to explain now. How about we sit on a beach one day and I break it all down for you and you return the favor with some of your stories?"

"Deal. Okay, we need to come to an agreement. I will not kill you; I will protect you and any family you have while we deal with Peter. Can we agree on that?"

"Yes."

•   •   •

The buzzer alerted them their guests had arrived. Casey buzzed them through the security entrance and two minutes later, they entered the apartment. He patted them down and removed the pistol from the taller man holding a duffle bag.

Showing them the stack of twenty-four disks he asked to see their money. They opened a duffle bag. Casey explained to them how the first disk would write the software to their computer, then they could access the rest of the floppies. He threw the duffle bag at Casey's feet. Stepping over it, Casey handed over the cases of disks. He returned the gun to its owner and the two men left.

David came out of the room and smiled. "Wow, that was easy."

"Yes, I've been dealing with them for six months, setting this up."

David called John. Not being one to struggle with conversations, he didn't know how to tell John about the situation he found himself in. The shock of realizing Peter was behind all the killings and attempted hits on The Family shook David to his core.

"John, what have you got for me?"

"Casey is clean. I am looking into Trent, from what I can find, he is very real and spotless."

"Okay, John, I need to roll, so just listen. Tell Phil when he checks in, we need four tickets. I am bringing Casey home for protection. We will need to keep it quiet. We need to talk to a Trent. I have his information. Tell Peter I had an issue in the basement and missed the hit on the Iraqis. Bye John." David hung up the phone.

Before they left for the airport, Casey needed to clean up and destroy an evidence of his assignment. They collected Casey's documents and placed them in David's backpack before running strong magnets over the computers and drives.

• • •

Walking through the departure level of the airport, David found Amy on a bench outside a bar. She jumped up and hugged her brother. David introduced Casey.

Sitting in the bar, The Russian who met Casey earlier stood up and exited, without Amy noticing. He walked past David, Casey, and Amy, then turned to look at the trio talking. He watched as they moved to a departure board hanging from the ceiling.

Amy pointed to the board. "David, the best flight we could get is to Berlin. From there we could either head to Guelph or Portadown, see where John wants to—"

David turned to see the Russian approach. Amy, shocked and confused, watched the Russian insert a knife into Casey's back. He removed it and inserted it between his ribs. Casey fell to the ground. Spinning around, David swung at the knife, knocking it from the Russian's hand.

Amy stepped back and tripped over a suitcase on the floor. A lady screamed as a man jumped on the aggressor's back. A crowd swarmed the Russian, knocking him to the ground. David dropped to his knees. He rolled Casey over. Blood was coming out of his mouth.

He looked at David. "Save my country, fix the problem," Casey said, then exhaled his last breath.

David stood as police ran towards the scene. The Russian now had three men lying on top of him.

Amy was still on the floor. "Amy, find Phil. I'll meet you at the gate." David said. "Go straight to the gate."

The police arrived and a team of paramedics arrived a few minutes later. David melted into the excited crowd. Everyone stood back to allow the police to handcuff the Russian. While the cops were busy with their assailant, David slipped through the crowd and disappeared. He headed to Gate Three.

Phil jumped up and waved at him. Holding a hat and shirt in his hands, he passed them to David, who went directly to the washroom.

When he came out, he had a new Australia hat and an Aussie rules football team jersey on. "We need to get on that plane, guys."

"When does it board?"

"Five minutes at the most. First class was just called. What happened?" asked Phil.

"We can talk later, but Casey is dead. The Russian identified him, I guess."

A few minutes later, they boarded the plane.

•   •   •

Two days later, David, Phil, and Amy sat in the office with John and James. The scene Amy witnessed at the airport still upset and bothered her. Relieved to be home and safe, they discussed the last job and the information Casey passed to David.

John contacted Trent and set up a meeting for later in the week.

CHAPTER TWENTY-SIX

Still in shock over the information David had learned from Casey, The Family planned their next move. When Peter called John for an emergency job, John acted like there was no issue. Peter had found the last of his group who sold government secrets to enemies of the state. Knowing that Peter was the issue all along, and that he had attempted many times to have David and others in The Family killed, John believed the last minute request was to get David to a job where he would likely be captured or killed. John received the job package. A murder suicide job on Trent and another DIA agent named Joe Hart. They would be in Branson, Missouri. There was to be no trace of them or the people they were meeting. John denied the job. He explained to Peter the timeline was unreasonable and they could not get a clean-up crew, David, and a surveillance team to Missouri and ready to act within thirty-six hours.

Furious that John would turn down a job, Peter controlled his emotions. "John, if you don't do this job, I will have every agency I know request government investigations and create charges against your entire team worldwide."

"Peter, I dare you to start an investigation like that," John said. Before Peter could reply, John hung up the phone.

A half hour later, Peter called back to apologize. John accepted the apology, then told him to give him a realistic timeline. Peter explained how stressed he was with the internal investigations, staff who worked on the other side of the line, and the issues around the world with terrorism and increased "non-government approved" drugs that were now coming into the country.

With a second plan to catch the last two men, Peter requested David and Phil fly to Washington in four days. Agreeing to the plan and the price, John offered to have David arrive a couple of days early and meet with Peter. He thought they could head out for a couple of bike rides to help relieve the pressure. Peter thought a ride would be a good idea.

Once he hung up on Peter, John called Trent.

"Hello Trent," said John.

"John, hello. What's going on?" asked Trent.

"Peter has put a hit on you and a Joe. Needs it done immediately. I assume you are either leaving for or are in Branson, Missouri?"

"Yes, we arrived about six hours ago. But how do—"

"Trent, I don't have time to get into that right now. You are a target. Peter is our rat. He was the one. I can't believe I am saying this. Peter was the one who tried to put us out of business. He was working with the Russians and cartels and he had his own men killed by us. He passed on information that had David kidnapped. I am not sure why, but he has turned on us and his government. Trent this needs to end and end now. Lucky for you and me, I have the team to do that. I just need the go ahead from you."

"Thanks for the call and the information. You do what you need. We need to meet. Listen, I will stay here. You take care of Peter in Washington. I will make some calls about this."

"Consider it done."

"I will call you tomorrow morning at ten, your time. I'll pass on what I find. You tell me your plan to end this."

"Till tomorrow, Trent."

"Goodbye."

•   •   •

In Washington, David and Phil checked into their hotel. Excited, like a kid on his birthday, David looked forward to being out on a ride somewhere that wasn't around Southern Ontario. Phil brought his bike, but his dad had him scheduled for a meeting.

They met in a Kmart parking lot outside of Washington D.C. where they compared bikes, David had a top of the line Trek, and Peter had an older Bianchi.

"I think you are getting paid too much for these jobs," Peter said. "I wish I had something so nice."

Heading south from Brandywine, they found nice back roads to explore. They passed farms and small one street towns. A couple other cyclist rode with them for several miles. The traffic was light and when they weren't sprinting to a stop sign to see who's buying lunch; they discussed the jobs coming up, the wars that were building and the weapons his teams inside foreign borders would need. Peter told David about the time he met President Reagan and his mandate to topple the Soviet Union. He told David how he was on the initial team that worked to bankrupt the Soviet Union and then manipulate the markets and the economy to destroy the country from within. That was back when Igor was an agent for both countries.

They had just ridden forty miles. David wanted to pound out the last fifteen miles, then sprint to see who was buying supper. Peter laughed and agreed with no confidence he would beat David twenty years his junior. Sprinting up a small hill, he slowed, waiting for Peter on the downward side. A car drove by them, giving them no room, and pushed David onto the loose gravel. David pulled his bike onto the pavement, raised his hand, and flipped the driver his middle finger. The car slowed, and David stood out of his saddle and sprinted to the car. The driver waved and accelerated away.

Peter caught up to David. Winded, he asked, "What would you have done if he had waited and got out of his car?"

"I don't know, Peter; you know I can get pretty mouthy when I need to."

A car full of girls drove up to them, slowed their car, honked, and yelled, "Nice legs and asses." Then drove away.

"Ask me what I would do if they stopped Peter," David said.

"I don't need to. I know I would be finishing this ride alone," he said.

A white van slowly drove up behind them. David waved them past, but the van waited. Peter turned and waved at them to pass. The van stayed behind them.

"What the hell is going on?" said David.

A car sped around the van and the cyclist. The van sped up and pulled beside the cyclists. David looked over his shoulder and noticed the driver wearing a balaclava. He swerved at the cyclist, pushing David and his bike onto the shoulder. The side door of the van slid open and a man in a balaclava pointed an AS VAL rifle at David and Peter. He shot three rounds over their heads. Peter swerved onto the soft shoulder. His front tire caught the loose gravel and Peter toppled over his handlebars, his bike landing on top of him. David held strong but had to stop when the van cut him off and stopped. He jumped off his bike, turned it, and ran to the back of the van. The driver met him there with a pistol pointed at his chest.

"What the fuck?" David reached for a small knife in his jersey.

"Keep your hands where I can see them. Put the bike in the ditch, and get in the van, now," the driver said with a Russian accent. David stepped into the van; the driver followed him.

Peter stood up to the muzzle of a gun in his back. His legs and elbows bled. He had small pebbles stuck in the cuts. He followed David into the van.

"Lie down, you two," the passenger said. David lay on his back. Peter on his stomach.

"What do you want?" asked David.

"No questions," the driver responded.

The passenger pulled out two syringes and injected David and Peter in the thigh. After a couple of minutes, Peter passed out.

"Is he out?" asked Phil.

David shook Peter. "Yes, out cold." Frank and Phil pulled off their balaclavas.

"First, can we go back and get the bikes, please? Second, Phil, could you have jabbed me any harder? And how did you know what syringe was the right one? They both looked the same to me."

"Yeah, just lucky I guess, right Frank?" said Phil.

"You guys were making good time. We thought we had missed you," said Frank.

"I know, for an old guy, he could keep a good pace. I was worried that you guys would be too late. We're what, five miles from the city line?"

Frank spun the van around and picked up both bikes.

"You should win an Oscar for your performance; Peter had no clue you were in on it. And I knew what syringe yours was. Trust me," Phil said.

"Frank beautiful Russian accent. You had me convinced."

"David, I thought you were dumping your bike when you hit the shoulder. I know how much you love that bike. If you had damaged it, I would have driven away."

"Frank, it's okay. I didn't know what you were doing. I don't think you did either. All right, how long before the serum wears off?"

"Three hours. I gave him a light dose. We can always use the heavier stuff for the flight to Portadown."

The three men drove with their new prisoner to a small private airfield south of Washington, D.C.

•   •   •

Peter woke up in an office inside a hangar, tied to a chair. David sat in the room with Peter. He was waiting for Phil to return to the airfield after dropping Frank off at Dulles Airport.

"David, you escaped. Free me too. What happened? Where are we?"

"You woke up Peter."

"I hear planes. Are we at an airport? David, free me. We can escape. More damn Russians?"

"Sorry Peter, I have nothing to escape from. I'm just waiting for Phil. We should be wheels up within the hour."

"David, what do you mean? What is going on?"

"Peter, stop the fucking act. We all know who you are and what you did. You piece of shit. I only wish they would let me finish you off."

"Who are they? David, I don't know what you're talking about. David, we have done so much together. We almost had all the foxes out of the henhouse."

"Peter, just stop. I killed innocent men and an innocent wife because of you and your lies. We all know you are the rat, you fuckin' piece of shit. You tried to have me killed by Russians, set up my family to fail and possibly die. I think you gave up our location the night my Granda died. If you did..." David hesitated. He stood up and walked behind Peter. He bent over and whispered into Peter's ear, "If you did, I would take years to kill you, and your sister, her family, your parents and every fucking cousin you have."

Sitting back in his chair, his face was red with anger. He shook with adrenaline, but he had to wait to kill this traitor. "You sent me to silence your co-workers and men that dug too deep into your connections. Well, guess what, you're heading to Northern Ireland, where an assembly of high-profile leaders are waiting to talk to you. If you're lucky, it will be life in prison. If I have my way, it would be death by me. I guess we will have to see."

"If I go down, so does the U.S. government and your entire family."

"See, comments like that are what will put you underground real quick. They are going through your office as we speak, looking for the insignificant details you missed. Everyone knows you're not dumb. But no one is perfect, Peter."

Phil entered the office. "Oh, you're awake. I guess it's time for a top up."

"Yes, shut him up please," said David.

Phil injected a chemical into Peter's thigh. He was unconscious five minutes later.

•　　•　　•

Peter woke in a dark room. The rag in his mouth prevented any noise from exiting his mouth, no matter how hard he tried. Chained to a wooden chair, he tried to tip it over but realized they bolted it to the floor.

The door opened, a figure, silhouetted by the light outside of the room, stepped into the dark room. Peter could see a machine shop beyond the figure in the doorway. The lights turned on, bright and white.

"You're awake," said Chris. Peter recognized him. He was the director of the CIA and his boss.

David stepped into the room and took the rag out of Peter's mouth. Then slapped him on the cheek.

"Chris, help me. What's going on? This is a big mistake. I am not a bad guy. I have given my life to the agency. Chris, how could you doubt my loyalty?"

"Peter, I don't doubt it because I don't believe it exists. At least to us. So, do you want to talk now or wait?"

"I want my fucking lawyer is what I want. You can't cage me up in this room like one of David's victims. I'll not be talking until I have a lawyer. If anything happens to me, there are—"

"We know, and those files no longer exist. Your friend at the Washington Post, well, one visit from James and he handed everything over. He agreed never to speak of your files or his meeting with James. Your sister? Well, she needed a little more work. David did an outstanding job there. We cleaned out your office. We emptied your house and burned it to the ground. John has a team right now; they are completing your fake escape to Russia. The six o'clock news will tell the story of a fallen hero who defected to Russia. No one is coming to look for you. No one. Not even your friends in Russia, Columbia, or Iraq. Sorry. There certainly isn't a lawyer coming. Maybe a priest, if you're lucky."

Peter dropped his head.

"Why did you do it, Peter? We gave you free rein. You ran so many successful operations. You had life by the balls. Peter, you were in line for my job when I retired. What happened to you?"

"I don't know, sir. We tried something years ago, and it worked. I guess you just see and do things differently when you have a foot in both worlds. You were the one who gave me the free rein to work outside the law. You knew about my operations, my underground connections. They should tie you to this chair beside me," said Peter.

Chris turned the lights off and left. Peter sat in darkness and cried. The door opened again.

"Mr. Vice President?"

"Peter, if you can give me anything, anything to help your case, I can shut this all down. You will do time, but you will live. Peter anything. Tell me, have you hidden any other files I can use to defend you? Is there anyone I can talk to?"

"I am sorry, Mr. Vice President. I have nothing to say. We all had a job to do. My role in this play has ended. I will bow out and meet my maker. I'm ready to die. I'm sorry, but I'll not talk about any other files or give anyone names. Do your worst or best. My lips are sealed."

"Are you saying there are more files or people to talk to? It doesn't have to end like this. Give me anything. Where are the files or names? We all have crossed the fine line to get to where we are. Look, there will be some public shaming, but you can walk free after a few years in jail, draft a book, and live comfortably. Just give me something."

"I would like to speak to David or John."

"Suit yourself Peter. We *will* find those files and people. I just hope they take the money and shut their mouths, unlike your sister."

The Vice President left the room. In the darkness, Peter fell asleep, the medication still floating through his body. David woke him.

"David, you have come like the angel of death."

"Peter, I am sorry. I'll make it quick; you won't suffer."

"No David, we need to talk first. Only you and me. I don't want anyone to hear this." David closed the door and locked it. He turned off the microphone, one of four, in the room.

"It is just us, Peter. I'm tired. What is it you want to say?"

"David, listen. I had my reasons for my behavior. We're all pawns in a bigger game of chess. Find Sergio. He will confirm a lot of this. David, our greatest enemy, is peace. The entire military complex believes that. It's all about profits. With war comes fear, with fear comes obedience. Retaliation, David, the days are coming when what we have done for years will come home. We need people like you, like me. We keep it in balance. Missiles and bombs don't win wars, what we do does. It's the people on the ground, doing individual kills, meeting the resistors, and selling weapons to fight from within. We run the actual wars. David, we do. I just got greedy. David, don't get greedy, you or your family. Stay small; don't get greedy."

"What?"

"I know what the actual leaders of the country are planning. Kennedy's assassination was nothing to what the future will bring. They are going to allow attacks on U.S. soil. They want to invade new countries. David, you know this. You know who runs the world. We are their muscle. Listen to me, you will see countries fall. Who do you think was behind the Soviet Union's collapse? Your granda and Igor started the collapse with the help of many others once Reagan became President, including myself. David, I'm ready to die because I don't want to see the evil rule our country."

"Peter, you are talking crazy shit, man. There is nothing like this, don't try to scare me. What did you mean about Kennedy? Granda was there that day, he told me. They dressed him as a hobo, and he stood by a bridge. He was the last line of shooters if the car got to him."

"Exactly, David. The people who planned his and his brothers' deaths are now running our government. You have seen enough to know that. Think about it. Talk to Sergio, if you can find him. Talk to John. There is so much they have hidden from you, stuff you should be told. David, kill me, but remember these two things. Within the next five years, they will blow up a building in middle America. Remember this, David, our, your greatest enemy is peace."

David stood behind Peter at the workbench. He filled a syringe with Digoxin.

"Peter, I hope you are wrong about all this. I hope it is just the meds making you loopy. We truly do not know who our customers are or their intentions. We just do their bidding, collect the money, and find inner peace. I know we are pawns and when they are done with me, they will deal me the same fate you are today. I just hope it doesn't happen for a long time."

"David, one last thing. Igor was not your sworn enemy. I killed him at an airfield. We worked together to the day I had to put him down."

"Yes, Peter. That's why you are here. We figured it out. Tom, remember him and his team? We hid him away. He survived and had plenty to say before he fell into a coma. Casey? The same thing only we screwed up at the airport. I assume you sent Alek to wait for me when I was sent to kill Casey. We had you figured out. Igor was going to die that day either with you or me, so—"

"He, like myself, was just trying to survive within the new world order. He was going to release information about all of us. One of us had to kill him. And yes, I was the one who sent him after you. I told him where you were staying the day he took you. It might come to a point where you will see death as the best option."

David left Peter in the room and walked into Scott's office. He was emotionally drained and fell onto the couch. "Where did all the big wigs go?"

"They said their piece, confirmed Peter was dirty, and handed him over to us. When you're ready, you can kill him."

"Okay,"

"Are you okay, son? Did he say something that bothered you? You looked defeated. He tried to have you killed many times. I would think you would be pumped to be the one to take him down," said Scott.

"I know, but some days I wonder if Mom was right about just having a normal life."

Scott stood up and walked over to David. "Remember what I told you the night we pulled you out of your bed? When you were a wee lad?"

"Aye, Uncle Scott, I do. Family is all we have; family is all that matters. Remember, family first. I know we take care of ourselves because no one else will."

David went back to Peter. Peter looked at him. "I have made peace, David. You need to, as well. About everything. Go ahead, do what you do best, kill and cause chaos."

He looked for a vein on Peter's left arm and plunged the needle into it. Nine minutes later, after three violent full body muscle spasms, Peter passed away. They would not return his body to the United States. Wrapped and weighted with bricks, they dropped his body into the Irish Sea.

CHAPTER TWENTY-SEVEN

With Peter out of the picture, Trent, Casey's other contact, researched and reached out to other countries to learn more about David, John, and The Family. He wanted to know about their strengths and weaknesses. He met with MI6, CSIS, and multiple militaries and agencies to see what they were all about. Trent did not realize how far The Family's reach was or how big those tentacles were. All the organizations wanted to continue and grow their relationships with The Family.

Satisfied with the investigation into The Family, Trent called John to schedule a meeting. A week later, they met in John's office. Everyone was out of the country working. John was the only one available to meet.

Peter was their first topic. With him out of the way, John gave Trent a small history lesson on The Family and some of their future plans. Even though The Family was very good at what they did, Trent pointed out they were falling behind on technology and knowledge of new organizations growing out of the fall of communism.

"With the world getting smaller, you and your team need to catch up with technology."

"Now you sound like David and Phil."

"Don't worry, John, I will help your team with that. I have done my research on The Family. I reached out to many countries and agencies. They all say we need you and want to keep your team around. You know how many of the militaries and alphabet agencies share information. We have been working on a few multilateral agreements. With more eyes on how money, people and militaries are managed, I agreed to be your point of contact for work for the U.S.A., Britain, Canada, and other countries."

"Okay, but here we go again. One point of contact. I am not saying it would happen, but that was how Peter was getting away with so much stuff. We need some form of a checking system."

"I fully agree and have already set up a check-in system to improve many aspects of how The Family will receive jobs. I will be the contact who makes the request, sends the reports, and confirms the job when they are complete. This isn't public news yet, but I have left the DIA and opened a shell company to separate all ownership and 'paper trail' of jobs from any government who requests The Family or any other organization's services. Within fifteen minutes of a job being offered, the requester will send a coded message to your office from the country or agency who requested the work. You will have a series of codes to correspond with each country and agency. All the agencies agreed to this additional step called the Cephas Clause."

They wrapped up other business items, then headed out for a meal.

Now self-employed, Trent's company's name would be Saltstone National. A week later, John received his first job.

· · ·

David received the page *'We have credit cards needing cut'* and they delivered a package to John. They all sat in John's office and reviewed the details of the job. Phil would assist and support David, as usual. This was the first job contracted through Saltstone National. Everyone wanted it to go well. They had a target; he was in London. He was a leader in a growing group from the Middle East, looking for support and funding to have Israel give back the land, he believed, they had stolen from his people. The IRA, certain religious leaders, and two government officials planned to meet him throughout his week stay in London.

David agreed to the work. Phil worked on the travel arrangements and a day later, the boys were on a plane to London. The hit was to happen in an apartment owned by a couple of prominent Muslim financial wizards and where the target was staying.

• • •

Phil had followed the target for two days. He was alone, with no security detail, no partners and wandered the streets of London doing tourist things, then would head back to the apartment at six every evening. Both nights, there was a delivery of food and female company.

Trent confirmed two IRA leaders had arrived in London. Taking out a couple of IRA leaders would be a bonus for David if he could time his hit right.

With trades going in and out of the service entrance, in the lower parking level all day, David could slip past security at the main door.

Phil tailed the two IRA members to the apartment building; they entered the front door where the doorman checked his visitation sheet. On the list, he directed them to the elevators.

Having completed his part of the assignment, Phil headed to their car to wait for David.

David, on the third floor, watched through a window as his targets enter the building. He walked to the elevator and hit the call buttons. When the doors opened, he stepped inside.

Charles, the IRA member scheduled to meet David's target, turned to look directly at David as the doors closed.

"Mate, you are—"

"Both of you put your hands where I can see them. When we get to the fifteenth floor, we're all going to exit the elevator and head to the apartment."

David had a gun in Charles' back while the other official, Henry, stood with his hands laced on his head. The doors opened, and the men stepped out. The hallway had paintings on the walls, brass hardware on the doors, and the thick carpet had a floral design throughout it.

They walked to the left and stopped at the third door. "Knock on the door. And one wrong move..." David said. Charles knocked as David stepped to the side to avoid being seen through the peephole. The door opened. In one fluid motion, David pushed Charles into Talib, his original target. Grabbing Henry by the shoulder, David dragged him across the threshold and into the entranceway. The apartment was bright, with windows from the floor to the ceiling. The sun shone on antique furniture, large plush area rugs and paintings, some stolen from the NAZIs after World War Two.

"Everyone take a seat," David said. He pushed Henry further into the apartment. Tripping, Henry fell and knocked over a vase.

"What is happening?" said Talib.

"Talib, this is David. He is here to kill us all. He has killed many of us and will probably kill many more before he is stopped," said Charles.

Charles sat down on the couch while Talib sat in a chair. It faced the couch. Henry lay on the floor, his hand bleeding from a chunk of the vase.

David kicked him, "Get up and go sit over there, you clumsy clown."

Henry slowly stood. Glancing at David, he walked to the dining table, a magnificent piece of furniture from Germany made in the 1800s.

"David, you don't need to do this. I have a surprise for you. The real reason for the meeting was to get you here. I have a friend who wants to see you really bad. He says you, or your family, are the only ones who can help him."

"I don't do small talk, Talib. So let me do the talking and I can be home for tea. Can the three of you please get on the floor?"

"David, you can take me alive. Let these two go. They were the bait. David, listen to me. Your job was to kill me. Not these two. Let them go and I'll trade you for something even better."

"David, you heard him, mate. Let us go. Sounds like you have a good night ahead of you if you do."

"Shut the fuck up, Charles."

"David, if I show you the gift and you like it, will you let these men go?"

"No guarantees Talib. Show me the gift."

"I need to get it. I have to open a door. That door down the hallway."

David backed up against the door. "Slowly. No sudden moves."

Talib walked down the hallway. David kept his gun on him while he glanced at the two IRA men.

Talib stopped at a door. "David, I am going to open this door slowly."

David nodded in acknowledgment as the door opened. Talib said something in a language David wasn't familiar with. Stepping back, Talib walked towards David and sat down in his chair.

"Come, come now," said Talib.

David pointed his gun down the hallway. He didn't know what to expect. An older man entered the hallway. He was bent over, with a cane in his left hand. Straightening up, he smiled at David.

David's mouth dropped open, shocked because of who was standing in front of him.

• • •

"I don't believe we have had the pleasure, David." said Sergio.

David looked around the room. Talib smiled. Charles and Henry stretched to see the man in the hallway.

"Sergio? What? How are you here? Why are you here? I could, should, will, kill you right here and now. I will take all four of you down."

"David, you said you would let us go if you liked the gift. You seem impressed," said Charles.

"What? Sure, just go. Go now." David waved his gun at them. He knew Phil would be very confused when he saw them walk out. He didn't care. Sergio stood in front of him, the most wanted man in the world, and Peter's old co-worker.

"Can I make us some tea, David? I think we all have a lot to discuss before we leave here."

Charles and Henry slipped past David, thanking him as they closed the door to the hall. David didn't even see them leave.

Still confused, he walked to Sergio. He was astonished how old Sergio looked. He was the same age as John but looked to be twenty years his senior. "Sergio? Is it you? There is a price on your head, and you stand before me. And in an apartment where I am supposed to be doing a job. I am so confused."

"David, I, we need your help. We want John, not you, to make us disappear. I'm tired of hiding and running. John can do it right. Talib, he wants out too. The world is going to change because of the madmen now running it, both sides of it, David. We want to grow older by hiding away from what is coming. We will tell you everything. Talib has information on Osama bin

Laden and his plans. Wait till you hear his story. David, I have information on your grandfather's death. I have all kinds of secrets about the governments you work for. All we want from you is safe passage to Guelph, then a new life created by John."

Talib brought a pot of tea to the dining table.

"Are you two going to sit and get comfortable?" Talib asked.

"Phil, Phil is waiting for me. I need to tell him I'm okay. He'll be worried the job didn't go right."

"He would be right in that assumption," said Sergio.

"David, I'll call down to the front desk. Where can the doorman find Phil?"

David walked to the window. "See the blue Ford Fiesta? That's him."

"Okay, I'll call while you two pour the tea. I'll get another cup," said Talib.

"David, can you close your mouth? You are catching flies," said Sergio. The look of shock was still pasted on David's face.

David put his gun in his hidden chest holster and sat at the table. There was a knock at the door. David got up and opened the door. With his gun in hand, Phil stepped into the apartment.

"Are you okay?" Phil asked. He looked behind David. "Sergio? What the hell?"

"I know, my thoughts exactly," said David.

In shocked silence, the boys sat at the table with their two targets.

"Okay, I have so many questions. I don't even know where to start. Where have you been hiding?" David asked.

"David, now is not the time. We will have lots of time to sit and talk. Briefly, I have been straddling the border between Iraq and Iran. I think trying to find me might have been part of the reason Mr. Bush started the war. Honestly, we wouldn't be sitting here if Igor and Peter were still alive. They would have destroyed your family to locate me. There are many who still want me dead. I just hope John isn't one of them. We go way back." Sergio took a sip of his tea. "Peter used me to gain the upper hand in the agency. Then he set me up on a job in Cuba. When Peter took over and became your sole contact, your granda never felt comfortable about it. After an attempt on my life in Berlin, I faked my death and went into hiding. But I panicked and missed a couple of key points. Those in the know picked up on my mistakes and never believed I was dead. So, I hid in Asia and then Columbia. They outed me in Columbia, and everyone came for a visit. We escaped by mere seconds and my friend here hid me."

"I need to call home and check-in. John will be waiting," said David.

"Of course," said Talib.

"This will be a strange conversation," said Phil.

• • •

John answered the phone on the second ring.

"Hello, John."

"David, are you okay? Is Phil with you? You are well past your check-in time."

"Yes, John, I know. Listen, we have a big problem. What would you say if I told you I could put my hands directly on Sergio?"

"Where is he, David? Do you know?"

"John, I'm not speaking figuratively. I can, right here, right now, hold on. John, I now have my hand on Sergio's shoulder and now Talib's."

"David, what the fuck are you talking about? How is this possible?"

David laughed. "John, if I knew how this was possible, I would be the best magician on TV. They both want protection. Can we do it?"

"What?"

"Yeah, Phil and I are sitting here with possibly the two, maybe the four most wanted men on the planet. Let that sink in. They offered to help us out, tell us anything we ask. In exchange, they want you to hide them. They say you're the best and only one they trust. Will you do it?"

"What?"

"I know, it's messed up. But this entire year has been."

"Let me talk to your dad. What do you and Phil think?"

"We both vote yes."

Phil nodded in agreement.

"Call me back in two hours."

They hung up. David sat back down at the table. "Okay, so here is my problem. I am here to kill you, Talib. The request was to return with a finger and photo for proof of the kill. I can have someone here in an hour to do makeup, no big deal, but I need a finger."

"First job with a new group, John wants to impress them," said Sergio.

"I understand," said Talib.

"I am glad you got to Peter before more innocent people died."

"How did—never mind right now. Yes, you're right," said David.

"David, a finger for my and Sergio's future. Being properly protected by The Family. A finger is a small price to pay. I have plenty," he said, waving his fingers.

●　　●　　●

When David called John and James back, John had a plan. The first step was to get the two men to Portadown. There, photos could be doctored and a physician could safely remove Talib's finger. Neither man had any family to worry about, so that made the transfer less of a challenge.

The next morning Phil went shopping and bought clothes, hats, and sunglasses to use during the transportation of the two men. John booked a private jet to be on the tarmac in Gatwick that evening. Scott would pick them up at the Belfast City Airport. The Family had not done a large extraction operation like this since a popular British television host wanted to be taken away from the limelight and Kenton helped fake his death.

• • •

When they arrived at the shop in Portadown, the family doctor was in the office ready to perform the removal of a perfectly good finger. He didn't agree with what they asked of him. But he never asked too many questions.

The first step was to remove the finger. It would need to be done with David's knife. A medical scalpel would be too neat. The doctor showed David where to cut to make it easy to repair. David made the cut precise and fast. Once the finger was off, the doctor gave Talib three painkillers, and the repair work began. Thirty minutes later, he relaxed in Scott's office. He wouldn't point at anything with his left index finger again.

Martha, an old friend of The Family who worked on some BBC shows in the 1970s and 1980s, came to the shop to do the makeup. With the painkillers helping, Talib kept a relaxed look on his face. David snapped a couple of Polaroids on a bare concrete floor. They wouldn't be expecting an Andy Warhol print from him.

The doctor left a bottle of pain killers and said he would return if it became red or full of pus.

• • •

Looking for confirmation of the hit, Trent had called the office, concerned about the delay in information on the hit. John had promised to get him an update after he spoke with David. With The Family's attention to detail, Trent expected updates.

David faxed the photos of Talib to John's office. Not the best quality, but all they could do until David could get the originals couriered to Trent's office.

After a phone call between the two shops, the team decided it would be best to keep their guests in Portadown for a week. David needed to be on the next flight with the evidence of the kill. Trent would meet them at the shop, in Guelph, to confirm the fingerprint.

David sat with Phil on the British Airways 747. His carry-on luggage had a finger and photos of a dead man.

He looked at Phil, "I'm a little worried Phil."

"Why? What's going on?"

"Brother, I think we're going to see things we never imagined. From the quick conversation I had with Peter and now Talib and Sergio, I think the Gulf War has opened the gates of hell. The world will never be the same. We need to be better; we need to look out for each other and The Family. I don't know what other information Sergio and Talib have, but I think it's going to rock all our worlds. We're going to learn there's more going on in the world than we're aware of, I think. I love them all and I don't want to lose anyone like we did Granda, but our dads and Scott are still thinking in the seventies and eighties. The world has changed. We need to lead the change for ourselves. I know we had that talk, but they're already slipping back into the old ways of doing things."

"I agree. It will be up to us to lead The Family deep into the decade and then the new century."

"Phil, you are the book guy. I think you need to become the computer guy too. John had some of those specialists, but we need to be up on technology, too."

"I was thinking the same thing. What about Amy? Could we convince her to take a programming course at university?"

"We need to try. That could be her future within the team."

A black limo picked them up at the airport and they headed to the shop to meet James, John, and Trent.

When they all arrived, they sat around the conference table. Trent had questions about the job. David walked him through the job as if he had done it. Beginning with the pictures of Talib dead on the ground, David spoke about how the kill went and slid the tip of a finger cross the table. The bag of ice was now just a half full bag of crimson colored water and a wrinkled finger. Trent took the finger out of the bag and studied it. Then he compared it to a photo he produced from his briefcase. He passed the photo and finger around the table. John took his time and studied it. He showed Trent the minute scar an eighth of an inch from the cut and confirmed it on the photo. Trent agreed with John's comparison. He stood up and used the phone.

With the job now complete and paid, Trent asked for extra time to discuss their future together. Everyone agreed that the top concern was the new Russian Mob, the Rodstvo, moving into North America. He told the crew how the new Russian Mob had no rules, no desire to work with others and were savages when it came to killing enemies. These groups already had deep roots in Los Angeles and Miami and New York.

With no respect to the old boundaries, John's concern was that The Family would find themselves in a territorial war. Trent agreed. He unofficially told John to reach out to some bike gangs and Italian Mobs to build alliances if it wasn't already too late.

Trent handed out secure cellular phones to the team with an extra six for anyone the Family thought would benefit from them. They were not trackable and worked anywhere in the world. Starting this new relationship, Trent wanted them to have modern technology and security. He wanted them out of the arms race at least the large military items they could still sell, but they needed to stay small, as they did in the eighties. Guns and ammunition, only. No more tanks, vehicles, or planes. They never moved drugs, and he wanted it to stay that way. What he needed from The Family was David's skills, John's business sense and the contacts and alliances John, James and Scott had built around the world. There would be people to protect, groups to support, and governments to remove. The Family needed to be his eyes and ears, his first line of defense and always his invisible partners. He understood they had other customers, but he wanted to be number one and he wanted them to downsize their client list. The remaining years in the century were going to be chaotic. He needed to know they would lead the charge when called upon.

With his thoughts out on the table, he asked if he could have an answer within twenty-four hours. John had questions for him. David did too. With conviction, he answered their questions. Once satisfied, Trent left. He would await their answer and if they agreed, he would have a constant supply of work for The Family, more than Peter ever offered.

With Trent on the way to the airport, The Family sat and debated the pros and cons of his offer. Agreeing on getting out of the large weapon and military business was a simple yes from everyone. The money was good, but the work was not always worth it.

"Hello Trent. We all talked last night. We are looking forward to a long, productive relationship with you."

"Good John. I am glad to hear that."

"We only have a couple of issues we can discuss now. If you have time?"

"Sure, go ahead."

"We will decide who we work with. Not you, or the U.S. government. We will not work with anyone that would be out to harm your country or any of their allies. But we will continue to work with our clients. If we ever hear of any operation against the U.S. of course you will be told."

"Makes sense and I'll do the same for you. I thought I would try to slip that in, but you have a great reputation with many organizations around the world."

"The only other thing is we need immunity to any government work happening to our clients."

"John, of course. It's a fine line to walk. I will support you. But you need to stick with what you do and what I know you do. Do not expand to drugs or large weapon trades that belong to us. Prostitution and carjacking are out too. Do what you do and be happy with it. I know we, and Britain, are thrilled with your special services."

"Trent, we need to meet and celebrate our new arrangement."

"We will. Thank you, John."

•   •   •

A week later, Sergio and Talib arrived in Guelph with Phil as their escort. Talib's finger, or base where his finger had been, continued to heal. John's doctor examined the stump and commented on the lack of swelling and how well the stitches were healing. Garth prepared two rooms for Sergio and Talib at his motel on Woodlawn, and he left the rooms beside them vacant to give them their privacy. Bringing the lunch daily, David would sit quietly listening to Sergio tell stories of his dad and grandfather or of terrorist attacks that happened around the world.

After six weeks, they renamed Sergio and Talib, Derik and Jason. Their final destination was being secured, and their new life in a small town south of Atlanta was about to begin.

CHAPTER TWENTY-EIGHT

The CIA, after six months, filled Peter's vacant job with a manager from the Berlin Embassy. Named Gerald Jenkins, he had spent most of his CIA career in Europe and Asia. He was an office jockey and hadn't been scarred by years of service in the field; he believed the CIA was doing the right thing around the world, at least on paper. His co-workers and friends called him Cowboy, not because he was wild and crazy but to mock his precise, by the book, cup always full attitude. He had risen through the company ranks by working hard, never questioning his superiors, kissing all the right asses, and not causing waves on any teams he was in or ran.

When the CIA announced Gerald or Cowboy as Peter's replacement, he was excited. His co-workers and those he used and stepped on while he climbed the corporate ladder were not so thrilled.

Wanting to bring pride and respect back into his department, he vowed to his staff he would never ask them to step over any blurred lines Peter had created. In the last few years, too many of Peter's co-workers and staff had disappeared or mysteriously died. He didn't want that for any of his people. Cowboy wanted them all to go home every night.

In his new office, he sat at his desk and looked out the large window to where his staff sat in cubicles. A cleaning crew had removed all of Peter's personal items. Cowboy's priest had come to his office, blessed it, and prayed for his protection and longevity in the position. The priest did his best positive prayer while he splashed expensive water on the furniture and carpet.

The first day in his new office, he had meetings to help catch up on a few assignments and operations his transition team had found. His goal was to work through the old case files and have them either archived or shredded. He called home and told his mother he would stay late to get extra work done.

Cowboy was the first into the office and the last to leave daily. He worked through the five filing cabinets in Peter's office. No, his new office, he would remind himself.

The third cabinet he worked through had files and documents from the late seventies and through the eighties. Reviewing each file, he knew a lot of rumors followed Peter to his grave. Cowboy had always worked well with Peter, even when he didn't agree with how Peter was gathering or destroying information. He thought Peter took too many trips and didn't spend enough time in the office, but he had only begun to walk in those shoes. They fit but were worn and tired.

Working through the file cabinets, he tried to open the bottom drawer to the third cabinet and noticed it did not open all the way. It wasn't by much, but an attentive person would notice that it was an inch and a half shorter than the other drawers. Cowboy pulled on the drawer; it didn't give. He took the files out and looked into the drawer. It looked normal. Going to the next cabinet, he pulled out the bottom drawer and the one above it. They came out to the same distance. Cowboy stood up and scratched his head. He checked his watch; it was almost midnight. He replaced the files from the bottom drawer and headed home.

Driving home, he thought about the cabinet. He stopped to get a burger and a pop. In the parking lot of the fast-food joint, he thought more about the drawer.

The lights were all out in the house when he pulled into the driveway. His mom forgot to leave the porch or kitchen light on for him again. Standing on the porch, he thought about the drawer, thought about the rumors of Peter being dirty. Not just crossing the line but being consumed by the other side of the line. He thought, *Maybe there could be something that held the drawer back, maybe some of Peter's truths held the drawer from opening all the way.*

Turning and walking down the baby blue worn porch steps, he went around to the rear of the house. The cloud cover and waning moon made it impossible to find the lockset for his key to open the shed. He took out his penlight and held it in his mouth. Pushing his key into the bottom of the padlock, he opened the lock, and the shed door and dropped his penlight on the grass. His hand reached into the darkness, searching for the cord to the light. He pulled on the cord. Nothing happened except the click of the switch.

"Dang-it! I forgot to change the bulb." He picked up his penlight and shone it on the shelves in front of him. Locating his dad's toolbox, he grabbed the rusty handle. Paint flaked off the sides of the toolbox when he slid it off the shelf. The last time someone had opened it was when his dad helped him fix the chain on his bicycle. He was twelve. That summer, they killed his father. He worked for the FBI; he was on assignment when the accident happened.

With the toolbox in his hand, his memories flashed back to the day they killed his dad. He hadn't opened that box of memories, hidden deep away in his soul, for some time.

•   •   •

Cowboy's dad, an office jockey for the FBI in New York, had chased a father and son assassination team associated with an old Canadian spy. He had never seen them; only known to him on paper and through an Italian Mob connection. He knew they worked for governments, organizations, and the underworld. His notes showed they were either British or Canadian or a bit of both. A hot tip came across Cowboy's dad's desk. The team he wanted was in Colorado. With a co-worker, they flew to Colorado and met with two other agents from the Denver branch. The four men rotated on the stakeout. They identified a CIA agent and the two men he met in a cottage up a remote road above Boulder. His dad's and his partner's shift ended. Handing the surveillance over to the Boulder crew, they headed back to the hotel. The steep roads were hard on any car's brakes. The written report, and the agent who came to console Cowboy and his mother explained, the brakes failed at a steep part of the road, and his father drove off the edge of the mountain in the middle of a hairpin turn. There were no survivors. The two men that took over the stakeout disappeared the same night, without a trace.

Cowboy locked the shed and got back in his car. He couldn't sleep for two reasons; the rawness of that memory and the need to investigate the cabinet further.

• • •

In his office, he pulled all four drawers out of the cabinet and carefully examined the shell. He took out a measuring tape and measure the outside and the inside. There was a quarter-inch difference between the inside and back of the cabinet. All the other sides were single sheets of metal. He tapped on the cabinet and pressed against the back. There was no flex to the metal. From the inside, he pushed on the back and sides of the cabinet. There was no movement on the back. He studied the cabinet, looking for a button or pin to hold a second sheet in place. He installed each drawer and repeatedly opened and closed them. They all closed tight, just the bottom one didn't come out as far. Trying different drawers in the bottom location, they all did the same thing. He flipped the cabinet upside down and studied it, then turned it on its side. Something moved inside the cabinet, a shuffle of paper. He looked again. Nothing changed, but he was sure he heard something move. He replaced all the drawers and locked the cabinet. The cabinet sat in the middle of his office. He walked around it clockwise then counterclockwise. Giving up, he tried a "Fonzie tap" on the sides, back and top. He heard a change in deflection of the metal when he hit the back and top. Unlocking the cabinet, he pulled out the top drawer and pushed on the top from inside. Something moved. He put both hands inside the cabinet and lifted. The top moved an inch, and the back fell to the ground. The sound in his quiet office was like a cymbal being hit by Neil Peart, Rush's drummer.

Walking to the backside of the cabinet, a false metal back lay on the ground with eight yellow interoffice envelopes lying on top of it.

"What the fudge!" he said out loud.

He looked at his watch, 6 a.m. He had spent the night in his office. Out of the five cabinets, three had hidden areas. He recovered twelve envelopes, twenty-three large floppy disks, and a handful of the 3.5-inch disks. There were photos, maps, and dossiers on many people.

He plugged a disk into his computer drive and found it locked. Luckily for Cowboy, the only person he hadn't stepped on during his climb to his new job was his only friend and the only one he trusted, a computer encryption specialist.

Cowboy cleaned up his office, grabbing his spoils from the night's investigation before he headed out. He would need to get home, shower, clean up, and be back in the office before ten. He filled his briefcase.

At ten, he returned for a team meeting; it was the first item on his calendar. He stopped in his office and called Stanley. They needed to talk, but not at the office.

•   •   •

Cowboy and Stanley went for a walk by the reflective pool in Washington and sat on the steps of the Lincoln Memorial. "Cowboy, you won't believe what I found on those disks." The list of discoveries Stanley found included several CIA black budget accounts, the bombing of buildings and cities, governments that were overthrown, notes about all kinds of illegal activities, many requests for hits, and a lot of weapon shipments. The money went to the same three accounts set up in Sweden, Egypt, and Grand Bahama. "Listen, I am worried about what I have uncovered. You know what happens when people find out more than they should. They get put down like a sick dog. Who knows about these disks, besides us?"

"Stanley, relax, no one does. Listen, take some time and organize the files, then we can find a quiet place to discuss them. If at that point you want to turn it in, I will do it without mentioning your name."

•   •   •

The following weekend, Stanley had three computers set up at his family's cottage near the Outer Banks in North Carolina. He and Cowboy both booked the week off work and met to review the documents, scandals, and full-blown conspiracies. Cowboy brought the documents and Stanley had the disks.

Stanley's only comment to Cowboy, on the way to the cottage, "Well, Peter, was filthy, not just dirty. He also documented everything they asked him to do. I guess he figured one day he might need those disks to clear his name or make a lot of money. Some of the shit he did came right from George Bush, Ronald Reagan, or William Casey. Cowboy. Listen to me. He had many people killed, famous people."

"I can't believe it is that dire. Next, you're going to say Oswald didn't kill Kennedy, Peter did. Dear oh dear, what a tangled web we weave."

"Cowboy, you will see it when we get to the cottage."

They arrived as the sun dipped out of sight. The cottage on the beach was stuffy and warm. They opened the windows and waited for the cool ocean breeze to cool the building. On the porch, they talked about work and politics until the cottage was cool enough to sleep in.

The next morning, Cowboy was up early and out for his four-mile run. When he returned, Stanley had his computers on, and the first series of disks installed. He had compartmentalized the material on new disks. Sorting through the material to make it easy to review.

"Where are the originals, Stanley?"

Stanley, one step ahead of him, had the bag of disks on the coffee table. "Right here, Cowboy."

The first day, they didn't eat. They spent fourteen hours together. They took notes, discussed items Stanley revealed, and shook their heads in disbelief. That night they went to bed exhausted.

The next three days were the same; up for a run, review the data. The only difference was they occasionally stopped to eat and drink.

On the fifth day, they reviewed their notes. Cowboy was like a child who was told Santa wasn't real. He was shocked, disturbed, in disbelief, and angry. "How could our government allow all this to happen? How could they be so corrupt? I knew there were pockets of bad or off-the-books people, but not to this extent. Stanley, we have proof that requests came from Presidents, Vice Presidents, senators, Congress members and many other agency heads."

Sitting on the porch alone, Cowboy reviewed his own morals and those of his country and the world.

He reviewed his notes, highlighting names and organizations. A series of names were constantly in the files. The Family, who or whatever that was; an Igor Volkov, a Russian contact from the KGB and freelance weapons and many other items, dealer; Sergio Garcia, a man Peter worked with and a confidant of Peter's until he disappeared with copies of most of the disks. Then there was the Irish bomb makers, Nigel and Dermot, the CIA and military, used them for jobs in Beirut, Asia, and many other places around the world. He found many names throughout the documents, but those names were constantly in files and written on loose pages.

Cowboy's goal was to locate and talk to each one of those people. The only name hidden in a file folder with a phone number was Gregory Kite. The note from 1988 said.

If you find this note, I am dead. Likely killed by one of my own for the sins I have committed. The documents are all real. The notes, files and reports are all real. I assume most of my primary contacts are dead as well. Look up Gregory Kite. He will clear my name and help find those named in these documents and on the disks. You can either continue to use these people or have them imprisoned for the work they have done. As of this note, January 13, 1988, Gregory's phone number was 555-964-1732. You can him find somewhere in Europe.

Peter Thompson

"Stanley, I'm crushed. I thought we were fighting for the good guys. After all these disks and documents, I don't believe there is a good guy on the planet anymore. What do I do with this?"

"Cowboy, live up to your name. You have all of Peter's contacts. You saw Peter's financials. We could do what he did for a couple of years and disappear as he did. When your mom passes, we go."

"Stanley, how can you say that? We pledged to protect this country and its citizens."

"So did a lot of the people on those disks and files. I appreciate you play the part of the good, clean guy, but I know what you did to get to where you are. Hell, I manipulated computers and personnel files to help you climb. You owe me this. You owe yourself this. What is the saying 'if you can't beat them? Join them?' Well, we can go one step above that. We can join them and then beat them as we walk away."

"I need to sleep on this. Let's not talk till lunch tomorrow."

Cowboy reviewed the notes and disks throughout the night and right up to noon. He knew the government and its agencies had skeletons in their closet, but nothing to the extent of what Peter recorded on the disks. The disks were Peter's, *get out of jail free* card. He couldn't believe Peter's involvement in the bombings and killings of so many people, known and unknown.

While walking on the beach, he thought about Keith. They were on an assignment last year together. Until yesterday, Cowboy thought Keith and his wife had defected to Russia. Now he knew a David killed them and David's handler received $96,000 for the job. They exposed a pastor and killed him, then arrested his staff. A bomb in Paris, a jumbo jet downed in Scotland. All by some contacts of Peter and ordered from those above Peter, all to hide some form of the truth.

Back from his walk, Cowboy joined Stanley on the porch in rocking chairs. They both were quiet and just stared out at the ocean. The waves broke just off the shore, umbrellas stretched across the sand with families on vacation or just enjoying the last few days of summer before the children returned to school.

"Stanley, I have to turn these disks in."

"To who? Cowboy, to who? Anyone in a position to help us was named somewhere in those documents or disks. President? President Bush's name is all over the documents. The Attorney General? Signed off on an enormous explosion at a wedding of six Muslim families by that Nigel fella. There is nowhere to go with the information except to use it for our own benefit. Come on, Cowboy, two years, and we're out with more money than we could ever make even if we worked into our eighties. Then we destroy everything, buy some property on a Pacific Island, and retire. Hell, maybe we can take down those people before we go. Until then, use them, use the government's money, use it all to benefit us."

"I don't know. I wasn't raised like that. It wasn't what I wanted from the agency. Gosh darn, what would my father think, rest his soul? My mother would be broken-hearted if she knew any of this, or that I was going to use it for personal gains."

"Okay, Cowboy, there is one disk left. I wasn't going to show you what was on it. But maybe this will open your eyes. Like the good book says, the truth will set you free. Come back into the house."

Stanley turned on his computer and inserted a disk.

"Sit, Cowboy, sit." Cowboy sat on a chair by Stanley's makeshift desk. "Here, read this report. I am sorry bud. This one is going to hurt."

Cowboy read the document on the screen. He shook, then cried. He wiped his eyes so he could finish the report.

Cowboy looked at Stanley. "You should have shown me this document first. I always wondered what happened to Dad. This changes everything. I need a minute."

Cowboy left the house and walked to the beach. His minute turned into an hour, then hours. He didn't return until the moon hung overhead.

Stanley had packed up his equipment and cleaned the house. He sat on the porch with a lit cigar and a large glass of whiskey.

"Well, that was a long minute. Are you okay?"

"I wish I had never taken this job. I have spent my life in darkness not knowing anything about this world. Yes, Jesus said, The truth will set you free, but he forgot to say there would be consequences to that freedom."

"Bud, have a drink and relax. I'm sorry. I shouldn't have shown you that last document."

"Stanley I'm glad you did. It removed the scales from my eyes. You're right. We need to take our piece of the pie. I think a meeting with Gregory is where we should start. Talk to him. See what he has to say."

• • •

Two days later, Cowboy sat in his office. He stared out his window at the bullpen. He had made calls and waited to hear from the names he rang. Stanley had done more of an in-depth search of the disks. He found deleted files that had been written over, poorly. The additional documents proved they needed to talk to Gregory.

Cowboy had sent out feelers and the responses back were not promising. Igor had died. Nigel was in France, very well protected. He presumed Sergio was dead. Then there was the group known as The Family. No one would give him information on them, just rumors and ghost stories. One person who returned his call told him to stop looking for them. "If you ask the wrong person the right question, both of you will be missing."

The number tied to Gregory's name was now a pizzeria in Conway, South Carolina. The owner knew whom Gregory was but hadn't seen him in years. Cowboy and Stanley continued to search for Gregory. The only lead was that he was in Europe. Finally, Cowboy convinced Stanley to expense the trip through the CIA, and go on a manhunt.

Stanley brought a laptop with him. He had hacked a computer tied to Peter. The agency hadn't taken it off the network or didn't realize it was still active. On it, he discovered multiple addresses for Gregory. The last one was a hidden away cabin in Switzerland.

●   ●   ●

After a week of traveling, they located Gregory's cabin. Stanley decided they should stake out the cottage before they kicked in the door. He took the first watch while Cowboy found a place to stay. The motel was twenty kilometers away and had a Canadian staying at.

Cowboy found a second hotel for himself and booked a room. Once unpacked, he relieved Stanley, who had stationed himself a half-mile away from the cottage. From his surveillance, Stanley noted one man, Gregory, living in the cottage. He had chopped a cord of wood and had a quick visit from a lady who dropped off food earlier in the day.

Cowboy watched Gregory prepare supper. The large cottage windows gave him a view of most of the inside of the cottage. Gregory ate his supper on the porch and wrote notes. Then when the sun dropped below the horizon, he went inside and to bed.

Cowboy continued through the night watching the cabin. Stanley arrived with a steaming hot coffee and a piece of toast the next morning and they switched off.

At nine that morning, a stranger appeared through the field and knocked on the door. Stanley saw the surprise on Gregory's face when he opened the door. It appeared to Stanley that the stranger forced his way into the cottage. Through the window,

Stanley watched as the stranger angrily paced the floor and vocalized his displeasure. He spent four hours with Gregory. After the first hour, he calmed down.

· · ·

James sat with Gregory. "How did you hide all these years? You are a fucking idiot. I told you not to leave the cottage. You were at the market early yesterday morning. You had a lady bring you food, and you spent the afternoon outside chopping wood."

"James, I am sorry. It has been my routine for months now."

"Listen, we have another two days before we travel. Stay in here. I can't watch you and the town for people who might not want to keep you alive. Just because Sergio wants you close doesn't mean I have to do it. I have been here for two days, and you have not done one thing to help me keep you alive."

"I have had no issues so far, James."

"No, I know. But you are this close to not having to look over your shoulder anymore. Don't fuck it up!"

James left Gregory and headed outside. The sun was overhead, and the day had a briskness to it, a reminder that winter was coming, and coming soon. He headed back through the field he came from. Circling around, he scurried across the road, protected by hedges and trees. James noticed earlier; he was being watched. Most of the morning sun had reflected off a pair of binoculars from the field across the road. Gregory saw none of it. A retired CIA agent who had forgotten how to protect himself.

Recognizing the person, as the man staying at the hotel in town, James crept up behind him and tapped him on his shoulder. Stanley jumped in shock and turned to look at James.

"You seem interested in my friend," James said. He reached behind his back and pulled out his knife.

"What? No. Umm, yesterday there was a beautiful lady there, and I watched her in the backyard. I am waiting for her husband to leave. We are having an affair."

"What? Now, why don't I give you, a Yankee, a chance to retell your story."

"Umm, I work for the CIA. That man's name is all over files I found. I'm watching him. And well, I don't know what to say after that. You might have more answers than I do. I guess we will bring him in to be questioned." He slowly reached for his bag.

James swung his knife and sliced through the sweater Stanley wore. He hit the bone and pulled back. Stanley's biceps muscle rolled up to where it connected with his shoulder and his arm went limp.

"Now why don't we start over. How did you find Gregory?"

"Peter, an old co-worker of mine, left some information when he retired. One note said to find that man you were visiting this morning."

"Uh-huh."

Stanley reached for his upper arm. James drove his knife deep in between Stanley's upper ribs. He fell on his back. James stepped over him and drove his knife straight down into the chest. He pulled his knife back. Stanley died two minutes later. James dragged his body a little further from the road, grabbed Stanley's bag, and headed to the motel.

James called John and reported to him what had happened. "This was the guy I told you showed up the other day. I believe he is alone."

"Okay, maybe we should pull Gregory tomorrow," said John.

"I'll search his hotel room and ask about any others in the town. I'll check out and move in with Gregory later." James hung up and headed to Stanley's room. Searching through the bag and room, he found a series of notes on The Family, and Gregory.

There was a knock on the door. Gregory lifted himself out of his chair. Opening the door, Cowboy stood on the threshold. "English?" he asked.

"Yes," said Gregory.

"Evening sir. My car broke down just up the way. Do I detect a Boston accent?"

"Yes, I'm on vacation here. Yours is an Atlanta accent, right?"

"Correct. Wow, what are the chances? Can I come in?" Cowboy asked. He stepped forward and pushed on the door.

"No, I think—"

"Gregory, I know who you are. I took over for Peter at the agency. You, for some reason, were important to him. How about we sit for a bit and figure out why?"

Gregory stepped towards the kitchen.

"Why don't we sit down here? You don't need a gun. We might be fighting for the same side." Cowboy placed his hand on Gregory's shoulder and spun him into a chair.

"What? Who are you?"

"Sir, they call me Cowboy. I took Peter's position and found his disks and documents." Gregory tried to stand, but Cowboy reached over and put his hand on his knee. "No, no, just sit there."

"Son, if you want anything from me, we need to go. I don't need protection. I have it. The real man that was here earlier will give it to me until, well, he won't. How about you? What can you offer me?"

"Would he be the same man who killed my partner across the street?"

"Likely the very one. If he comes back here and finds us, we will be lying in a field with your friend. So, I will ask again. Will you protect me?"

"I will if you are worth protecting. Tell me, my dad was an FBI agent. The last document that man lying across the street showed me was what convinced me to look for you. Before we leave, do you know the names John or Kenton? They were the men Peter met with the day my dad died."

"Is this all about revenge?"

"It's about a lot of things. But the one thing I really want to learn about is those two men and the group they are with."

Gregory stood up. He looked out the front window and took in a deep breath. He turned to Cowboy and whispered, "Let me tell you about The Family."

END

ABOUT THE AUTHOR

Stephen W. Briggs is the author of *Family of Killers—Memoirs of an Assassin*, an Irish organized crime thriller.

Born in Northern Ireland and raised in Canada, Stephen is married and the proud father of two, twenty something boys.

He enjoys daily walks with his wife and two dogs, Basil and Winston, on a variety of trails around town.

His only addiction is cycling, something he does regularly. He has been told that he owns too many bikes, that is a matter of opinion, mainly his family's. The longer the ride, the better for Stephen. He uses the time to create new story lines, develop characters or just listen to music.

NOTE FROM THE AUTHOR

Word-of-mouth is crucial for any author to succeed. If you enjoyed *Lies Lead to Death*, please leave a review online—anywhere you are able. Even if it's just a sentence or two. It would make all the difference and would be very much appreciated.

Thanks!
Stephen W. Briggs

We hope you enjoyed reading this title from:

BLACK ROSE
writing™

www.blackrosewriting.com

Subscribe to our mailing list – *The Rosevine* – and receive **FREE** books, daily deals, and stay current with news about upcoming releases and our hottest authors.
Scan the QR code below to sign up.

Already a subscriber? Please accept a sincere thank you for being a fan of Black Rose Writing authors.

View other Black Rose Writing titles at www.blackrosewriting.com/books and use promo code **PRINT** to receive a **20% discount** when purchasing.